Amy

William A. Clifford

authorHOUSE®

AuthorHouse™
1663 Liberty Drive
Bloomington, IN 47403
www.authorhouse.com
Phone: 1-800-839-8640

Published by AuthorHouse 6/03/2014

ISBN: 978-1-4969-1709-6 (sc)
ISBN: 978-1-4969-1708-9 (e)

Library of Congress Control Number: 2014910195

A my came into being in response to a challenge. Many years of pain and suffering, led to a comment to the effect of, not suffering the female variety of pains.

This was met with agreement, but started the thought process. Could this comparison ever be laid out, in conclusive reasoning.

As an empath, that is someone who feels the symptoms of others, I have a grand base of understanding, the trials of the afflicted. I feel I need to explain, how this came about.

It started at birth. Too long in the birth canal, resulted in a slight damage to the brain. That in and of itself, would lead to a premature deterioration of the area affected. But that was the beginning, of a lifelong series of events.

Every time a noise was heard in our house, someone would say "He's fallen again." I didn't have to do much, in the way of moving, or communicating as a child, for there was always somebody close at hand, to take care of me. Whatever I wanted, was brought straight away. I was taken any place, I might like to go. I was the third child, with siblings six to eight years older than I.

It was always "Look at what he's doing now!" I didn't learn to walk, or talk early, because I never had the need, until another came along the next year. The following year brought another. Now I had to fend for myself, in getting the toy I wanted, or any such thing. As was normal for developing children, I had my share of the usual falls and slips. Tumbling down the stairs was a favourite trick. Not that I particularly liked the activity, it was just something, I had the occasion to do.

The outings were where the noteworthy spills began. The first, I remember clearly, at about three years old, was the walk to Sulphur Springs, a favourite place to swim and chase water creatures. We were just arriving at the spot, right by the bridge, when I heard my mother call out, "There's a car coming. Get over!" and over I got. Dutifully stepping aside, and off the edge of the bridge. Fourteen feet below, I stopped. I had landed on the concrete slab, poured to stop erosion. There was only a couple inches of water there, and I wouldn't have made many waves. I don't remember how I felt, I was to busy figuring out, where I had gone wrong. The instructions were clear. I had followed them to the letter. I think, now, I might not have been in the group so told. I did receive a good deal of attention, but I didn't like the extent of the activity, needed to attain it.

I had run ins with toys, that needed unusual treatments and vehicles of the full scale variety, which started my collection of stitches. My first grade inoculations, gave me a paralyzed arm, that was the preview of my inherited condition, diagnosed in my thirties. That kept me in bed a week, or two, with a cushion under my arm. At least it seemed that long. The condition, first thought to be arthritis, was fibromyalgia.

Our grandmother had a cottage, that my father's brothers and sister, would share time at. We liked going up to the cottage, on Fawn Bay, of Lake Couchiching. We got two weeks, for our time and sometimes, we would have the aunts and uncles stay for the day, when our arrival would overlap their departure. My dad would stay for the weekends and go home, for the weekdays. I tried my hand at waterskiing, which did not go well. We had a rowboat, we called Pogo, after the comic strip, which was popular at the time. We would take it out, if it was still afloat, and have to bail our way back home. There was a sand beach, that had been trucked in, for a public access and play area, and there was a dock, and boathouse, along the waterfront.

We would walk to Rama, to the general store, for treats and walk back. Cutting through the pastures brought us face-to-face with menacing cows. Little kids needed little to frighten them. So sometimes, we would walk along the road, to avoid them.

On one occasion, I had bought a treat for the girl next door, visiting her grandparents. On the way back, I dropped it and ruined it, so my sister, went back, to get another while I, at three and a half, was told to keep going. It was just down the road. My sisters both went back and left me alone. I wasn't worried, since I had been there, many times before. Things got frightening, when a big red Cadillac convertible stops, to drop off two teenagers, with a pellet gun. The boys started shooting, fence posts and signs. When they saw me watching them, they thought they would scare me and started shooting at me. I hurried on toward the cottage and when I felt a pellet hit me in the back, I fell down in the grass and ditch, hoping they would be afraid of the trouble they had just caused, and leave. They, at first, just laughed about it. My laying still in the ditch, had the desired effect, and they left. I stood and ran home to tell the story, and the police were called. My description of the car, and the boys, led them to a cottage, not far from ours. The scar from that incident had some problems, later in life, as it would swell and become inflamed. Eventually, I had to have a cyst removed from that spot. The boys lost their gun and were grounded, but did not get a record from it, to my sister's frustration.

We were out for a ride, in my sister's, boyfriend's car. Along the way, we saw a train stopped, with a crowd gathering. A car had tried to beat the train to the crossing and had won the race, but not by enough of a lead. They did not survive.

Things would step up a notch, when we moved to the farm. I had the usual childhood diseases, that came with the era we lived in. One that caused some concern, was scarlet fever, or so I was told. It was quite fortunate, that there had been great strides in medicine and that episode only caused my parents to worry, and not any noticeable problems. We did, as a family, miss out on the polio outbreak, thanks to that vaccination, that gave me my stint in bed, as previously mentioned.

The adventures on the farm were epic and I was, at the same time, unlucky to have them and lucky to survive them. Many children lost there lives to these experiences on the farms, that I lived to tell about. In fact, they had succumbed to these things, one at a time, where I survived the whole collection. People would do these things for a living, stuntmen, or fall guys. I did it for free, but not by choice.

We walked to school, in the first years on the farm and it was the usual three miles uphill, both ways, as your grandfather might tell you. In fact, it was one of the most beautiful journeys for which I could have asked. There was the short-cut, a half mile through two adjoining farms. Then there was the long way, about two miles of hills, across bridges -no concrete to land on here- and past forests, that begged to be explored.

The schoolhouse was of the one room type. They were slowly being closed down, as modern schools were built to take their places. Several grade levels were in that classroom.

The path to school, opened the way for misadventures. One spring, we were coming home and stopped on the bridge, to see the flooding water pushing through that narrow span. We would watch one side, then run across to the other, to see how long the floating sticks and branches, would take to come through. Being overexcited got me and my older brother a soaking, when I fell in and he had to go in to save me. No injuries came of that, but it did have a place in the list, by virtue of the potential severity it possessed.

Another incident was on the shortcut. It was winter and the stream was frozen over. There had been a quick thaw, with an equally quick freeze. The ice, therefore had layers thinner but not noticeable, as there wasn't water running close enough underneath. We started across and heard some cracks and groans from the ice, but the first of us got across okay. Not I though. I found the water that 'was' flowing underneath. Right in the middle of the stream, I went through. Up above my waist was where the water stopped. The stream was only deep during the middle of spring, so the big danger was hypothermia. I headed back the eighth of a mile to the house. I made it in plenty of time but, the pains in the muscles started then and for a little while, were quite intense. They would come back, now and again, over the years.

I didn't have too many chores around the farm, because my father had wanted us to have a carefree childhood. He went off to war, when the country needed men, to keep the fighting overseas. So, for the three little ones, as we were called, the little times we gave our efforts were more our choice. My elder brother had some chores to do, but still managed to get into trouble with us.

I remember riding, with my little brother and sister, on top of the hay wagon. Coming in off the front south field, the tractor dipped down then climbed up from the shallow ditch. Turning onto the lane, the wagon tipped the load forward a bit in the dip, enough to send us tumbling into the gap, between the tractor and trailer. We could have been killed, as others in that situation have, but we came out with only scratches, from the straw and bruises, from the drawbar. That lesson learned, we did not have occasion to ride in again, at least not on a full load.

Playing in the barns was always fun. We would have all sorts of adventures. Climbing up and walking the beams, of an empty barn. When the barn was full, building forts and playing in them gave us hours of business away from mom, letting her have some peace. Well at least until one, or another, would get hurt. The lofts of baled hay and straw reached two or three stories high and the falls from them were terrible. There was a pile of wood, at the bottom of an access hole, which I was thankful for, when it broke my fall and saved my neck a few times.

We had beef cattle and a bull was a necessity, for producing the inventory. I found myself cornered by our bull, Ferdinand, who at times could be gentle. Weighing as much as a small car, he posed a great hazard. As I realized my situation, so did he, and started to come at me. What made him get offensive all of a sudden, I never could figure out. He started to charge and my only escape, was through another access hole, in the wall of a hog pen. I made it to the hole and fell through. I landed on my head, folding my head to my shoulder, and my shoulder, sideways to my knee. I was unable to walk properly for two weeks, or so it seemed.

Riding in from distributing posts along the fence line, I slipped off the rail of the pickup truck, hitting the rear wheel and tumbling down the hill. More often, the fall from the truck, would be off the tailgate.

We had two dogs. Benny, was a border collie and Saber, was

a king shepherd. Saber liked to follow us behind the truck, as we would drop off the fence posts. He first picked up one end, and then the other, of these eight foot wood posts. Finally, he would pick up the post from the middle, and with his head high, would trot along behind us as we yelled to him to drop it. He kept trotting along, so proud of himself. When he stood on his hind legs, he could put his front paws over the doorway, of the farmhouse.

I was playing tug-of-war with Saber, with a thick rope I had found laying around one of the outbuildings. I looped the rope around myself to get a better hold. Big mistake. Saber would pull the rope and, as I got closer to pulling him over the line, I would turn around wrapping the rope round my chest. This gave me my footing in the rut I was using, successfully, to pull him. He gave a tug on the rope, pulling me off balance. On the ground, he knew he had me and dragged me over the line to win. Animals don't always get the meanings of our rules, and he was going to enjoy his victory, by dragging me in tugging motions, as I attempted to extricate myself from the rope, which was tightening around me. The rope was twisted and snagged, keeping me from getting loose. It started to crush me, so I had trouble breathing, and couldn't get the volume in my voice, to call for help. Mom had just come to get me to come in, when she found us in the struggle. Saber stopped as she told him to and she scolded my stupidity as she unraveled the rope.

I was eight, when we moved to the farm. Eleven, when my dad died of lung cancer. I remember him standing out, looking over the back forty at night, after the animals were fed. I would stand beside him taking it all in. I like to say he was 'outstanding in his field'. When he was sick and grouchy from the cancer, I remember thinking "Why don't you just die?" A few weeks later, he did. I had an enormous feeling of guilt, from that comment. That time I said it out of anger. I would say it again, out of compassion, to someone else, on a later time. My father also had the fibromyalgia, along with his cancer. He suffered from that for thirty three years. He was a chain-smoker, lighting one on the last. He smoked nearly a carton a day. The physical wounds and the psychological, weighed heavy on me, most of my life.

After Daddie died, we sold the farm and moved into town. During the process of moving, we had to take one school bus and transfer to another. I missed the bus one morning, as I often did, with one of the others. I'm not sure whom it was. They elected to stay put and I decided to hitchhike in to town. Benny, as he always did, would follow me well in advance and come back occasionally, to check my progress. No matter that he was told to go home. He was coming with me and his mind was made up. We weren't going a route we had been on before but that didn't stop him. He would act as scout and report back. Reporting back meant checking to see I was still coming and then going on ahead. A car stopped to give me a ride and the man seeing Benny, asked if this fellow was with me. I said yes, and he stopped to pick him up. Now Benny is an excitable dog. In the car, between the space in the back of the station wagon, was stacked trays of eggs. I couldn't calm Benny down and he ran from front seat to back space nonstop. I apologized to the driver, who seemed unconcerned, as Benny stepped on eggs with each trip. Amazingly, we arrived at the street we were moving to, without breaking a single egg. I took Benny to the house, locked him inside the sun porch and headed off to school. I expected high honours, when telling the story to my mom. Good thing I hadn't held my breath waiting.

Bicycle falls were common and even being hit by cars, started a trend. I had ridden with a friend, that went on to become a celebrated, professional, football player. I was sitting on the handle bar of his bike, when my foot slipped into the spokes of his front wheel, tossing us head over heels, onto the paved road.

Riding through the neighbourhood one day, I crossed a street intersection, while looking back, in conversation. A startled woman was just able to stop, as she hit my bike.

Now this was indicative, of the outcome, of the birth canal passing. I had started to have concentration problems. I was slow in motor skills and memory recall as well. I did not suffer any injury in this incident, but that wouldn't be the case in future car related experiences.

My little brother had a motorcycle when he was fourteen. We would ride it around the property, in and out of the ditch and around the house. A few spills here weren't too harmful but when I was driving, I didn't have control for trying more to just hang on. The bike went faster the more I tried until I would run into a bush. When I think of the hurts that really seemed big back then, I laugh. There were bigger fish to fry, deeper holes to fall into and tighter spaces to squeeze through.

We were sneaking around, trying to get to our objective in a war game and I got into a culvert. I had been through it before, with no problem. The trouble this time was that, I had grown quite a bit since then, and I got half way and couldn't move. I was panicking. It is hard to hear screams under eight inches of stone and asphalt. Finally, someone went looking for me when I didn't reach the target. They got me out and when I could compose myself, we had a good laugh, but I had a real fear of close places after that, which I had to face to overcome. I still have problems with that, no matter how much I face it.

One summer we had to paint the sun porch and dormers. We started scraping down the old paint and sanding the edges that were too tough to get under. I had to go up on the ladder to start on the dormer and half way up I froze. I couldn't move, not up or down. Every effort was wasted. My big brother got mad and told me to come down but I could budge. I was only three feet up. It was totally illogical. I had played thirty feet up with very little real fear. Now I could fall off and not get hurt much at all, but I was frozen with fear. A totally irrational fear gripped me. My brother realized it was useless, to bully me down, so he climbed up the ladder and squeezed between it and me. Then he took my arms off the ladder, and put them around his neck. He then lifted me up off the ladder rungs and climbed down.

I later faced this fear by getting a job driving overhead cranes in the steel mills and got very good at it, sixty feet off the ground. While waiting for a lift to be made, I would even lay on a board I put across the controls right on the edge of the cab. Later they would put windows in, to air-condition them, and take away that thrill.

Back to the painting, we got the job done but I had to stay on the ground.

I think we did everything full out, until fear made us stop or, at least, slow down.

My little brother was driving before me, on his motorcycle. He got into a bit of trouble since he was two years, too young, to get a license. One day he came home pushing his bike. They had laid fresh gravel on the road he would take, back home and he lost traction. Parting ways with his bike, he looked sideways to see his bike doing cartwheels beside him. I can still picture that clearly.

I always wanted a motorbike but my mom, ever encouraging, laughed saying I was too uncoordinated. Thanks mom. I probably was saved a whole chapter of pain, with her stance on that.

It seems that ever since cars got into the hands of teenagers, there has been a tradition of wild driving and fearless drivers. I was no exception but the difference, in my case, was that I was a survivor. Sometimes though, I wasn't so sure that was a good thing. Usually I would not take anyone with me, on those adventures. I gave a lift home, to a couple of my brother's friends, one of which had tormented me with teasing and ridiculing me. A slow lane of traffic baited me to pass. A truck was coming away down the road but I knew I had time. I floored the accelerator and passed four cars in that line. The truck loomed large ahead of us, and the boys dove to the floor, in the back seat. I made it with room to spare and I'm sure those guys needed to change their clothes, when they got home.

I didn't always make it and became too familiar with auto body shops and emergency wards.

Walking didn't save me from harm though and while returning home from a visit to a favourite girlfriend, I met up with a guy even cops didn't want to mess with. He asked me if I wanted to fight and since he was with his little brother, I asked with whom. I was swung around by the hair while being kicked in the face. A car happened by and stopped it but I wasn't sure it was over. In the hospital I waited for my mom to collect me. She had to have somebody point me out to her, as she could not recognize me. She was a nurse so I should be okay with her at home. In the morning she woke me and apologized, for not waking me throughout the night, which she was to do to prevent shock from taking me, but was in too deep a sleep herself and frankly, forgot me. But I survived so don't have much to complain about. Isn't that what people say at times like that?

I repeated a lot of the mistakes I had made. I did have a problem reacting. It would not be until I was in my mid twenties that I could start to have better reactions in emergencies. It was in my forties when I could finally get a hold on the skills of controlling a vehicle in a skid and I was quite good by then. I always joked that, I took the crash course in driving.

had become close with God, and prayed often. I put my life in His hands, many times and He pulled me through. The angels may have feared to tread but they went in with this fool and stayed close by. Because of these times, I was deeply connected to God and even when I couldn't agree with the church, I always knew His voice.

You now, can see the path my life has taken and though the examples are few, the incidents were not.

Some workmates would peg my age at eighty five when I was in my early thirties, because of the twisted form I could have some days. They knew my story and understood my suffering. I never minded the aging since I had already been living that part. I would say I am growing into my years. Later I would seem to reverse the aging with some of the treatments and learning how better to live with it.

I was forty when my mom died. My brother-in-laws and I turned forty that year and we all took a trip together to celebrate. Later we went back to that same area for a summer camping trip. It was on that trip we got the call that mom was taking a turn for the worse. We left camp as it was with the others to watch it and headed back home. We were there in time to say goodbye.

It was when she was in hospital and suffering so that I asked God to give me the pain she was feeling to let her rest for a while. He did not give them then and I learned later, that the suffering is necessary when one is dying, to make them let go.

Later. when I was nearing sixty, that is when He gave me that gift. Some would call it a curse but, when you know what your friends are facing and can relate to them they can be comforted better knowing that you know. Imagine feeling the mouth pains and drained aching of someone experiencing leukemia. An empath will feel it for a short while and it will be over but the patient still lives with it. A child breaks a bone and it gets to you just enough to know. The disease you have been carrying, this fibromyalgia mimics all pain and all diseases, but is only an inconvenience compared to lupus, or cancer. Sure you can be disabled by the pain, until you learn how to handle it. You know it is just a mimic and you can push yourself through it. You still need help and encouragement but it doesn't kill you and it doesn't make you stronger unless you fight it.

This brings us to Amy. After that comment and accepted challenge, I prayed to God to take part of me and create a new person psychically connected to me. Not just psychically connected but psychokinetically connected. This way I know what she knows and I feel what she feels. When she goes through puberty and experiences her first period, I would feel it too. When she has a child, I could experience the pain. It had to be that way, or nothing could be definitively answered.

My wife agreed to this idea and was willing to be part of it. I had enough extra weight to give a hundred pounds to make this girl and my wife would shed some with me to help this come about. God will answer a prayer if three agree. He would also forego that if the prayer benefits others and not the one praying. That is why you always should be happy when others pray for you.

I proposed the experiment in my prayers and gave the details of the circumstances. He had done this before, when He created Eve. This would allow Amy to be created at an age when she would be more able to understand and deal with the knowledge she would have access to through my mind. She would be at an age that would be starting puberty and then have children before my life was over. She would basically be me in a females body but have the capacity of a separate mind and mental decision freedom. God always insists on the freedom of choice. Giving Amy the knowledge from my brain and my wife's, she came equipped with the basic information you would need as a young teenage girl and the protection the knowledge of societal pressures and pitfalls can give. The big drawback is the premature access to carnal knowledge, that would give a prepubescent girl.

When and where, do you draw the line. One good aspect, is the wisdom that came with that knowledge. Wisdom learned through the mishandling of the knowledge, that comes with natural maturation in teenage boys and girls. Wise beyond her years, people would say. You have heard people say that of someone, haven't you? Imagine a teenager knowing and comprehending all that at sixtyish couple would know and gathered through all those years.

There were other stipulations that had to be observed. Because, in this day and age and the country we were living in, a girl of twelve, or thirteen could not just appear and whose circumstances would be accepted in time to let this experiment continue successfully, Amy had to be passed off as a victim of amnesia. She would also have traits to make her identifiable to us if anything were to happen to her. She was not born of the flesh but created, so she would have no navel. She needed a possible extraneous circumstance to explain that. Therefore she would have definite, but not extremely, pointed ears giving a hint of an otherworldly connection. A possible tie with the half believed faery world would give some thought to either explore or cover-up this trait, and so the story begins.

Chapter One

The Finding

The garden was feeling empty and a mist was in the air. It was mild for the season. The decorations and furniture were stowed in the garage and the pool was covered for the winter. There was still plants covering the fish pond and the waterfall was still running. The soothing sounds of water over the rocks made you relax and move without expectations. I duck to miss the lantern swinging on the holder by the door to the garage. Everything is as it should be in my mind. Halloween is over with no damage to the place or for the neighbours' either.

I walk around the garden. I'm looking for the things I might have missed. The faery houses and gnomes can stay out. There isn't a whole lot of space left and they are very durable. There are the leprechauns and some lights. I guess I'll take the lights in but the wee folk can stay out.

If there was anything else to do, I couldn't think of it. That happens a lot. I call it sometimers. Sometimes your on top of things and sometimes, well you just aren't even there.

I have a long list of things to do but finding the list is number one on it. Remembering to write one should be. I feel dizzy again. That happens often. The one thing that took me off the workforce, vertigo. I drove heavy cranes and other machines that meant I would need to be in charge of my faculties. Vertigo came on when I nearly lost the vision in my right eye. I could compensate for a while but then it would hit me quickly without warning. That the company could not allow. They kept me on for a while, but the other problems worsened. When I could get my pension base raised, they said it was over and I had to go.

I had always joked that it took three years to get in that place and thirty-two years to get out. I did feel they did right by me. I could not have had that chance in any other country.

I feel it again. It is much stronger. I think I need to sit down.

Oh wow. That was...What was that? I feel like I passed out. I'm checking myself for other symptoms. Other sudden onset symptoms. I lost consciousness and was dizzy but that's all. No numbness or blurred vision, at least not more than usual. I stick out my tongue and it is straight. No other sign of stroke. There is one thing though. My clothes are loose on me. I mean really loose. I have lost a lot of weight! Incredible...!

I hear a noise behind me and am conscious of being in two places at the same time. This is incredible! My prayers to God about that experiment in human existence has come true! I turn to look into the eyes looking into mine. The connection is materializing. It is forming slowly to allow us to prepare ourselves. I can feel her thinking the same things almost. She is not fully aware that this was because of prayer. She feels it is strange that she feels the wet grass she is on and the hard cobblestones that I am sitting on.

I try to stand because I realize she is uncomfortable with me sitting on the hard stones, but I can't yet stand. I am still too weak. She is too. I feel her trying to stand. She is sitting there naked and it is just too cold for that. I get myself on my knees but that brings excruciating pain. There is not much flesh protecting me from the rough old stones. I crawl onto the grass and pull off my jacket for her. She isn't that cold that she is suffering. Her youth and new senses have protected her from the cold. The jacket is short but not on her.

We help each other to stand on wobbly legs. I think about what she has to go through and she understands my concern and my thoughts. She wants to get warm now as the cold is starting to grip her. We get into the house. Right away I feel her enjoy the warmth. I suddenly remember my wife. She is usually vacuuming but, there is no vacuum on. Amy assures me that she is alright. She can feel my wife now and she lets me know what has happened in here.

I hear her in the bedroom. The dizziness that I felt, hit her too. She went to lay down and was lying on the bed. I told her what had happened and she looked at me, as if I was crazy. She didn't remember the prayer, or even us talking about it, but she looked at herself and knew I must be telling the truth. She also, had lost weight, and she had not been working on it like she wanted. She realized I must be telling her the truth. Nothing else could have explained, what she saw.

I told her I had to get Amy some clothes.

"What would she wear?" she said.

I said I have some things that she could use left over from our son's wardrobe.

I went over what has to take place, to get Amy some I.D.. How she would have to feign amnesia and go through the medical exam and Police questioning. How we will have to be involved in the story of finding her unconscious in our yard.

I knew my wife was not ready or able to go that far. She already had enough to do. Her mother was ill and she didn't know how long she would linger. She was tired and longing to be able to retire. She had lost hope of getting the life she wanted and I was not able to help the way she would like. This is too much for her to go for. This is stupid. What did I want to pray for this, for? These are her thoughts. Amy was relaying them to me.

So, finally I said to her "Look at your body. You have a chance to get off the blood pressure meds. You will feel and look younger. As well as the weight, He took years from us to give to Amy. We will still be sixtyish but feel fifty fivish. We can have Amy live with us, and get some help in coping with things, while she goes to school."

That helped. She did feel better and little by little, she was gaining her strength and composure back.

I told her, Amy and I had common interests, and she shared her talent with her, too. Amy would help us keep space between us, if she lives with us, a little insulation from each other. "Amy can translate your thoughts and desires to me, so that I can anticipate them." Oooh, she liked that. That is a good thing.

"How long would this go?" she asked.

I said it would take some time to assess her health, during which we would volunteer to take her in. It would take about a year, or so, for her to go through the courts and CAS, while they look for her parents. DNA tests will disprove any claims. Her willingness to live with us, and our record with children and the CAS. My disability would not be a big factor, since she is able to care for herself, and I would be available, anytime there is an issue. All this reassured her and helped her open up to the idea.

Having a daughter in the CAS role of caregivers, will help the process and eventually, Amy will get identification that would move things along for her.

All this time, Amy was listening to our thoughts and conversation. She let me know, how I was proceeding in my wife's view.

She asked "Why did you call her Amy?"

I told her that in French, 'amie' means friend, and with the psychic connection Amy is closer than any friend could be. It was also short for amethyst which is the stone I am sending with her.

It was getting near time to take Amy to the hospital, or police station, to start the process. She was comfortable and warm. She had eaten food from the fridge, while we were talking. She did not have to be near us to know what we were thinking, or let me know what was in the mind of my wife.

I was very nervous and anxious, about having to talk to people. I usually have nosedives with my energy level, when I am like this. Having family with me helps avoid that, sometimes. This time was not so lucky. I had to sit down quickly, and Amy shoved a chair under me as I staggered. This connection can be a real blessing, as well as the true purpose it has.

This helps me decide where to take her first. The hospital will have questions, but not to the intensity the police station would. It would make better sense to take her there first. Amnesia and her physical health, would have to be checked, and the Police will be brought in there. That is the plan then. I will have the energy drops in either location, so that will be easier to stay close to her in the hospital.

She will be asked a lot of questions, and will be examined for sexual assault, as well as physical injuries. They will be suspicious about her clothing, especially when I say, she hadn't had any on when I found her. She had not washed so the evidence from her being found outside on the grass, will be substantiated. They will also see whether she has been interfered with sexually.

I am even more nervous for her, but I know she has a steadier mind than I.

This is going to be intense.

Marie, my wife, is going to be shaken by this even at home, since she does not have the psychic connection, with either of us. It is good that this is Saturday and there will be time to settle things down for us. More so, for Marie, because she will not know what is going on with Amy, after I leave her. I will be able to tell her, but she can be calmer, if she doesn't have to worry about her.

There are many things going on in our minds, so we must get things moving. I kiss Marie goodbye and Amy and I go out the door. We wish each other good luck as we climb into my van. Being able to communicate in thought rather than speech will take some time to master, but for now it is going along fine.

We look to the house together, as we drive away, to wave goodbye to Marie. It is a tradition with Marie and I, to do this each time we leave, but Amy did it without thought, just as if she was me.

Thoughts were still, as we drove away.

Chapter Two

The Presentation

We drove up to the Children's Hospital and parked underground. We walked silently to the yellow elevators, that will take us to the Emergency department. Our thoughts are still, as if there is nothing to do but walk, nothing awaiting us. We rode up the elevator and got out on the second floor. We turned and walked down the hall, around the corner, and across the ward to the emergency desk. It was as if, we had both walked this route many times before. I had. Amy was using my memories, as if they were hers.

When we got to the desk, I presented the nurse with the story, and gave her my ID card. She looked at Amy and asked for her card. I explained, that she had no ID, or anything else, when I found her.

"Did you check her clothes?" she asked.

"She had none on." I explained.

"You found her nude, in your backyard. Why would she be in your backyard, with nothing on?"

"I really don't know why she would, but that is how she was found, lying on the wet grass." I said, acting frustrated.

"Was she conscious?" she asked.

"She was just gaining her wits when I noticed her." I told her.

"Your clothes are dirty and wet. What caused that?" she added suspiciously.

"I had fallen, and then I got dirtier, trying to help her up to her feet?" I related the scene.

"Was she hurt?"

I shook my head "Not that I could see. I brought her here to make sure. She did not know where she was, or who she was. She was cold, so I gave her some clothes my son had left, when he left for the west years ago. Then my wife thought I should bring her here first."

"First?" She asked.

"I had thought to take her to the Police for their help, but my wife said that you would bring them in while you examined her." I had a feeling things were looking more benign to her as far as I was concerned.

"Alright, fill out this form, and we will get her checked out as soon as someone is available. Have a seat over there and we will get started trying to sort this out." she said clinically. She picked up the phone as we walked away.

The usual bustle of the emergency ward went on, without us knowing how much was caused by us, but we did know, this wasn't an everyday occurrence. We started filling out the information, when a nurse came and took Amy away to check her vitals and get her story. She was asked if I had been in any way, threatening to her. How did she come to be in my yard? Who she was and where did she come from? Did she have any memory of anything, prior to being found in my backyard? Did she feel any pain anywhere? The questions were seemingly constant and we both felt overwhelmed by it all. I was hearing them as if I was right there beside her.

I see a policeman walk in and up to the desk. He was directed my way. I tensed up as he walk toward me.

"Mr. Wrent? I am officer Sarin. I would like to get your statement on the appearance of the girl." He tried to make me feel at ease. "How did you come to find her?"

I told my story, just as I had to the nurse. I said I had not seen her before and it was good that I found her when I did, as I don't usually go into that area, when everything was put away for the winter. I was just making sure, I had put it all away, when I saw her.

"You said you had fallen. What caused you to fall?" he asked.

I explained my disability to him in detail.

"You said your vertigo had started, when you nearly lost the sight in your right eye. I noticed you have some problem with your left eye."

I went into detail about the surgeries on my left eye this summer.

"How is the sight in your right eye now?"

"I just had that checked, and was given a clean bill of health, on that one." I beamed.

"So you have no trouble seeing to drive?" He looked kind of unsure looking at my dilated left eye.

"No." I answered. "I have no problem as long as I concentrate on my driving. I usually let my wife drive, when we are going into busy, or unfamiliar areas."

"Did your wife come with you today?"

"No, she stayed at home." I stated. "She doesn't like being here, when she doesn't feel she has to."

"Well, I am going to have to ask her a few questions." he warned. "I will have to come by your house, and look at the yard where you said you found her. Now I will go and get the girl's story and then we will see where we go from there."

I nodded and he stood and walked back to the desk, where he was directed to where Amy was being examined.

I made sure Amy would not tell him, word for word, what I had just said. The doctor had finished looking her over saying, "Well everything looks as it should." When the officer came in with a nurse, the doctor gave him the rundown on what he had found. She had only been seen in areas where there was concern. Amy was still dirty from laying on the lawn, so they felt they had a good impression, of how she was found.

"How did you come to be in the backyard, where you were found?" Officer Sarin said pointedly.

"I don't remember anything, before I woke up on the grass." she said. Which was true, as it was only then, that she came to be. "I saw Mr. Wrent getting up off the patio, where he had fallen, and he came to me when he saw me, and put his jacket over me and helped me to my feet."

"Had you seen Mr. Wrent fall?" he posed.

"No, he said he had noticed me, after he fell."

"What is your name?" He tried to catch her off guard.

"I don't know. I can't remember." Amy answered simply.

"Do you know where you are now?" he wanted to see how much she has retained since she came to.

"I am in the Children's Hospital."

"What city are you in?" he queried.

"I don't know." she looked at him straight in the eye.

"Okay miss, I will see what the doctors are thinking and we can get you taken care of, as soon as we can."

She watched him walk away and looked around the room. From where she was, she could see mostly, just curtains and a chair or two, some medical equipment on wheels. She asked me what that was, as she looked at it. I could see it, only through her eyes. I told her, that I though it was a machine to monitor IV lines.

The things she was seeing, were all new to her, but she could rely on my memory, more and more.

I asked her, if she could feel, what Marie was feeling. She told me she could, and she told me what she had been doing since we left. She could feel me relax a little, after hearing that. We are still in our separate areas and keeping each other company, just through our thoughts. It was still a lonely feeling, not being able to be next to her.

I told her funny things I would do, with my kids, when we were in waiting rooms. She recalled the memories, and laughed to herself. We suddenly realized, that this might be a problem, when they do an EEG, or a MRI test, or any other test, that would show brain, or nerve activity. We will have to be ready and careful, about stimulating the senses, when she is being tested.

The doctor and the policeman came back to me, to let me know what the next steps will be. Amy will stay in hospital for observation for a few days before being sent with CAS. I will be notified, if I was needed for anything. I had to leave my contact information and then I could go home. Officer Sarin was going to follow me home, and interview my wife. I tensed up at this, because Marie was not fond of getting surprise visits, even if they should be expected, and she did not like being questioned, especially when it involves something I might have orchestrated. Amy told me to relax, as it will not go on forever, and this too shall pass. I could feel it was God, talking through her, and I felt his touch on my soul. I was at peace at this.

I went out to get my van from the garage and meet Officer Sarin in the emergency entrance area. I had to wait for him to come out. When I saw him I waved and returning my wave, he went and got into his cruiser.

Amy sat, for a while, in the examination area until a nurse came to get her admitted. Then an orderly came over, to take her to the ward she was to call home, for the next few days. She felt alone, even though she was as close as a thought, from me and could see and feel every move Marie, and I took.

This is taking parenthood, a huge step beyond normal. Our kids were always in our thoughts, but Amy knew our thoughts, felt our anxiety and I felt hers. It was like being in two places at once, for me, but it was like being in three places at once, for Amy.

We knew what we were getting into and now, were aware of how it was going to be for us, for the rest of the time the two of us, were alive. If you think this was a crazy idea, welcome to the club.

Chapter Three

Scene search

I pull up in front of the house, and back into the driveway, as I usually do, and the cruiser pulls up to the curb. Officer Sarin steps out and walks up to meet me. We head to the side door.

Stepping inside, I take off my shoes and head up the stairs. Officer Sarin seeing the ladder asks if we are doing some renovating, as much to announce to Marie, that he was with me, as to get an idea, what had been going on, when this all started.

I told him about the paint peeling on the ceiling above him, and my son-in-law helping to fix things around here. I told him about the new floor in the kitchen, painting a picture of quiet domesticity.

"Was your son-in-law here, when the incident happened?"

"No. He has been doing other jobs and gets by here, once every week or so, when we need a hand. He works two regular jobs, as well as his repair and renovation jobs. He is quite busy." I laid out the picture of a life, to hectic to notice the goings on here.

"Sounds like a busy life. I guess he would be away from home a lot." he offered. "Does he have a chance, to have a family life at home?"

"Oh yes. His life is coordinated by cell phone, and he works fast. He is home, between the regular jobs, and for dinner. Then he gets a day to relax, here and there. They have CAS children to care for, and he gives blood, and platelets every month."

"He sounds like Superman." Sarin was impressed.

We went into the living room, where Marie was working on her crafts. She puts her work down and gets up, to greet the policeman, as I introduce him. He asks her about her project and she describes what she is working on.

"What were you doing when the girl was found?" he stepped into the job, for which he was here.

"I was doing my housework and I felt dizzy and went to lie down on the bed. I don't usually have that feeling, but it was so strong I just had to lie down, and the bed, was the closest place I could reach." she explained.

"Did you lose consciousness?" he asked with a concerned look.

"I don't know. I might have. I lay there, until my husband came in, with the girl." She did not want to get checked. She just wanted to stay home, and do her needle work.

"Do you think you should get it checked out. I could run you over to the hospital. They would check it out faster, if I brought you in." he offered, sincerely concerned.

"No, thank you. It might just be a cold coming on. I didn't have any other symptoms and I don't like running to the hospital, for every little thing." she pleaded. "I just want to relax. I will go, if it happens again, but I don't think it will."

"You said, the same thing happened to you, in the yard, around the same time. Didn't you, Mr. Wrent?" he plied.

"Yes, I did have the same thing, at the same time. Perhaps we had an earthquake. That causes feelings like that." I suggested.

"I didn't feel anything today, but I will check for reports about that. Has this happened to you before, Mrs. Wrent?"

"Not that I can remember. Not for a long time, in any case." she replied.

"Mr. Wrent said he has vertigo. Do you think that you have had anything like it? Light headedness, or the room swaying, or spinning?" he seemed to think there might be something deeper, going on, that could explain something to him. There are too many odd things happening at the same time, in the same place.

I had to hand it to him. He was alert to what was background, but could tie into the main point. He was searching for possibilities.

"I would like you to describe what happened, when Mr. Wrent brought the girl in." He had better get on with the statement, before he gets to far into the how, or whys.

"I heard him come in the door and he had someone with him. I heard him climbing the stairs, and I started to get up. He came to the doorway of the bedroom, which is the one, right at the top of the stairs. He must have heard me getting up, because he stepped right into the bedroom. He started to tell me about her as she stepped in, naked, except for his jacket. He went and got a blanket around her, and told her to have a seat in the kitchen. I asked him what was going on, and who she was, and where she came from without any clothes. He said, that he found her that way, in the backyard, lying on the grass. He said she couldn't tell him anything, because she had lost her memory of everything. She looked cold and wet and bewildered, so I told him to take her to the hospital. He said he was thinking of taking her to the police, but I thought she could get looked at, faster, at the hospital, while you were on the way there." She ended the story there.

"Why did you take her there, instead of calling 911?" he postured himself a bit.

"She was not suffering with any hurt. She seemed healthy physically. So we thought to take her there and get her looked at where she could be thoroughly examined." I explained. "911 was not something we needed to do, in this case. I think we might have got to this stage sooner, but that wasn't in our thoughts, at the time."

"I would like to look around, and see where this all took place. Can you take me to the backyard, where you said you found her?" I nodded, as he posed the question and headed toward the side door.

"I was just looking in the yard, to see if I forgot to put anything away, that might get damaged by the weather. I had been to the back there, in the corner, and came up to the pond here, and when I got to the patio, this is where I fell. It had been wet by a light drizzle. I felt dizzy, and I fell. I felt dazed, like I had passed out, but I wasn't sure if I had, as there was no change to let me know time had passed by me. That is when I saw her, laying on the ground, in the middle of the space there, between us and the pool. That was the only thing, that suggested I may have passed out."

"You said you went to the back corner there, first. Did you not see her then?" he looked puzzled.

"No. That confused me too. I had just passed that spot twice. I may have not been looking in that direction, and that is my blind side. But, I should have, at least, seen something as I passed by, sometime along there, but I did not see her. Either she got there, after I fell, or I walked right around her, without noticing. She was cold, but not very cold. I saw her there and saw she was naked and then I tried to get up, but it was painful on my knees. So, I got over to the grass, to try to get up there, and as I did, she was trying to help me, as I was trying to help her stand. I took off my jacket, when I was on my feet, and put it around her. It was long on her, because of her short frame, and it did well to hide her."

Sarin looked a little off, at my description, but was following along well enough. "I got her inside as quick as I could. Just so she would not be exposed to anyone looking in. I did not know if anyone else was in the yard, that might have caused her to be there like that, but I wasn't going to wait for them, to get further hold on her."

"Okay. Lets just stop here while I look around for any other sign of her coming into the yard." He walked slowly walked along the path I had taken. He looked carefully for any signs of footprints or a struggle. He saw where we had helped each other up. After confirming with me that that, was the spot, he walked slowly on. He walked around a couple of times, watching carefully as he went. He then asked, if I had my left eye open, or closed.

I said it was closed, for most of the time, so that I could keep my right eye focused, on what I was looking for in the yard.

He then walked around the yard slow, but a little faster than before. This time, he kept his left eye closed, and looked at the edges of the yard, as if looking for things that might need to be put away. He looked from side to side along his right just as I had done. After getting to the point where I said that I had fallen, he said that it was quite possible, that with my blind side to her, I might have walked around past her, without being aware of her laying on the grass. It was a slight chance, but still plausible, that that is what occurred.

I felt a little easier, as this gave her a larger window of time, for her to have a conceivable explanation, as to how she came to be there. Even though the amnesia took the need for the explanation from her, there is a plausible reasoning, to theorize her previous existence. Now things were not over by a long shot, there was a possible excuse, for me to find her, in the way I had.

The policeman spoke into his radio handset, mounted on his shoulder, and gave an indication that he was near the end of his initial investigation, in this location. He asked if there was any further information that he need to address, while he was still here. No, was the response. He advised them, he would finish up here, and call back for further instructions.

Officer Sarin thanked me for my cooperation, and said he will file his report and continue with the investigation. He was going to be our contact, until there is any change in the case, that would have it taken over, by another department.

He excused himself and returned to his cruiser. He sat in the car for several minutes writing out his report. I expect he would get it all down, while he could still get to us, to add any evidence he would need. That proved to be unnecessary, as he radioed in and then drove away.

I was inside watching as he drove away. I looked at Marie and said that, at least that part was over with.

Marie looked at me troubled. "Why did this have to happen? How has it happened? Are we going to have to have police questioning us all the time? Is this going to take control of our life?" She looked near tears.

"You remember what I told you, about my comment weeks before, as we sat on the porch. I had made the comment, that I wish I could have this happen and with the thought that God, would take flesh from us, and form another person, to be connected to me psychically, you had agreed, because we both were hard pressed to shed extra flesh. Now the thought that my prayers, with your offhanded agreement in the concept, would be agreeable to God, that He would bless us, with this experimental existence, is nearly unfathomable. But, you know, God does move in mysterious ways and you should always be careful what you ask for." I put my arms around her and said "This will be involving us for a little while, but we just found her, and there are many reasons that could have led to these circumstances. It will keep some people busy, investigating her, and that is a good thing, as people need the jobs. She told me, that she volunteered for the job. God had asked for someone, to volunteer, and that it would not have happened, if there were no souls wanting to accept these conditions."

"Who will take care of her now?" she was worried now.

"The system is there to take care of her. It doesn't matter where she goes from here. I will always be in her every thought, and she in mine." I didn't want to sound obsessive, or overprotective of her.

"So, you're going to let her just go?" She was accusing now. "You aren't going to take care of her, yourself?"

"No, that was not the intention. I am just supposed to suffer her pain, and feel every emotion she has, as well as the consequence, of any action she takes." I was lecturing her, to see what she has a mind to do. If she wants to have her in our lives, she is going to be the person, to make that statement outright.

"Well, I think we should have her with us. She is as much a part of us as any of our kids." She was ready to demand we take her in. "I think we should have her here, with us. I think we should tell the police, that we want to take care of her."

This is what I wanted to hear her say. I can make the request, or offer, to the CAS, when they take over her care. "Okay dear, I will tell them, that we would like to have her stay with us, until her parents are found. We have to let the system run it, and search for missing person reports, to have her parents identified and contacted." I laid it out, for her to see the progression that needs to be followed.

"Okay, lets do that then." She has settled that for a while and all is well.

Chapter Four

Diagnosis

Amy is sitting in her room at the Children's Hospital. She is bored a bit but is finding things to pass the time.

The doctors are baffled as to what caused her amnesia, but just as there are examples of different cases like hers, she doesn't have any symptoms, that would indicate a cause. There is one thing that could. Severe shock is likely the cause. She has no physical wounds, and no evidence of a nervous trauma. She is quite normal and stable, in her mind. She is, for all intents and purposes, a very normal young girl. She is not morose, not giddy, excitable, or fidgety. She remembers everything, that has transpired since she was found. One thing, so far, that makes her stand out, is that her ears have a definite point on them. That was found, when one doctor was searching for any head injury, that could have caused a loss of everything, that has happened in her life, up until when she was found on the grass. She could have witnessed a horrible crime and shut it out but, she has blocked out her entire life, except her motor functions. When the chief psychiatrist sees her, she may make sense to her, but that will be tomorrow.

A range of tests are ordered for her and that might have more information. These are repeat tests for some but new ones as well.

She has no sign that she is hiding anything. She has no alcohol or other substance in her blood. She is not acting depressed. The only thing that seems likely to cause her TGA (transient global amnesia) is emotional shock. There is no sign of stroke. She was found wet from the mist, but was not overly cold. Considering she was found nude, she could not have been in the cold water of the pool or fish pond that were in the yard where she was found. One thing is good about TGA is that it is usually a short term memory loss. She should show some improvement within a few days or weeks. Although the memory returns, some portion may be lost, but that is not likely to be a very large portion.

She can start recalling from my memory some general knowledge to be consistent with this type of amnesia. The only thing she can't recall, is family, and personal history. This will be unusual. Normally, there is some evidence of identification, but she had none. She did not even have clothing to help link her, to missing persons reports. The only thing they can use to identify her, is her picture. When there are any responses to claim her, they can be checked through DNA, except for cases of adoption. That, could be checked through adoption records and the claimants would have to show some evidence to support their claims. Pictures of her with family. Identification cards, or forms from schools, or medical examinations. Dental history and immunization records, will also help. Seeing that these, do not exist, they would have to be forged, if someone was trying to profit by gaining control of a young girl. She would be watched closely by the health officials after returning her to claiming parents, because of the recurring incidence possibilities. These would be things like, another memory loss, migraines, stroke, or epilepsy, to name a few.

This is an unfortunate situation, necessary, to establish any form of an identity. She will need to go through this and other forms, of historical examination. With her normal functioning levels, she may not be required, to live in a long term facility. She may be released to family, or foster care. This is where we have a chance, to gain custody of her, and eventually, adopt her.

Having her here with us, is the best scenario. She could assimilate into our family and social groups. She would be protected, but this is not going to be a sure thing. There are families already in place, to which she could be assigned. There is a shortage of foster families however, and that would work in our favour.

The examining doctor, to whom she was assigned, came in to tell her what has been progressing thus far. He explains the type of condition she has, and warns her of some things that might come from this. He informs her, of the promising aspects of her case and tells her to let him know anything that might return to her. It could be little things. Things that my not seem important, but may give clues, to other facts that can help put pieces together. He says it may take a while, but things will come around eventually.

She says that she would like to be called Amy, because Mr. Wrent called her that to help her know when he was talking to her. She said that that was because amie, was French for friend.

He put that on her chart, and said that, he thought, that would be a good thing to call her.

She smiled at him and said "At least I can hear a name that means something to me now."

The doctor told her about the further tests, that they have lined up for her, for tomorrow and the name of the doctor he will be consulting, and to whom the case would likely be given. He says that her patience might be tested, but that they can't rush her through this. He touched her hand, and saying goodbye, he walked from the room.

Chapter Five

Through Time and Space

Since we first met on the lawn, Amy and I have constantly been exchanging thoughts, thoughts of reassurance, thoughts of directives, memories and love. I had to let her know that, to me, she is my daughter and Marie was sending those thoughts as well. Marie could not hear Amy's thoughts, but she knew Amy could hear hers. We all knew, this is a blessing and a curse.

A curse, because we can't keep anything from Amy. Even to protect her from some fleeting ideas, that can flash through your mind. Ideas that can sting and wound a girl, who has taken on a role, that few have ever had, and fewer have ever wanted.

There are those to whom this gift was given but, it was normally that they heard the thoughts of others, not converse back and forth between them in thought. There, also, have been those, who could convey their thoughts back and forth through telepathy. Amy, however can do this and feel all the senses I feel. I also can feel all Amy's sense. Feelings of pain, joy, sadness, arousal, repugnance and every other feeling a person could possess.

The Corsican brothers come to mind, where one would cut himself and the other would bleed. They would seem invincible to those who would view them individually. In fact, however, when viewed together, their weakness was exposed and to kill one you would stab the other.

This is not true in our case. What one feels, they both feel. Marie's feelings are felt by neither Amy nor I. Amy would only know only Marie's thoughts. Marie is not connected psychokinetically to either of us.

It is a bit of a convoluted situation. The purpose of the whole idea was to show the differences and similarities to both Amy and I so that the comparison could comprehensively be established and revealed.

The conclusions found here would be challenged by many, but they would be set out for those to accept or reject just as people can accept or reject the very existence of God Himself. This is likely why God would make this happen. He knows and purposed the freedom of choice to teach those who would be taught and leave all others to remain in ignorance of these conditions. Just as they would choose.

One will only find truth, if one is open to believe it, when it is found. This is the same now, as it always has been, and always will be. This will remain, until the end of time, or until God, Himself, changes that.

Amy is thrilled now at the way the progress is being made. She has asked to be referred to by a name of her choosing and that was accepted. This has shown her that she has some level of influence and control of some aspects of her being. She sees now, that she has the freedom of choice, that was always supposed to be there, from God's creation of life. The one thing that man has fought against, since the beginning. Man has always tried to deny others their inherent right of choice.

I have brought my family along with exposure to my religion, so that they can know that choice, but that they will have that choice to make, for themselves, whenever it is their choice to make it. I have always tried, to pass this on in this way, because that is the spirit of God's law. If I was to tell them, to believe in my religion, I would be forcing my will on them. I would be attempting to enslave, my own children. For this reason, I came to God and chose Him and I have since that time been graced with His guidance.

We are now on a journey, that will be wondrous, if we are open, to it being so. From age to age, it is a gift to age. One that many are never given the chance to enjoy, by someone trying to direct their own version of life on others.

I have, for many years now, been at peace, with my own mortality. I have experienced so much, through faith, as well as through ignorance. There has been in me, an acceptance of death, a willingness to go on to another life. My purpose, though, has not been fulfilled and I continue on my path. I am ready to encourage others on theirs and walk with them, as I am asked to do. Now, though, I have someone linked to me, for better, or worse, from their beginning at an age far advanced from the normal birth. We are connected far closer to each other, than God had intended. The success and failure, has been already exposed, but the results will, still have to be realized, none-the-less. Just as Jesus' life, was laid forth long before his birth. He still had to follow the path laid out before Him.

All of us must live our lives, just as it ours to live, and our end will be the same, whether we choose to forgo it now, or continue on it's course. Look at the adventure that awaits us all. There are new places to go that are only for us to enjoy in our own way. There are people to know and love. Meetings to enjoy and partings to suffer, are only for us to have.

How many times have we asked for something, only to turn away when it is there for us to get.

Chapter Six

The Gauntlet

The day started with an under flavoured breakfast, but a bright sun peering in the window. There was no time to sit in the glow of the day as an orderly walked in with a wheelchair.

"I don't need a wheelchair. I can walk." Amy protested.

"The hospital does not want you walking until you have been cleared by the neurologist just in case you fall. We don't want a lawsuit on our hands, or an injured patient." he stated firmly.

"Where are you taking me now?" she queried, trying not to let her anxiety show.

"First we are going for an x-ray, then for an EEG. After that you have an MRI and then to see the psychiatrist for an evaluation. You have a busy day ahead." He smiled and said "Don't worry. None of this is going to hurt. You will only feel the chill of the room. Are you claustrophobic at all?"

"I don't know. I can't remember anything about myself." Amy looked a little nervous now.

"Oh, that's tough. Well we will try and make this as uneventful as possible." He tried to calm her. "What tests did they give you on the weekend?"

"They put we me on a table and the room was dark. This big machine was over my head. It clicked and made a whirring sound. Then they put me on my side and did it again."

"That was the x-ray. They want to take a couple more pictures of you with that. What else did they do?" he was getting her to relax by getting her busy with the conversation.

"They put me on another machine and slid the table part into a tube."

"That was the MRI. I don't know why they want to do that again." He was puzzled by that. "Were you scared at all by that?"

"No," she replied "that didn't scare me."

"Good," he said, happily, "then you don't have claustrophobia."

"Oh, I wasn't sure what that was." she wanted to sound naive. Young kids don't always know things like that and it helps her to play the part more convincingly.

"The fear of close spaces." he explained. "How old are you?"

"Twelve, I'm twelve. Hey, that's something I remember!" she squealed.

"Great!" he shared her triumph. "What grade are you in at school?" He thought he might get something else to come back to her.

"I don't remember that." she said, disappointed.

"Do you remember what school you go to?" he tried again.

"No," she sounded down, "I don't."

"Do you remember any faces that might be a friend or a relative?"

"I can picture faces but I'm not sure where they are from.

They could just be people I've seen here." she made herself sound a little confused. She has to delay progress somewhat, for they have areas which can't be explained and that has to be real. Once they can establish that she has no physical impairment causing her memory loss, then she can get on with being placed away from the hospital.

"Why don't you try to draw the faces so that you can concentrate on them? Maybe they will help you remember. Well here we are at your first stop of the day. I'll let them know you are here and then I will be back later to get you." he assured her.

She waited patiently for them to come and get her but, there were a few more serious cases ahead of her. It was an hour and a half before they came for her.

"Sorry to keep you waiting, Amy. We had some accident victims we had to get done first. Be glad when your tests are delayed. It means you woes aren't too serious. No matter how bad you feel, you can always find someone whose problems are worse. If that holds true, you will be alright." She hoped to set her at ease. "My name is Cynthia. I will be doing first tests for you and then Doug will come and take you to your next appointment."

"The first thing we will do is get those x-rays. They want a couple more at different angles, just so they don't miss anything. Now you can get up on the table and on your right side. Now lean toward the edge of the table, just a bit."

The x-rays were like that. Oblique angles and this way and that way. She took several and said "This is a good thing. It means they don't see a problem and have to search more carefully. They will keep going until they find the cause or rule out all the possibilities. Be glad when they rule out things. They have to be more thorough and get more accomplished."

The next test she went for was the EEG. All these wires, a lot of things she recalled from my memories were the same but some were different. She didn't feel the pain she recalled from my first EEG. They did not rub the spots for wire placement, quite as hard. Every step was explained to her as they proceeded. She did have some fun during all this since there was so much attention on her.

Soon she was on her way again. She had no sense of time and I didn't bother to look so she could wait until they passed a clock. Doug was taking her over to the other side of the building. The psychiatrist's office was decorated like a den more than an office. It seemed relaxing and warm.

The doctor grilled her on the story and the missing memories and after what seemed to be an eternity, Doug came back to get her.

"There is an opening in the schedule for another test." he told her. "This one is called an angiogram. They didn't think they could fit any more in but, they have had some cancellations. This one they inject a dye in your arm and scan you to show if there is any bleeding inside. It won't be too hard on you. It will just feel like a slight bee sting and it will be over before you know it."

"I don't remember what a bee sting would feel like." Amy shuddered at the thought of what it might feel like.

"You'll be okay." Doug did not want her thinking about it more since there was no other thing he could think of to liken it to and that didn't matter much now. "You are my last fare today so I'll stick around and get you back to your room."

"That's great, Doug. I'm getting tired and very hungry. I

haven't had anything to eat ever since you picked me up this morning."

"That's too bad, but that will make the food here taste better. Won't it?" he laughed to ease the mood.

"Well yes, I guess it will." Her stomach growled and made her laugh too.

Doug pulled into her room and helped her out of the chair. Bowed and kissed her hand, at which she curtsied. They both giggled and off he went.

It took another thirty minutes before her dinner arrived. She was so glad to see it. It was a bit confusing for her to be hungry, while feeling how I felt after my meal, an hour before. I was feeling the strange sensation as much as she was. It was like getting the munchies real bad after having a huge salad while on a diet course. Your stomach can't hold another bite, but your craving pizza, because the taste buds didn't find anything in your meal. I've had it before but not to this degree.

After she ate, she felt drained. The sun had set before her meal came. So, she laid back put the blanket over her and watched the lights of the traffic on the escarpment. I felt her slipping off to sleep.

I have a lot of trouble getting to sleep at night, and this time I was feeling her energize, at the same time I was working to get tired enough to sleep. It was a losing battle. I was still awake when my wife got up in the morning at eight. This is like being back on shift work.

Amy awoke around the same time. The ward was bustling with meals and meds being shuffled and sorted. With me being up all night, she really didn't feel rested. This is a real catch-22 situation. How are we going to get this straight? She feels my energy low and I hers. I start to bob my head after just an hour and climb into bed. Hope my sleep will help her feel better, but I dread the night coming.

Amy was picked up for an appointment with the neurologist. Her driver this time, was a volunteer. He spoke a bit but, not like Doug had, just basic pleasantries. The trip seemed to last forever. This one must have something bothering him.

Once at the doctor's waiting room, she was announced by her volunteer and left in the middle of the room. She wheeled herself over to a table with some magazines. She selected one and leafed through it. She felt me resting and it was affecting her, giving her a refreshed feeling. She was young and did not need much sleep, but now her sensing me sleeping, gave her that feeling she missed when she first awoke.

She heard her name called and was about to set the magazine down, when the woman calling her said she should bring it with her if she would like to finish it. So she was pushed down the hall around a corner and into a small room.

"The doctor will be with you shortly." the woman said and left the room.

About ten minutes passed before the doctor did get there. He had her chart and looking at her briefly, introduced himself and went back to reading her chart. "There is some good things we have found out from the tests we ran. We could not find anything that would cause your memory loss. Nothing physical anyway. We will repeat some of the tests in a couple of days."

He had her do the sobriety walk to check her balance. Looked at her eyes and ears. He then had her stick her tongue out and uttered a "hmmm." Asked if she felt any numbness, saw flashing lights, or if she had any trouble speaking, or walking when she first stood up, the day she was found.

With no response to all those examples, he repeated his interjection. "Hmmmmm." Finally, he spoke "I'll send you back for now and I'll see you again in a few days after we've done those tests again.

"How long will I be staying in the hospital?" You can't get an answer unless you ask the questions, she thought.

"We won't know for a few days. My guess is at least two to three weeks."

This was not what she wanted to hear. She knows it is necessary, but she really would like to get out of there.

She wasn't picked up for an hour and a half. When she returned to her room, her lunch was there waiting. It did taste good this time.

Chapter Seven

A Visit

Marie and I had been going about our usual routine. Although I knew Amy's thoughts and followed her progress the whole way, I felt I had to see her and Marie felt the same. She was, after all, our daughter, though not publicly. So after we had our breakfast, we headed down to the hospital. Traffic was light. A good start to the day. We parked and walked over to the elevator. We had to stop at the lobby to get directions to her room.

"Are you her parents?" the receptionist looked on her screen.

"No," we tried to get the right thing to say, while she kept her eyes on her computer. "we are the people that found her. We wanted to see how she was doing."

She told us the floor and instructed to go to the nurses station. We got to the ward and got our directions. We have to report back, after our visit in case she revealed anything she might remember. They are hoping to get her reactions from any connection outside the hospital. Sometimes seeing people can trigger memories to return. We got the rules and were shown to the room. Amy was sitting looking out the window. She knew we were there but did not give that away. We greeted her and sat down next to her bed.

"We brought you some clothes we thought you might like. Since we knew what you had, we didn't have any restrictions, and who knows where they are going to send you from here. We would like to offer to be your foster home." We spoke loud enough for others to hear. "There is a beautiful room all ready for you. Although, it is small."

"Thank you so much! I would love to stay with you, if it was possible." We had rehearsed the exchange in our minds, and it came out rather well. "I am going to be here another two or three weeks, the neurologist says. I am glad to have some clothes. Thank you."

"Maybe they might let you leave earlier, if they knew you had a place to go." I hoped that someone were able to hear the conversation. I always thought that was rather hokie, when they did that on TV, but here I am, doing the same thing. We talked leisurely for a while so Marie could get Amy's thoughts, since she is the only one of us who could not hear the thoughts of the others.

Amy knew what Marie wanted to hear, and so she could keep up, without any waste of time searching her own thoughts about the subject. It appeared that we were long time friends, but only going through the brief history we wanted to portray. Anyone could see we were quite at ease with one another.

"There was an announcement on TV about you. They were asking for anyone with information about you, to call the police here, or in their area, with details and any identifying marks, that they could prove the connection with." Marie said "They showed your picture and it stated amnesia victim on the screen. I heard it on the radio too."

"I wonder who would come forward. I am starting to remember things, that I tell them about and they are optimistic about a full recovery!" she said adding to me in thought, that she is careful to give general knowledge and obscure views of things she might have seen someplace.

It will be interesting to see who does come forward, with the false claims. I thought to Amy that they have only seen her ears and not her missing navel. We silently chuckled about that. Most people will be thinking of birthmarks and tattoos.

We have a chat for a while longer. Then we say good-bye and head to the nurses station, to give them a report on what went on in the conversation. We mention our willingness to be her foster parents, until her real parents are located. They say they will put that in her file. Having done our duty to the staff, we go down the elevator to the parking level.

When we get home, we call Officer Sarin and tell him about our visit and that we offered to take Amy in until her folks are found. He said the CAS will be called in when the doctors are ready to release her. He gave us the contact number and suggested we phone right away to get clearance from them.

After we were done with Sarin, we called our eldest to tell her all about what went on and asked her to mention it to her case worker. We hadn't told the kids about our finding Amy before we cleared it with the police. Now that they have put out the notice on TV and radio we could talk to them about it.

"I saw that on the morning show! She was in your yard naked?!" Grace was astounded at the story.

"We don't want that known to anyone outside the family. It

could affect the results of the police investigation." We had to get her understanding the importance of this secrecy.

"Yes, she was lying on the grass in early November. She was cold but not very."

"How have you kept this in this long?!" Grace was a little unnerved by this. "Did they tell you that you couldn't talk about it?"

"They didn't say outright that we could not tell anyone. But, we didn't want it spread far and wide in case we woke up to find news crews at the door. There are things about her that should not get out and that part about her being found nude is one important factor. There are others that the police will use to screen the people calling in to claim her."

"What did you think when dad brought her in dressed like that?" she asked her mother. "Was it a shock?"

"I couldn't believe what I was seeing! She was a small girl. Short enough so that dad's jacket came well down on her thighs." Marie retold the story right through.

"Have you told Faith?"

Marie grunted in answer. "I had to tell you so we could get things going with the CAS. We will call her next and then we better call Nicholas. We have more to tell. A lot more but, we have to wait until things get sorted out."

"Well, okay, I'll call my worker tomorrow. It should be simple enough, since you were cleared before. I'll see what you need to do and then I will call you. Are you sure you want to be her foster parents?"

We both said "Yes." at the same time. "When you get all the details you will know why."

This is quite exciting and exhausting. With emotions and

dealing with authorities, it is draining my energy. I have to go lay down and nap. Marie, on the other hand gets so she can't sleep, or relax. Her mind is racing. She hates taking pills to get to sleep and only does that as a last resort. There is no way around it. Amy needs an identity. She needs to go to school and get health care. So, we are trapped in this circus. So far, there hasn't been any news people coming around. They will though. It is just a matter of time before they find out where she was found.

When I wake up from my nap, Marie is laying beside me. She's not sleeping but she is tired and looking it.

"Have you talked to anyone while I was asleep?"

"No. I didn't know who I should talk to and what I shouldn't say." She looked like she was frustrated with the whole secrecy thing.

"The only things we cannot say is that she was naked when I found her, and the things that could positively identify her, the pointed ears and the missing navel. All the other things we can talk about to friends and relatives we trust."

"Well, I don't feel right telling people about it." She was tired and she needed some down time.

"Just relax and I'll warm up some milk with a bit of Bailey's in it. Then you can rest." That is something she uses when sleep isn't coming and she can't go on. I made her the drink and she half dozed for a while. While she rested I called Faith and told her the story. I told her all about the hospital visits. Faith is no stranger to those. It surprises me that she doesn't have her own parking space next to the emergency. She and her kids, as well as their father have plenty of time in the local hospitals and a few outlying ones too.

After talking to her I had a drink to ease my anxiety before I called my son. I talk very easily with my daughters, my one son-in-law, and it puzzles me why it is so hard to talk with Nicholas. I know I am more relaxed talking to women, or to strangers, but with him it is too tense. I had that with my dad, now that I think of it. Is it that I don't want to let them down or feel judged overly by them? My dad was an easy-going guy and so is Nick. What is it about them? I have had trouble speaking to others but that doesn't worry me as much as my relationship with my son. I am the diplomat of the family. I diffuse situations at work and with my own family. I don't get it.

I called Nick and told him about it.

"You've got to be careful, Dad." he said. "She could be just using you."

"Do you believe in miracles, Nick?"

"No, Dad, I don't." he was short with me. "What has that got to do with it?"

"Just keep that in mind for future reference. There will be a time when I can reveal more to you and the girls and then you can consider your stance on that."

"What is that supposed to mean, Dad?" he was laughed his incredulous laugh. The one he often uses when he thinks I'm being ridiculous.

"Just keep that in mind for now." I said. It bothers me when he does that. Marie sometimes is like that with me.

"Well, I gotta go, Dad. I've got work to do." It is the way he ends most calls. It is that, or someone needs him. It is why we don't talk often. What can you do?

I need a drink again. It takes one to get me able to talk to him and one to recover from talking to him. I can go months without wanting a drink or having one with company. But, with him, I NEED two. It is either that, or a tranquilizer.

Chapter Eight

The Inspection

Grace had called her case worker at the CAS. There is a shortage of homes for children and a shortage of case workers, also. Arrangements were made for an inspection of the house and Marie and I. We busied ourselves straightening up the mess I have in the basement. Marie is glad it is finally getting cleaned. I need to get help to finish the shower drain in the basement bath. It will have to do until there is more definite resources to do the job.

We had to get a police background check done. That was easy. Marie needs that every two years or so, for her job. It is something we are glad to have done. There have been too many incidents, where a crime has been committed by somebody, that should have been excluded from the situation, long before the event occurred.

We have everything ready, for when the worker gets there. We see the car pull up and we check the time. Very punctual. As she comes up the drive, I get an anxiety attack. I can't have a drink so I take one of my Atavan tablets. I sit in my chair in the living room while Marie answers the door. She's not happy to be the one to greet the woman, but she knows how I get, when I sit that hard in my chair. The guys I worked with, knew what to do and even when, it was starting and would help me to a seat close by. Marie is not that intuitive. She still works and doesn't see it happen so often.

She brings her into the room. I try to stand but it is too soon. I fall back in the chair and that wasn't a good impression. The two ladies talk about the process and the regulations. Marie ensures her that I am not like this all the time, but that it comes and goes. I wouldn't require the child to assist me. They get up and Marie shows her the room, where the foster child will be sleeping. They go over the room thoroughly and then the bathroom and finally, they return to me. I stand this time and steady myself on the TV cabinet. She sits and goes over the report. She gives us a list of things we need to change, and what we should expect from this point on. We agree to make the necessary adjustments and she gets up to leave. We are both ready to collapse in the chairs as she walks down the drive to her car.

We need to make more room in her bedroom, for the chair and desk she will require for her homework and studying. All medications must be stored in our room away from where she would have access. They must be in secure containers. All this is done within a few hours after the CAS worker had left. They will come back for a final inspection before the girl is brought to us. We know this is what happens with all foster homes and are confident there won't be any complications to come forward.

We also know, that if we were to want to adopt Amy, it will take years for the court to decide on that. All avenues must be taken to find the child's biological parents. Until then, we will have some support for taking care of her, and she will get a temporary identification card and a health card. She will be enrolled in school at the level appropriate to her age, and after an assessment period, she will be advanced, or put back, to the level she is suited for, according to her results. After learning that, I was nervous she might not have that good a time, or miss high school altogether.

She can expect the trial of her life, to be going to university as a preteen. Amy has, after all, my total knowledge and that of Marie as well. She has excellent recall and at about 200, an IQ which is higher than mine. She could take it slow purposely but, that could harm her by distracting her and she would be bored with the programs she already knows inside and out. The things we are thinking, from such a little bit of stimulus is scary. Amy and I are doing it in silence, and Marie and I out loud.

"I can't do this." Marie spits out suddenly. "I have to stop."

That leaves it to Amy and me. That is fine with us, because that is what we do. Marie doesn't like talking much to me. Amy and I get along very well, discussing things at length telepathically.

She throws me off a bit, thinking about someone walking by her room. She is attracted to them and it caught me off guard because I did not see the person. That is amazing to me. I thought I would see everything. That is not the case. It was so fleetingly quick that I could not even perceive it. I have a recall handicap and apparently, that gives her just a little bit of privacy. If she would picture the person in her mind, I would be able to see them. But, Amy is having fun with me and not picturing them at all. She is so thoroughly and completely enjoying this, that she starts to laugh out loud in her hospital room. A nurse looks in the doorway, to see what is causing her laughter. Amy puts her hand across her mouth and the nurse steps in. She sits down by Amy and urges her to reveal the humourous secret. Amy can't help but snicker through her fingers so, that she could have sprayed the nurse. She can hardly reveal it, without jeopardizing our situation and the connection we share.

"I saw something go by so quick, I couldn't see what it was, and it surprised me, and made me laugh"

"Good girl, Amy." I said aloud, but soft enough that Marie could not here. "Quick thinking."

There is something that I totally missed, but it will be good for her, to have something to keep from me. Eventually, I will see her thoughts about this person and the image of them. I was quick enough to feel the attraction and it was a physical feeling.

It dawns on me, that she really could go to live with someone else, and still keep me informed, but I don't want that. It scares me. I really need her, to come and live with us, and I feel that I don't have any control over her future, and neither does she. I feel sick at my stomach. Amy feels it also.

The nurse sees Amy's expression. "Are you alright, Amy?"

"I just realized that I don't have any control over my future. That scares me."

The nurse puts her hand on Amy's shoulder and says "They won't do anything without asking for your concerns. The court will consider your feelings, about any situation, before they make any judgments, on what is to happen to you. That is the law that keeps you safe."

We both relax slightly, but we both still have that helpless feeling. How can we accept anything contrary to our own plans? What if my health problems give the CAS, or the court, any reason to keep her someplace we don't want? I have the most problems while I am around authority, or determined people that stand against me, intimidate me, or unwittingly threaten me. They could rule against me, and there, I have no say. Amy has a say and through her I have a say, but that is still only one voice.

I have to get this fear out of my mind. I have faced all my other fears head on. This one, though, is long away yet and too far to face. We have to get our thoughts on something else. Amy relents and pictures in her mind the person she saw. "So, now you tell me." I think to her. Well, I was afraid that might happen. Are you being influenced by someone else's desires, or is this of your own mindset?"

Amy assures me, it is her own feelings. "I don't know what these feelings mean. Are they bad feelings?"

"No Amy. They are not bad feelings. You must never believe that those feelings are bad. The actions you take because of those feelings, could be good, or bad. Don't think yourself to be anything less, for having those feelings. They are natural to you. Others may not agree, but we live our lives and not theirs. You may not always feel that way and I hope never to influence your feelings, one way, or another. You are just starting your life and you need to get used to those desires and what they mean to you. Don't rush it."

Chapter Nine

The Circus

We hoped there would be a long quiet time, to adjust to the newest chapter in our lives, but that was not the case, and it was cut short today. The morning paper is just outside our door on the porch. We must step out onto the porch to get it from behind the door. When Marie steps out to get it, news trucks are just arriving. She grabs the paper and jumps back inside. Closing and locking the front door, she runs to the bedroom and wakes me with an urgent shake. I don't sleep well and am usually up around eleven. Marie is used to an earlier eight o'clock rising. "The news people are here." she nearly barks at me.

"Just wait here while I get up. If they can't understand the sign on the door, they are not good people to talk to. I'll give them a note to make them feel a little sympathy. If they can't come back later to talk, then when you are ready to leave, I will go out and lead them away from the house and then you can get out quick."

We hear the knock at the door of the house next to us. The neighbour comes out and has no clue as to what they want. They are grilling her about Amy. She says, "I don't know no Amy. You got the wrong house." She goes back in and closes the door. That isn't like her. She usually would want to know the story from them. A minute later her husband comes out and confirms his wife's statement. This time they followed the news crews out to the street. Now that is more like them.

The crews come around to our door. By this time, I have written a letter, which I hand to them and close the door. The letter reads, "I am ill and will not be able to answer your questions, for another three to four hours. I will be glad to give you a statement then, but not before. Please do not bother the neighbours, as there are some with serious health issues, that you could worsen if you persist. Please come back later, when I have had time to stabilize myself. Thank you."

"It worked. I don't believe it they are going back to their vehicles." I call to Marie.

We ate our breakfast in peace. After that, Marie got ready to go off to work. She took the opportunity to get away. "I'm going shopping and then I'll stop in and visit Mom." Her mother is in a care centre suffering from dementia. She can't remember visits, but the girls still go and take care of things that need to be done and take her out for coffee just to give her some different surroundings and fresh air. Then Marie will go to work and hopefully the reporters will have their story and will leave us alone.

I relax at the computer and play a few different games, to get my mind working and sharpen my focus. I clear up my inbox, check some of the items I need to get clear on, and then get some tea. The news people should be coming back soon, so I get dressed and take my meds for the morning. By this time, I am usually getting out of bed, but today I am almost ready to go back. I see the reporters arriving and decide to get this over with. I greet them at the front door.

"Mr. Wrent, you are the one who found the girl. Is that right?"

"Yes, it is. She was in the back yard."

"Was she unconscious when you found her?"

"No, she was just coming to when I noticed her."

"What was she doing in your back yard? Did she say? And how did she get there?" They were firing questions faster than I could possibly respond.

I hold up my hands to get them to slow down. "She did not know why she was there, or how she got there. She didn't even know where, or who she was. She has amnesia."

"What was she wearing?"

"Is this for fashion news?" I joked.

"We heard that she was naked when you found her. Is this true?" They weren't amused by my humour.

"She was, yes. I didn't see any clothes around and we could not find any in the area." This was all the details I was going to give them. I had to sit down. My reserve was just about shot. "That is all the details I can give for now. I need to rest. Goodbye." I stepped back and closed the door. I knew they weren't going to accept that, but I couldn't go on anymore. I sat down to rest and fell back in the chair. I can only take so much. I was completely drained, but my mind was still racing with the speed they were firing the questions at me. I hate it when I am left like this. I can't relax, or recharge, when my mind is going a mile a minute.

I know they are going to bug the neighbours, even though I

asked them not to. The good thing is that they were not home when it happened. All the neighbours were away. The place was deserted. It was a Saturday afternoon, at the beginning of November. There were several people, from all over, digging for the story. The details that can protect Amy, are the ones these people are trying to get out in their news shows and papers. That they would let me close the door on them, surprised me. I was expecting them to push me right into the house, but they just let me go. I certainly was appreciating that. I guess Canadian news reporters are like the rest of us, a little more polite, a little more patient. At least, they appear to be today. They may not be so kind the next time. You see them on the news going after politicians and people accused of wrong doings, and they are nearly trampling each other as well as their prey. If we are to get through this, we need to keep those details quiet and out of the newsman's hands.

Amy sighs and I know what she was thinking and feeling when I started to calm down. When it was all happening, I completely forgot our connection. I did not feel her feeling the stress with me. Yet, she was. She was right there with me, the whole time. She even lost track of what was going on around her. It was as if she was deep in thought, as if she was daydreaming. I know that I believe God is with me like that, and so much so, you can't feel Him, but He is holding you up, through those harshest times. I can feel it has tired Amy as well, but not to the extent that she has collapsed like I have. She does sit back on her bed to relax. Up until now, she had been sitting on the edge of her bed, leaning forward, as if she was watching it all through a window, or on a monitor.

Just as she settles back, she realizes there is someone watching her. She looks up at them. "Are you with us now? You haven't heard us at all, it seems. You have an appointment. So, when you are ready, we can go."

This could be a big drawback to our connection. Can we function and concentrate on what is happening to ourselves, as well as feel what is happening to the other? We are going to have to work on that. This could be as bad as talking on a cell phone, while driving. It is possible, but not practical, or safe. In some things, it is okay. In others, we could get so caught up in the others affairs, that we forget our own.

I feel a spasm. Amy is having cramps in her abdomen. Her period. It is something like a mild IBS (irritable bowel syndrome) pain. I have heard they can get severe and some feel them more in their back. This is her first. It is comparable but not even much more than the pain I feel everyday. I can see that it would be bad for somebody that doesn't have constant pain in their life. I suggest Amy should tell the nurse about it, to get supplies for her. I imagine there will be similar situations where the feminine pains will compare with those that men feel, yet not as regular. Although men don't have pains like this which are exclusive to their sex. There are things that do compare.

The news people are finished bothering the neighbours all around us, and are starting to leave. It is good to get the stories out, to find the people concerned with the stories, but this particular tale has no other persons connected with it. However, we can't let that be known.

What would happen if we told the actual, real story. In this day and age, it would be the same as the middle ages. It would be a witch hunt. Church groups would not believe God would be a part of such a thing. It would be deemed blasphemy, heresy.

Scientists would want to study her and dissect her. She would not be viewed as human, and her life would be in danger every day. She would be hounded, or even locked up. We feel we are enlightened, intelligent beings, but we would kill things, that are not as we are. The fact that she has no naval shows that she was not born of man. Her ears are pointed to give her a supernatural aura about her. Those two differences are enough for some, to hunt her down. They can be an evil omen to some and a blessed sign to others. They helped me to recognize that she was the one for which I had prayed. The acceptance by God, Himself, to the experiment I had devised, to know just what difference there is, between pain felt by women and by men. Are we really that enlightened? I have serious doubts about that.

I get up and go next door to my neighbour and closest friend to apologize for the press. They were away when I found her and would not have any idea what they were being asked about. If they had seen it on the news, they would not have placed it in my yard. I should have told them about it when they got home, but he was so sick, I was afraid to get that close that I might give him a cold or anything else. He has leukemia and after his chemotherapy, he has no immune system.

Reporters, telemarketers and poll takers never think about the suffering people, on the other end of that phone line, or the other side of that door. Many of us that are in vulnerable situations, don't want to give up our homes, and try to enjoy them as we always have. Now we fall prey to the canvassers, sales people, con artists and others that think nothing of taking the life savings of the defenceless.

I confide in my friends next door because I had discussed the premise with them earlier that year. I tell them how it all came about. I tell them of the hurdles she is facing. The realization of the dream and prayer. I know them and trust them with things of such importance. They are deeply affected by the news. It is almost to a point beyond belief. They will share our secret and not divulge any part of it. I hope that does not weigh heavy on them, as they travel their own obstacle course.

I just get back inside as the reporters are returning yet again. I am not ready. I grab a glass and pour a drink. Marie was safely away, so I can handle this my way, without worrying about her having objections to what I say. We care to offer the truth in everything we do, but sometimes, I was taught, the truth and total accuracy, is not the path to take. We want to be fair with those with whom we deal. That is not happening here. There will come a time when this news will get out, and be told accurately, but that is not this time.

I go to the door and let them in. I herd them into the living room and sit them across from me. Their questions are answered, with the story we have agreed upon. I give them some things here, and there, that will quell their desire for more. The more simple you are, the less you can get wrong. This could go so wrong for us, if there were any eye witnesses. There are none to be found.

I feel Amy's sighing, as the news teams leave the house. This was intense for her. While she was paying close attention to what was going down in our living room, she seemed very distant and unable to answer the queries pointed at her. This will keep them guessing, as to what is truly, wrong with her.

The feelings I had been experiencing, were separating me from her thoughts, just as she was intent on listening to me. Is this experiment to succeed, or is it to endanger us over the minute details, so hidden from us? To share in this way, in touch with every little aspect of each other's existence, will overload our processers. We have, they say, a mind so intricate and powerful that our computers cannot come near us. I have, however, felt much like my computer, with a slow internet connection, syntax errors, and even hard drive crashes. How can I hope to isolate the opposing information. Having her feelings in one sector of the brain, and my own in another. Still yet another problem is stemming from the retrieval of all the stored memories, by both Amy and myself. Think of your own memory recalls. How many times have you been unable to recall an idea, and your mind goes blank? This is routine for me, but I hoped to not share this trait with her. It is the fibro-fog, a phenomenon associated with fibromyalgia. What other problems, everyday occurrences for me, will affect her?

When I was looking for a wife, I had certain criteria she needed to have, to correct flaws in my genetics. I had no thought, then, that this disease was hereditary. I did luck out there though, because my wife did not have that in her biological family. That is to say, the people in her family that suffered this ailment, had married into the family. In my hunt for a mate I had got derailed in my train of thought, and did not fully inquire about hereditary traits. I had a general idea of her genes, being right for the part but, hormones were throwing me off the track.

The hospital was keeping the press out and protecting Amy from them. How long that will be? I don't know. For now though, she is left to follow the doctors' orders.

Chapter Ten

Legalities

Thus far, we have known about the generalities of fostering and adoption. Now we have to get all the details ready to go forward. As I have mentioned before, my daughter is a foster parent and she has gone though the adoption process too. We have all the paperwork ready and we are waiting for our meeting with the CAS representative. Grace has come over to help us prepare. The case worker is to come soon and the nerves are on end. We are just concerned about the physical condition of our house. She is not a baby, but she has to have a room of her own. She needs a space conducive to studying and homework. All this we have prepared. I bought the things needed years ago, for a guest room. Everything is in new condition. The house has been thoroughly cleaned up, to Marie's delight. The project in the basement is orderly and neat. My office is also spruced up. Even the garage has had a fuss made for it's condition.

It is just after Christmas and the place is covered with snow. A spot has been cleared for the arrival and a spare space as well. This is the second inspection and it has to be good. I am confident that all is well now. I still am on edge anyway.

Grace sees the car pull up and recognizes the driver. She has dealt with her before and says she is easy to get along with and will help us through the hurdles all the way. Much of the funding has been pulled from them and it means an overload of the system. We should be alright though. We went for training. This should be the go ahead moment.

When the door was opened and our guest entered, I felt anxious again and quickly sat down. Grace and Marie ushered the woman in and we all sat in the living room. We handed over the final batch of paperwork. She looked it over and said it was all good. We then got up to do the inspection of the areas of concern. When she told us to relax now and that everything was just as it should be, I thought that I would pass out. Sometimes the relief can be worse than when the pressure is on.

We signed all the papers now and it will be up to the doctors as to when Amy will move in. Our rep told us that there will be some financial help while she is with us, to cover necessities for her. That will make it easier. It will make Amy feel good to know that we won't have any hardship in having her here.

The case worker congratulated us in completing the arrangements and thanked us for taking Amy in. She said good-bye and walked out to her car. Grace got ready to go. She needed to get back home, so now, we were alone with our thoughts. We looked at each other and hugged for a while. It was all done. The rest should be easy now.

I felt Amy's response and heard her thoughts as well. I relayed them to Marie. She looked at me strangely. She still had trouble realizing the concept we were facing. The fact that Amy could communicate with me from so far away, without a phone, or the internet. It confounded her. She stood back and looked into my eyes. I had not changed but that idea didn't help her to come to grips with it.

I told her that she could send a message to Amy as well, through the same process. She could not get the response that way. I told her that it is better that way because it was very difficult to function and concentrate on what she would be doing. Until I get used to it, myself, I would not be driving unless it was crucial that I do.

"It is that bad?" she asked. "How will you get around then?"

"I will be cycling where ever I need to go, and if I had to drive, Amy would concentrate on what I am doing and be helpful in focusing my thoughts."

"How is Amy doing now?"

"She is doing well. She is waiting for the doctor. She wants to talk about being discharged. The nurses said she would probably be getting out soon, because they need the bed for other patients. Sometimes I wish they would not say that because then you are waiting anxiously for the doctor and if you aren't released, it really makes you feel bad." I was wrapped up in the feeling Amy was now, and I remembered my stays in hospital. They always do that and it makes everybody feel the same way. They are either anxious to go, or anxious to have to leave. "They will be letting her go soon though." I said emphatically.

"They are giving her temporary identification papers and health card through the CAS." I added. "That is what I was hoping for. I think she will get permanent ones through the court, when she is not claimed."

"We will have to get her in to see our doctor to have her added to her roster, I think." Marie said, thoughtfully.

"The specialists she was seeing at the hospital will still be involved with everything she needs looking at, but I think you're right. We will need her added to our benefits through work too." I am getting anxious to have her home now. "I am having antsy feelings for her. I can't wait to get her home. It will be so much easier to become adjusted to our thought exchanging, when she is here with me."

"What do you mean? You can hear her from anywhere. Can't you?"

"Yes, but here we won't have different worlds to overcome. We will just have here and we can get a more intimate thought connection and fine tune it, with less input at the same time."

The doctor just walked into Amy's room. "Good news! You are going to be released today. I have signed the orders and the CAS will be picking you up and taking you to your new foster home. I will see you back here in a month. You will get a form in the mail. If, however you need to see me, you can call my office and we will get you in as soon as possible. Okay?"

Amy shook her head. "I will see you in a month then."

"You seem to be much older than your years. Let us know if you have any problems whatsoever." The doctor walks out.

Now Amy is getting excited. She can finally get on with the purpose of her existence. Nobody else knows just what their purpose in life is, but Amy came with the knowledge of just why she was here. She is, quite simply, here to help me experience the pain of being a woman. I had no intention of getting a sex change because that would not reliably have the real results we are looking for. Only this psychokinetic connection will enable me to feel the real experience through Amy. Plus, I am not so inquisitive to go to that extent. I am fine just as I am.

Chapter Eleven

Coming Home

Amy was sitting on her bed, dressed and waiting. She was not going to hold this procedure up, as far as she could affect it. When the nurse and a volunteer came into the room with a wheelchair, she sprang to her feet.

"Whoa, don't go making such sudden moves like that." the nurse admonished her. "You don't want get dizzy and fall, now. Just when you are getting set to leave us. That would be a horrible thing to do. We are giving you a ride to the main doors where your driver will be waiting. Make sure you have all your belongings. Don't leave anything behind. Have you got everything?"

Amy nodded her reply.

"Okay then, we will get you to sit in the chair and Philip here will escort you downstairs. Good luck, Amy. I hope we don't have to have you as a patient for a long time." She turned and left the room after handing some papers to Philip.

"Alright Amy. Have a seat and we will be on our way." Philip directed her.

Amy put her feet up on the footrests and leaned back to enjoy the ride. As she was wheeled through the ward, she waved good-bye to all the nurses and other patients she knew. Down the hall and into the elevator, she was whisked. Then out of the elevator and down to the front desk. A woman was there showing her identification and she turned to be introduced to Amy.

"I will be driving you to your new home. They will be expecting you and you will get to meet your foster parents." the driver stated.

"I already met them. They were the people that found me and brought me in here."

"Well then, this won't be hard at all, will it?" she said as she pushed the wheelchair out to her car which was parked right outside the doors. "Are you okay to get into the car, or do you need help."

"No, I'm okay. I can manage." Amy got into the car and waited for the driver to take the chair back inside. When she returned and got in the other door, she said "Have you got you got your seatbelt done up?"

Amy looked at her, then she recalled my strapping her in when I brought her down. "Oh yes." She reached around for the belt and bringing it over snapped it into the receptacle. "Okay, it's on."

With that, the driver pulled away from the curb and down the ramp to the street. Amy could not recognize, from her own experience, the road they were taking, but she recalled my thoughts and saw the route was familiar. This is getting so exciting, she thought. Linking the scenery to my memories was a good test of the rapid recall she would need in the years to come. There are vast streams of information to rifle through my mind, but as she rode through the city, it was like watching a rerun of a movie she had only seen once before. There were multiple memories of this route, but only time enough to call one to her mind. This will get easier and faster as we progress along our journey, together.

She sees some stores that she could not get from my memory and some she would like to go in to shop. They passed by others in the same area, that were familiar. I told her the others were new and I hadn't been at them yet. She said aloud "Oh, okay."

"Excuse me?" the driver looked over. "I'm sorry, I missed that."

"Oh, nothing I was just thinking out loud." Amy looked embarrassed. I told her not to worry. Many people do that.

The driver nodded as if to say she understood, and drove on.

She turned off the main road and up passed rows of bungalows. She pulled into the familiar driveway. She shifted into park and got out to walk Amy to the door. Amy was half way out of the car when her escort was by her side. "I'll walk you to the door and meet the guardians, and leave you with them."

When I opened the door to let her in, she gave me a big hug. "It has been so long since I saw you. I'm so glad to finally get here." She was almost bouncing with glee. It surprised her driver.

I reached out to introduce myself and thank her for bringing Amy to us. I was careful not to say home. I didn't want to sound too familiar with Amy, but with her giddiness, it was difficult. "We visited her in the hospital." I explained. "We got pretty close."

"Oh, okay. It isn't often the first meeting goes this well." she offered. "Well, good-bye Amy, enjoy your new home."

The chauffer pulled away, but we did not notice. We were yakking up a storm. It is funny, given that we can converse psychically, that we would be running on talking aloud, but Amy remembering that Marie could not hear us that way, knew better to include her and bond with her mother.

Amy had memories of a past life, and also, the time she spent in the afterlife. She did not have that taken away from her, before she came to us. That is against the normal procedure. Since she was starting off as a twelve year old, she needed some skill in communicating, that she would have developed in her early years. I was quite at ease with the passing from this life. I was ready for many years, now. So, it did not cause me any harm to know her memories of that. We would talk of these things, later. For now, we must bond as a family, in the time we're in. Marie, especially, needs this bonding time. This is our daughter, in fact, if not publicly. We have to make up for those early years we missed.

We talked of life with our other children, of our grandchildren and the places we lived. Amy, of course, could learn all of this from the annals stored within us, but the telling of it all, brought the important emotions to those memoirs. Without the emotional connection, it would be like reading a set of encyclopaedia. Amy has already learned of these things, during her time in hospital. Now, she can feel the love and tensions, related to the excerpts she knew. The two ladies went on a cruise down memory lane.

I, as I always do, got restless and had to leave them to talk. I left the room and went into the den. I have several interests contained in my sanctuary, that can keep me busy for hours. Later, when Marie is at work, Amy and I can share these hobbies.

She will help me do the things which I find extra challenging. She will, also, share Marie's hobbies. She will be able to mediate with us, in our relationship. She can help us remember the things we enjoyed doing together and the promises we made in our beginnings. Her schoolwork will not be much of a challenge to her. She recalls all of the facts and figures that Marie and I have learned, as well as the things she knows from her past life.

That is our next order of business. We must enrol her in school. Because she has no records from other schools she would have attended, she will have to take some tests to determine her placement. She will likely be tested at the school that our granddaughter was going to. She, however, won't be there. She has had some problems there and is going to attend classes elsewhere. Amy is not likely to be placed there, so the sharing they could do will be missed.

We have four grandchildren in her age group. Three of them are girls. They will be excited to have an aunt their age. My mother had an aunt close to her age and they stayed close all their lives, emotionally, if not physically.

It will get to me every now and then, the complications of our situation. We didn't even want a pet and now we have a daughter, in school. I'm sixty-one and retired. Marie is fifty nine and wanting to retire. I am disabled and not fit for work. Marie is able physically, but she is tired and is caring for babies at work. A whole lot more than she expected to be doing, at this stage in her life. We've known others who started families all over again, and we thought them insane for it. Now, we are facing the same challenges as they, and embracing it. We are insane! That is all there is to it. We're crazy.

Amy laughed out loud at this thought we shared. She told

Marie what I had been thinking and although she laughed at it, it unnerved her. She did think that and dreaded thinking further on it. She steered Amy away from that talk and into a more comfortable topic.

They turned now to the travels we had made. I turned to building my miniatures. It was scary to do since I lost vision in my dominant eye. I had trouble doing these altered kits before, with both eyes healthy. This will surely keep my mind still. I have a 1932 Ford sedan that I have cut down the roof height by six scale inches. It is 1/87th scale. The model is 1 and 1/2 inches long when finished. Yes, this will envelop me.

Amy is a pretty, petite, young lady. Her figure and appointments make her look much older. If it was not for her diminutive stature, she would draw too much attention from men. Although, it may not be that safe for her after all. What might save her though, is her complete lack of interest in the male populace. The image she showed me of the person she had seen going past her room in the hospital, was a female nurse. Nothing came of her crush. It had remained a secret between us. I had thought our connection might have caused this. My desires forming her desires. She told me flatly that this was not the case. In her past life, she had been a lesbian and these yens were carried over into this lifetime. She did say that she was not going to forego motherhood. This was denied her in her previous existence. She will have a family, this time. Since the social acceptance of homosexuals has made it easier to pursue that goal. I warned her that, although society in general has accepted them, some individuals, and certain areas, may not follow the crowd here.

It was getting near ten. That is when Marie gets ready for

bed. She brought Amy down to her room and pointed out where things she might need are. While she was getting ready, Amy came in to see what I was doing. She knew but wanted to see it firsthand.

"It will look nice when it is painted. The paint will hide all the faults." I showed her the joints with the small gaps. "I think these will fill with paint. They are small enough."

"That colour will look nice. It might have been one of the colours used by the manufacturer, but with black fenders. I worked on cars with my brothers in my past life. It never dawned on them that I liked the same girls that they liked. They were always setting me up with their pals. It bugged them that I wouldn't accept the boys' advances and proposals. They used to say, 'What are you teasing them for?' I wasn't trying to tease them. I just didn't know how to tell them. It was so nice, when I went away to college. I met girls there that were like me. We were always shunned by the straight girls, but we were safe while we were together. We sometimes got beat-up, when they got one or two of us apart from the group. That was how I died. When I was finished school, I got a job working at a factory, in the office. One day while I was on my way home, I was confronted by some guys in my neighbourhood. They didn't belong there, but they had one of the girls from school with them. She had told them I was a lesbian. So, they raped me and beat me. Then they threw me in the river nearby. When they found my body, they could not tell what I was. My body was swollen and disfigured, by the beating, and the garbage in the river."

"I'm sorry that happened to you, Amy. That shouldn't happen to anybody. The trouble is that there are still people like that around."

Marie was standing behind her and put her hand on Amy's shoulder. She had only just learned that Amy was gay. "They don't just target gays. They go after anyone that they decide they don't want around. They went after my granddaughter, too. She is straight as far as we know. They were jealous of how pretty she was and tried to drive her away. The thing is that, with all the protective measures we have, the victims don't report it, and that won't stop it."

"It still isn't a perfect world," I offered, "but we are still working on it."

"God knows, and He's helping us deal with it. We just have to pray and give our problems to Him." Amy professed. "I think I need to go to bed."

"Good night, Amy." Marie said, and kissed her on the cheek. She then came and hugged me and kissed me as well.

I gave Amy a hug and kiss, and both of them headed to their rooms. It has been a long day. I should be tired. I have taken my medications, but as usual, they have not started working yet. I checked the containers and I was right. They weren't there. In cases like this, it helps to have some red wine, or an Irish Cream. It helps you to relax and lets the meds work. They do not recommend alcohol as a sleep aid, because it doesn't give you a long sleep, but one that is disturbed easily. You shouldn't use alcohol with prescription medication. However, if you are accustomed to the meds and use alcohol to just relax so your mind so it is not fighting the sedatives, it is your call and you should use it sparingly.

I found an Irish Cream in the bar and opened it. Just thinking of this liqueur helps you to relax. It's soothing texture and light easy taste immediately puts you at ease. I must be careful not to be a bad example for Amy. She is only twelve and you can not expect her to be oblivious to your habits. As I am mulling this over in my head, Amy interrupts my thoughts to ask me to keep it down. I did not remember that she is always connected to my thoughts as if I am talking out loud. Well, that is just great. Not only must I keep my voice down for Marie, who sleeps light, but now Amy is affected by my loud thinking. I feel like screaming. I hear Amy giggling over this. Really? Think it over and be careful what you ask for, you might just get it. I put my head down to view my project and went to work at it.

Chapter Twelve

School Daze

Amy and Marie were up by eight o'clock. They had their breakfast and were getting ready to go out shopping. Marie wants to get Amy some new clothes for school, before she needs to go to work. She calls in to find out when she will be needed at work. That done, off they go. There are lots of stores all around us and Amy mentions the stores she saw yesterday. They have some good choices and are getting in the door just as I am dragging myself out of bed.

"Good morning." I said sluggishly.

"Just," Marie replies, "you just made it. It's ten to twelve."

"Oh, that doesn't surprise me." I mumble.

"Can you take Amy over to see the school and make an appointment to have her enrolled, please?"

"Just as soon as I can drive safely." I usually take a considerable amount of time to get to that point.

"You may as well relax, Amy. He won't be ready for a while.

In the meantime, you can try on those clothes while I get ready to go."

"Okay Mom." She replies. Amy closes her bedroom door and gets into a pretty dress that looked like she was going to the prom.

"Oh Amy, that is beautiful on you. That one you can save for special occasions." Marie was glowing at the sight of her.

"You mean I can't wear this for school?"

"No dear, that is too dressy for school now-a-days. Put on those pants you got with a blouse and a sweater." she instructed.

Amy went and changed and while she was changing, I texted Grace to see what her girls are wearing. Marie came in to kiss me good-bye and called her good-bye to Amy. I went to the door with her and saw her away. That gets me another kiss. I go to the living room window to wave. Amy comes into the room looking more casual.

"Is this what they wear to school?" she asks.

"That is what Grace's girls are wearing. You'll find out from the school what their dress code is. I will take you over in an hour. Until then, what would you like for lunch?"

She goes to the kitchen to check out what's there. I know what she's doing, what she's thinking, so it leaves little to talk about. She pulls out the peanut butter and pickles, and asks where the bread is I am about to answer her, when she says, "Thank you." That could get annoying fast. I think about asking her to talk out the conversation to give some semblance of normalcy. "Okay, we can do that. I guess it could look pretty freaky with us not talking. We could have people amazed by doing things without communicating, like precision stuff."

"Did you like that combination in your past life or are you just taking a chance?" I wondered at her meal decision.

"I don't remember that fine a detail from that time. I scanned your thoughts and its seemed like a good idea. You like to eat some weird mixes. Mashed potatoes and corn sandwiches? Peanut butter and banana sounds good. Oh, steak sandwiches, that sounds real good."

I didn't know if she being was sincere in her judgement, but she didn't give any indication in her thoughts. "I always wanted to have someone that could read my thoughts and work with me to get things done. I didn't realize how consuming this way of communicating could be. So many things are bringing up caution signs and red flags, marking a problem coming. I think it is a bit too much at times."

"Yes, it is. We are so open to each other that we won't have a private moment or a secret from each other." she looked seriously put off by that. "It is going to mean we will have to come to terms with this before we go much further. I think we should do those things we might do in seclusion in spite of the others judgement or repulsion. Like you and Mom having sex. That would be too much for a normal kid to come in and see, but it needs to take place, so we have to act like this is something we won't be able to see and let Mom think it is that way, or she wouldn't be able to, or want to."

"Amy, you are wise beyond your years. Will it be possible for you to ignore these things?"

"I will just have to make believe and condition myself, just as you will when the time comes that I will be taking part in those types of activities." she continues, "Like the Japanese. They have so little space, that they condition their minds to have their space within, and not allow the outside crowding to entre into their minds."

"You're good at searching our knowledge. Sometimes I can't recall things that well. It does help me remember when you find those thoughts. It brings them to the forefront of my mind." I feel much more calm, now. She can really set me at ease. "You make me more confident that we can see this through."

"Since I can access every part of your memories, I have to look at it like a romance novel, pure entertainment." she is convincing.

"Well my child, let's be off to get you an education. We may need to make some adjustments as we go along here. They will have to place you where you fit in and that may be beyond the scope of this first school." She seemed ready for that. Marie and I are in our late 50s to early 60s. The knowledge we have to add to what she came into this with, will allow her to progress quickly and reach deeper into the fields she chooses to study. "I can see a doctorate in your future. Picking the right field is the key to being happy in your work. Look at all your choices and test them out in these first days. Be honest with yourself. I knew a guy with a doctorate in Mexican music. It didn't entre into his work life, but it would make his future endeavours bright, as he gets through the earn a life phase, to where he can direct his path by his own hand."

"I understand. What might get me excited may not be what pays my bills. I will be able to choose the main field that I think is a good earning potential."

"Yes and no. You never know what will be in demand once you have completed your studies. Sometimes engineering graduates, even with a doctorate, may have to drive a cab at first, until the demand builds for their area. Also, it may take so long that they become to old to attract an opportunity." I know she can see my point, but she seems taken aback by this. "That is not always the way though, so you just have to look at things closely before you decide."

The school isn't too far, but we have to cross a busy main road, so it gives us time to finish our conversation. We park out front and walk up the long path. I ring the bell at the door for someone to admit us.

"You can't just walk in?" she looks surprised.

I tell her about the shootings and abductions that have shaped our current security measures. This shakes her up. She lived in a time that could be brutal, but this time does not look much better even with more general tolerances. We are let in and I introduce ourselves.

"Oh yes, Mr. Wrent, you are Briony's grandfather. I thought I recognized you." we had met when I came to get the grandkids on several occasions. "Come on in."

We were led into the office and met the principal. I told her of the situation and asked what we would need, to get Amy into the school system. She asked for the records from her previous school and once told they would not be available until she can be reunited with her parents, she understood with whom she was meeting.

"You are the girl in the news. We can test her to see where she would fit in, but for now we can put her in with children her own age." We went over the requirements, for needles and other such things we will need to get. It was fairly simple and won't be too hard to get done. We thanked her, stood up and walked out of the school.

"How do you feel about the school so far? ...and the principal?"

She shrugged and looked at me out of the corner of her eye. "One is as good as another. You learn what they want and work with that. It's pretty much the same as a boss will be. I won't really know until I am here for a while."

Imagine. You live one life and after a beautiful beginning you end up being murdered for your choice of a quiet lifestyle that may otherwise have gone unnoticed. Then you volunteer to step into someone else's dream. You don't lose your memory of that past experience, and now you are starting over with an attitude like that. You are not yelling about how 'life is not fair' and 'who are they to push us around?'. You are patient and open to the possibilities. You are more of an adult at twelve than some are at fifty. Amy smiles at me. "Thanks."

We go back to the house and start making the appointments we need. While I am doing that, Amy looks through my collection of magazines. "You have wide range of interests. Boats, cars, architecture, landscaping, hot rods, miniatures, and military stuff, history, astronomy, ...boy, you've got tons of stuff here. How do you find time to do all this stuff?"

"I take time to do it. I don't have much else to do, at least not until you came. Now, I have to follow through with the dream and record it. I just have to see it through to fruition." I walk in to join her. "I would be glad if you could get some interest in some of this, and maybe help me see it through with them too."

"I can help. Sure, I'd be happy to. You can teach me how to do these things. I'm sure I could use these skills for other things. Your dad liked this stuff too, didn't he?"

"Yes, I inherited it from him. Your brother and sisters weren't that interested. No, that's not quite true. They had some interest but I didn't help them much in fostering it. I was unsure of how to do it right and by the time I got around to doing anything about it, they had lost all the interest they had. I still hesitate from ignorance and fear of making a big mess with nobody around to help me straighten it out. I tried to rekindle the interest for them but they have moved on. I expect the fortune I've put into it all, will just get thrown out the window. Some of it is too far outdated. Some of it is very collectable. You have to know something about it to recognize it."

"You never know, Dad, I might pick up where you leave off. A girl needs hobbies too."

"It would be nice to pass it on to someone who might care about my dad's legacy."

In the next few days, we gather the things she needs for school. Her sisters help get things for me when I wasn't ready, and Marie handles a lot of it. Amy is excited to get to work on learning what kids are like and meet new friends.

I have an appointment at the hospital and with her not being in school yet, Amy asks if she can come with me. It's nice to have somebody with me, so I gladly accept her company. She may see something that she could aspire to. I go to have blood taken for an iron processing disease called haemochromatosis. I go to the blood disorder clinic. This is where Leukemia patients are too. Amy helps me get my wheelchair out of my truck and pushes me into the outpatient lab. She noticed a change in me when we got in the door of the hospital.

"You didn't need a wheelchair when you came to see me. How come?"

"Mom was with me and she can strengthen me by just being there."

"And I can't?" she challenged.

"You do but I will have long waits here and they are used to seeing me in a wheelchair. While I have my own chair, we will need only one for you. This is why I still use my chair while you are here with me."

"Okay, you're forgiven." I was taken in a few minutes later and Amy waited in the waiting room. When I came out, she took me to my appointment upstairs. I loved having her here with me. It is lonely going through this and Marie doesn't like going with me. Amy watches me do the familiar things I have to do. I fill out the questionnaire on the computer and wait for it to be printed out.

"Lets take a spot by the window. I can't hear them call my name sometimes, so I sit close and stay in the way."

"Why stay in the way?"

"If I am in the way here, I know they will find me. In the old hospital where you were, I had to stay there and not go to the waiting room because they can forget you there. Out of sight, out of mind." She could have gathered this without my telling her but we have to keep it vocal to train us to act more normal. "That is why I stay in the way. I also move around a lot, for the same reason."

"I see," Amy said, "so do I have to move around with you?"

"No, with you here, I won't feel the need to move around. I can sit here with you and admire my daughter." I beamed at her.

"And I will be here, for you to admire." she grinned at me. "Does it take long?"

Now I know she can recall this without my answer, but it really helps to talk out loud to her. "What, admiring you? Some days it can take hours. Other days we are in and out in no time.

The really great advantage with having you with me, is getting from here to the hospital side to get my phlebotomy."

"Why would you need a lobotomy?"

"Oh, you are so my daughter. Just like your sisters, you can really dish it out. They will love talking with you when we can get together." I hear my name called and I wave to the girl who called it. "Amy could you help me over there."

Amy jumps up and pushes me to the girl standing by the scales. I introduce Amy as my foster daughter. I get up and onto the scales and my weight is recorded. Getting back in my chair, I tell Amy to follow her to the room. "Have you seen anything that you might like to do here for a living?"

"Not yet." she trilled.

"My doctor is likely to inspire you. She has a great manner that instils you with a sense of ease and wellbeing, no matter how you felt before. I like my doctor. For a specialist, she has the manner of an angel."

We are shown to a consultation room where we will wait for the doctor. She doesn't always come in, so we just have to wait patiently. Sometimes she will tell them what she wants done for me and when she wants me back. We are waiting for about ten minutes this time when the doctor arrives. She greets us warmly and I introduce Amy.

"Your numbers are right where we want them so I'll have you back in two months. You can go for your phlebe today and I will see you in two months. Nice meeting you, Amy."

"Okay, now we go back to the front desk and they will give us a time for the next appointment. After that, we go down to the lobby and across to the hospital side. Go out the door and turn left, then right and straight down to the desk."

At the desk I hand over the doctor's orders. The girl behind the desk gives me an appointment sheet. I turn to Amy and off we go to the elevators. I tell her about the vertigo I feel sometimes when I am here. "It feels like an earthquake. As if the floor is bouncing. That is another reason I need the chair here. The last reason is that they use such thick needles for the phlebe, that it is easy to reopen for a while after. If I put too much weight on my arms it would pop open again. In the chair I have more time for it to heal."

After navigating the halls through to the hospital, we reach the main door elevators. We get off on our floor and wind through more hallways, to the blood disorder clinic reception desk. I hand over the papers and we go to the waiting room across the hall.

"Why aren't we waiting in the hall this time?" Amy wondered.

"Well, the desk is right outside of this one and it is very open with windows so they won't miss us here. Everybody waits here and not two or three other rooms, so I am confident they won't forget me. I do wander out there if I am restless, but it doesn't make much difference here." We wait for twenty minutes this time until a nurse comes to get me. Amy pushes me down the hall behind the nurse. We get to the room and I move into the lounge chair. I prop my arm up with the pillow from the chair while the nurse gathers the supplies. She comes over and checks my blood pressure and pulse while taking my temperature. She asks the questions before proceeding. Have you been admitted to hospital? Do you have any allergies? and all the rest. Now comes the needle for the IV. I look at Amy to see how she handles the sight. I point out the spot on my arm where they get the best flow, and in goes the needle, and out comes the blood. As it fills the tube I watch Amy. She does very well. She is calm and not disturbed by it. Her mouth is not watering. "You're doing real well. Maybe you can go into healthcare."

"I might do that. It's a demanding job and there is a great need for nurses and doctors. I thought about it while I was at the hospital getting checked out."

"What were you in the hospital for, Amy?" the nurse asked.

"I have amnesia and they were checking me out for what caused it." she replied. " I was found in Mr. Wrent's backyard."

"Oh! I think I heard about that on the news." she looked up at me. "You found her?"

"Yes. I was checking my yard for things that needed to be put away for the winter. When I got dizzy and fell. When I was getting up, I saw Amy. I took her down to Children's Hospital and got the police in to find out who she was. They still don't know who she is or where she came from."

"You still don't have your memory back?" she asked Amy. "So is Amy your real name?"

"No. Mr. Wrent has been calling me that because 'amie' is French for friend. So I asked them to call me that. I didn't have anything that would tell me who I was or what I was doing there."

"Wow! That's more excitement than I would ever want. They haven't got any response from the news stories yet?"

"No." Amy was a little agitated at the excitement she was causing. "They haven't told us about it if they have."

"Are you okay, Amy?" I asked.

She looked at me and told me without speaking, that if she let it get to her it would be more real than if she wasn't bothered by it. "I am surprised that we haven't heard anything and I just realized that. I guess I was caught up with being with you guys and getting ready for school, that I forgot all about me and all that I don't remember."

"I'm sorry. I didn't mean to bother you." the nurse regretted the pain she caused her. "I won't say anymore."

"No. It's okay. I just hadn't thought about it with all the excitement I've had. I just really had forgotten all about my troubles. Its good to forget them, but sooner or later you will have to face them."

It hit me that the more this story goes, the more it becomes a part of her history that, although fabricated, is real for the people caught up in it. It will be her reality and not her alibi. God said to pray as if it was already answered, already fact. That is what we did and that is what we have. Something only the most trusted of friends and relatives will know as being an alias reality. As a kid you are taught to tell the truth until you have things that should not be told and then you are taught to lie. Sometimes it is to save someone from harm. Next its to hide your problems. Where it goes from here relies on your ability to accept the lie as fact, truth. A person could do some serious damage to themselves by thinking to much about this. So our brain tells us not to question. It blocks out the truth and replaces it with the lie. A policeman told me that when I was in a car accident and told him I saw a green light and drove into the path of a truck. I said the truck was red and he told me it was blue. My brain had confused the colours to protect me from accepting that I had run a red light. One of the eye witnesses had said the driver of the car, my car, was killed. The many realities that come from perspective and a need of explanations for actions we cannot accept. How can we accept any story as fact? How can we believe what we are being taught? We have to weigh the need for truth and the need for protection from the truth, or the support of a tale to see us through a difficult trial. Does it really matter what we believe? Everything we choose to believe is relative to our needs. What we might hear from someone suffering from Alzheimer's or dementia is fabricated but is reality to them. The need to correct them is something, those close to them feel is strong. The reality we see doesn't matter to the sufferer. When they are gone, will our protests matter. No. Nothing will matter. Whether it is truth or lie, it will not matter. In Amy's case there won't be anyone coming to claim her that can provide proof of who she is. A simple blood test would prove that we are her parents. Does God need to be cited in this creation? Only by us, the recipients of his blessings. We thank God for the prayers He answers and the prayers He doesn't answer. It is all good which ever way He chooses. We must not bear false witness against others. We must not blame someone for something they did not do. But we must talk our dreams into reality. Pray as if it has already been answered. Can you see the difference? I have struggled with that question, that paradox, all my adult life. God tells us though, to be as a child, accept with an open heart as a child might.

Amy stands watching the phlebotomy without another word. She contemplates the facts and the fantasies connected with her story. The items I chose to help me recognize her as an answer to my prayers, are the only thing that can tell her that all of this is true, all of this is not a horrific plot to enslave a young girl. The fact that she can draw information from both Marie and I, but only share with me in the same fashion, tells the truth of her existence. The story we need to stay with to protect her from those that would not accept the truth, is talking it into reality and not bearing false witness against someone. Only Amy and I will suffer from the ramifications this experiment will bring, and we are the ones who volunteered for the job.

"It looks like we are done. Let me get this off of you." the nurse is removing bottle. She comes back with some gauze and tape for my arm. "Now put pressure on this for about five minutes." She pulls out the needle and I push down on the spot. We have to protect that spot, because it is the only spot we have been able to count on, for a reliable blood flow. She comes back and puts the tape over the gauze. "Okay just keep the pressure on that for me." Away she goes to check the other patients in the room. Most of them are here for Chemotherapy or a transfusion. Sometimes there are more of them giving blood. Haemochromatosis is not a rare condition, but you don't hear of it until someone close to you has it. Leukemia is not a rare disease and you hear a lot about it, mainly because it is so serious. Haemochromatosis however, if not treated can lead to Leukemia. The nurse returns, "Do you have some juice with you?" I shake my head. "Alright I will get you something." We need to replenish the sugar in our blood, but I forget to bring juice with me, when something else is occupying my thoughts. My pretty daughter is responsible for my mind's occupation this time. It isn't that she is at fault. It is that she is more far important to my thoughts.

"I didn't feel the injection so much, in that arm." Amy said.

"That is because I am used to it in that spot. I joke about it opening up and pulling it in. At times I don't feel it at all."

"So this is something you need to have done regularly for ever?"

"Yes. It will only change if they take the iron too low. Aunt Cath says, I am lucky to be having it done here, where they watch it closely and are careful not to let it go too far, one way, or the other. She said she had a patient that she had to set up for home care, that had been taken too far and now has worse problems because of it."

"What kind of problems?"

"She didn't go into that. It wasn't necessary that I knew. She just wanted me to appreciate the care I was getting here. She had trained as a nurse here and then moved to the states. She got her masters down there. She now prepares patients for homecare. They do many things different there. I'm glad we live here in Canada."

It has been about ten minutes and I feel safe enough to get into my chair now. Amy pulls the chair in front of me and I get up carefully and swing around to sit down without putting too much weight on my arms. Both arms had been poked. The right one at the lab and the left one here. I say goodbye as Amy pushes me to the desk. We stop to get the appointment for the next one. Once in possession of the appointment sheet, we head back to where we parked. I usually do all of this on my own. It feels so nice to have someone with me to help. I won't, however, ask someone to do this when they would be taken away from their own schedule. Amy was free to learn about this firsthand. Therefore she was perfect for the job. I always wanted to be two people so I could get it all done. This is basically what has happened here. We get down to the truck and, with the chair packed away, we were off.

"Where do we go now?"

"It is a tradition now, that we pick up a pizza for dinner. That is what we will do but first, we will get some groceries, since I have a helper. I don't usually shop after the phlebe, because I am not to do anything strenuous the rest of the day. No exercise, no work, no shopping. Today, I will pull myself along in my chair while you push the cart and handle the groceries. This way we can free up some time tomorrow, for another job I need to get done with a willing helper." We drive over to a grocery store and take care of that chore. With that done, its off to get the pizza and then home.

The foster parent system allows visitation for the birth parents and grandparents, but in our case, there is no one known to the CAS, so there is no regular visitation. There is a visit from the case worker to make sure all of Amy's needs are being taken care of and no problems have come up. When we get in the door there is a message waiting from Amy's case worker. I check the message and call her back. We set up a time to meet and get up to date on the progress. I always wanted a job that would give me a sense of contributing to the community. Although this is a bit of a contrived case, it still qualifies and I feel great to be doing it. When I was retired with the disability, I was pretty much denied the chance. It is a relief that I can have a function that gives help to others, in spite of not being able to be a reliable employee.

When Marie gets home from work, she doesn't like to talk about much. It is stressful at work and in traffic on the way home. She is glad to see she doesn't need to cook anything and we get settled quickly into our dinner. With the relaxation, she is open to talk and asks Amy how her day with Dad went. Amy recounted the days events and said how she enjoyed the experience. She comments on the pizza and shopping. They talk easily and without any effort like she was an old friend. In so many cases, where a child is put into foster care, there are resentments and rivalries, and some sort of rebellion. They have been taken from situations by force, or given up like they were being abandoned,

I don't know if we could cope as well, in that situation. This is actually our own daughter who has chosen, while in a free spirit form, to come and be, not only part of our family, but part of Marie and I that even our other children could not be. It is such a blessing to be in a relationship of trust that deep and that permanent. Whether she stays with us in our home, or if she leaves to live a separate life, she will be conjoined to us in every ethereal sense, as well as have a regular familial connection.

The next day starts off with my girls, going out to meet the girls that Marie is close to and gets together with regularly. We are preparing for our annual vacation trip to the Caribbean. Amy will be staying with Grace while we are gone, and Marie had to introduce Amy and share her, with her friends. The girls are their usual and Amy gets an insight into the experience. The visit is filled with the hilarity, that Amy could only hope to have, with her own friends someday. It is short but a fully eventful time. Marie would normally go straight to work, but must get Amy back so they leave a little early.

I am up and at the computer, doing my habitual exercises to help get my mind going, and checking e-mail while my body tries to catch up.

"Hon, when is that appointment with the school for?" Marie calls from the doorway.

"Its Monday morning at ten."

"You'll have to get up to go with me."

"Yes. I'll get up. Just call me when you wake up and I'll get going then."

"Okay. I have to go now. She wants me in for twelve."

I get up and go to the door to say goodbye and kiss her. "Okay. Bye."

She heads out and Amy and I go to the window to wave goodbye. Its the little things that help keep straightening out your relationship, resetting it every day. As long as you both make it a point to mean it every time. If it gets too hard, you just remember why you got together in the first place, keeping in mind what it takes to build a relationship with anyone. If you fail with this one. What makes you think it would be better with anybody else?

Amy likes that line of reasoning.

"So you saw the girls. What a hoot they have. Its like that almost all the time they are together. It always helps to keep a little insanity in your life, so you're satisfied with the things that drive you there."

"I am so glad to have folks like you. You're great"

"I know." I beamed.

Amy laughs. It is only your decision to enjoy life, that makes it possible, to take the steps necessary. Never take yourself too seriously, because no one else will.

The weekend was filled with visits from our girls and the grandkids. Amy can relate to both generations. She is as mature as her sisters, but is the same age as her nieces and eldest nephew. The younger one is still off on his own wave length and heads for the Lego blocks in the basement. The grandkids don't know the truth about Amy and won't until the official search is called off and we have adopted her. They tell her about the classes, and teachers they have, and all about the work. The older girls and boy, have already started working at jobs in the area. It is like a mad house, with all the chattering going on. It is a stark contrast to the visits the following day. Oma is brought over for some time away from the home and getting together with the sisters, her daughters. She thinks Amy is one of the grandchildren and we don't try to correct her. Her dementia is quite in control now and that won't change for the better. The visit is good for everyone and it is soon time to take Oma back. The sisters return after dropping her off, so they can exchange thoughts on her health, and set up the duties, for her appointments in the coming weeks. Amy listens in but keeps quiet, satisfied just to observe and get a more in-depth idea of our family life.

Amy asks me later about my side of the family. I tell her that, although we don't see each other often, I feel close to them and we enjoy the times when we do congregate for a special occasion. I know they feel the distance more than I do. I liken it to the example she cited earlier about the Japanese. I can feel them close as long as they are okay, health wise. When there is something wrong with one of them, it makes the distance feel much farther. I don't travel on my own very often anymore, so I have to rely on someone else to take me. She says that she will volunteer when she is old enough to drive. "I thought you might." I say in turn.

After the visit is over and they have left for home, we talk about the plans for the morning, and Amy's day at school. I tell Marie about the pending visit by the case worker that week. "I scheduled it for Tuesday evening. We don't have anything planned for that day, and it will be after Amy has been to school." Marie is not pleased with the arrangement, but admits that is the best time for all concerned.

In the morning, I get awakened gently, as she always does. We get ready and as we go, we find that we all are quite nervous. We feel like we are all on test. None more so than Amy, as she is getting the culmination of all our feelings mashed together right in the middle of her shoulders. It is like she is being hugged, really tight, and stuck so that she can't get loose. I stop and go to her. I put my arms around her and squeeze and slowly release, rubbing her shoulders as I do, to symbolize the release she needs. I give her a light hug before letting go and a kiss on the forehead. She is more relaxed now and smiles. I could feel her tension and now her comfort. I go to Marie and give her a hug. She is not that open to that as Amy was. She can't stand someone closing in on her when she is nervous, so my hug is short, and I quickly stand back to give her space.

Ready to go, we get in the car and head off to the school.

It turns out to be not quite as bad as we imagined, but not by very much. We all remember school first days. Marie and, I from both the parent side and the student. Amy, from her past life, so generously left to her.

We have all the paper work and Amy had all her shots, a full set, as we had to make up for no records. We knew it was right for her, but CAS were concerned about overlapping some she may have already had before losing her memory. We went with her down the hall to meet her teacher and to leave her there. After that we could leave, still regretting having to leave her. She is twelve for Pete's sake. Its not like we were leaving a five, or six year old. It is still as hard no matter how we reason it. I can feel Amy, she is glad to start, but wishing she had more time to prepare. Although, no more preparation, would change the ordeal.

Marie drops me off and goes to work, and I stay at home with my thoughts, and listen to Amy's day.

It is like something you wished you could do as a kid. She had an answer ready for every question that was posed. She didn't try to monopolize to the class, but when asked she replied and when no one else would attempt an answer, she would offer.

I remember in class at that age, I would never have the answer, and could not recall it, even if I knew it. I hoped she would not be bullied, by those that didn't like to participate. There was always a couple in class, that would pick on the smarter kids. Unless you were their friend. So newcomers were open season. There is a zero tolerance to bullying, but many kids would not report it, for fear of more bullying. It was a catch-twenty-two situation.

Amy was prepared. She had experienced it before, in her previous life. The life she was allowed to remember. The life that was taken from her. She did not talk to the teacher after class. She got away as quick as she could. She did this solely to keep the others from accusing her of grandstanding, to get the teacher's favour. When she was approached after school, she was friendly but acted shy. She told the kids she had no idea how she came up with the answers. She said she did not even know what grade she was in, or who she was. The sympathy angle gave her an edge against the tougher ones, while gaining the support of the rest. A hurdle well overcome. A couple of them walked along to the street, where I was waiting to drive her home.

"I couldn't do much today but listen to your day. You aced the whole experience. Tomorrow the teacher will most likely ask you to stay after class. That will make it easier for you to handle the crowd." I was proud of her and felt justified for it.

"I figured you weren't getting much done, because there were no distractions. Go and do things. The distractions can help me to not always be ready, with the textbook answers. I hope that might make me more like them." she admonished me. "If you are doing things, I can still function."

"I'll try. I am a bit interested in the process we're going through. It is a sight I would love to have been able to have, when I was in school. It is what teachers want to see in their class. That's why they dote on the ones that participate. I think that could weigh against you, if the teacher dotes on you. When you are called to speak to teachers after class, it might be a good idea to discourage it before it starts to develop."

"Yes, I think that might make them aware of the connotations, of over emphasising my involvement. I hope they can move on that testing though. That could help me get with a class for which I am more suited."

"That will move along once they see how you are behaving and coping with these classes. Exams are going to start soon and your performance will stir up their interest in helping you along."

"I see your point. I will try to make some friends here with some of the girls. When they see I am not after their supply of boys, they won't feel I am a threat to them. They won't know my interest is in them, until I let them and I won't do that. I will leave that for when I am settled, and have close friends to call on."

"I hope I can go about my regular things. I'll have to watch that I, don't get distracted by you. You do command my attention."

"Mom's too. At least her thoughts today, have been about how I was doing." she enjoyed the interest, but didn't want to demand it.

We had parked in the driveway and finished our talk. We got out, got the mail and went inside. I put the lights on so Marie could see to park. She used the lights along the garden wall to help her get over close, but not too close to the wall. That gives room for another car to pull in, or for me to get out.

During supper Amy and Marie caught up on the days events.

"I couldn't handle that," Marie said with a shudder, "when they would pick on us. They made fun of us because we didn't talk right. We had a lot of that all the way through school."

After dinner we watched TV while we talked more about that. It showed in the TV shows we liked. It was more about the relationships, than conflict and action. We didn't try to solve the game show questions, we knew that we had the reasoning to get those. We watched shows that focussed on making friends, and getting along in the world, with closeness and compassion. These are the things we valued more than reality shows, that polarized relationships.

Amy did her homework during a lull in the evenings entertainment. She returned for tea with us and watched with us a bit, then went off to bed. The shows being over, saw Marie off to bed and I to my den. I always stayed up to allow Marie to get to sleep, before I came to bed. She had to work and could be called in first thing. So I let her have a chance to sleep. I have a limit though. If I am falling asleep in my chair and getting ready for bed doesn't wake me up a bit, then that is it and I am coming to bed. Have you noticed that brushing your teeth, wakes you up, because you are massaging sugar into your mouth? I no longer get rested from Amy sleeping. I think that was a sensitivity we had, because of the new relationship. It was gone after a few days. I expect that being hugely aware of everything each other does, will lessen in time. I will know when she needs me though. She can raise my attention instantly. That is so strong, I can't imagine it becoming muted. I do a number of things to pass the time. I play the games that help get my mind working in the morning. I check my e-mail. I build tiny models of hot rods, houses with landscaped dioramas. I write poetry and songs lyrics. I have even started writing a book. My wife is sceptical about its popularity, but she likes the poems I write for her. Sometimes I am too successful at putting off sleep and I am still awake when she is getting up in the morning. I have pills to knock me out, but they are a more natural drug, and I sometimes resist their effect.

In the morning the girls are up at seven. Amy has to be at school for eight and Marie won't let her walk. She did the same for our granddaughter when she was at that school. It was mostly the weather but I think that was always a ruse. I get up around ten and get some breakfast. Marie is knitting for charities, or customers, usually friends but some through other connections. She fills her time with that, or crocheting. She reads quite quickly and will go through a couple of books a week unless she does nothing but read. In that case she would read a couple books a day. That is when she is sick and can't do anything.

Marie gets up to have her lunch and get ready for work. She asks what I have to do. I tell her my plans and she suggests something else, she would like me to do while I am out. She knows I am cycling today and says it isn't really important. I like to get as much cycling in to give me exercise. Winter always seems to throw me off my routine. I like to keep up during the winter, but there is something about Christmas, that starts something to go awry. We are going away in February and I need to get toned up for that.

The afternoon went well and I accomplished what I needed, and the extra Marie asked for. I nearly forgot about Amy and a shift in my attention let me know how things were going for her. I checked my watch and decided to meet her on the trike and she can walk home with me. The weather is good today and not too, 'anything' for a change. She has been asked to stay after class for a chat with the teacher. I wait for her near the doors at the front of the school. I can listen to the teacher explain that the exams will be starting soon and she would like Amy to not worry if she can't answer the parts from before her starting the class. Amy assures her she will try her best. A short chat was all it was after all. Amy sees me waiting and lets me know she will not be long.

"How did you get on with me not hanging, on your every thought?" I inquired.

"It was good. I had a little distraction when you were getting out for your ride, but I think you were affected by the cold."

"Yes, I did feel the bite a bit, but just for a moment until I zipped up the pockets on my jacket. I did keep my mind on what I was doing because I almost forgot to check on your day."

"That is the way it should be." As we moved along, me riding slowly and Amy walking briskly, we chatted about the day and her classmates. She didn't have a problem with anyone as yet. The ones she talked with today were curious about her health treatment. There was some questions, that she had to tell them she wasn't allowed to talk about, but few she couldn't answer. It was her identity she had no recollection of, that intrigued them the most.

"They were all like 'So, what's it like to not, know who you are?' and I told them I had just felt I would let that, work itself out and I would just, go with what happens."

"That is a good answer and a good outlook. Few people could handle that."

"I get that from you. You are so laid back and just taking life as it comes, in spite of all that has happened to you."

"It took me a long time, before I could take back that attitude." I objected.

"Well I don't have to take that long, to follow your example."

"Good point. People that are pushed usually become the most patient. I like to say 'Be patient, or become one.' Words to live longer by."

Every now and then, one of the kids we pass, would call and wave to her. That was reassuring. We get home fairly fast. "You could go walking with Mom. She walks really fast, and likes people with her, to keep up."

"I think that would be good." she looked ready for the challenge right then and there.

The case worker is coming tonight and this time I think we are ready for her. I would like to hear what she has heard from the authorities. We go through supper, busily talking about the school experience. The knock at the door surprises us. We were so busy talking, we lost track of the time.

Marie answers the door and brings the worker into the living room. Once seated, we get right into exchanging our information and our view, of how things are proceeding. We are told that the responses were not helpful, or hopeful, for the police. The doctor's appointment is coming up and we don't have anything in the personal category to spark memory return. The CAS is going to talk to the school, to see if anyone there could recognize her. We set out a plan of actions to take, on our side and the worker's side. We send her off with our assurances and sit down to talk about the meeting and what we need to do, to satisfy the CAS. After the busy talk, we get ready for bed.

Marie can't sleep with her mind racing. She is like that every time she has too much happen, or has too much going to happen the next day. It will be a long night.

Chapter Thirteen

Friendly Fires

Amy has been invited to the homes of some of her classmates. She is both excited and concerned. Some of the girls get along with her, but not with each other. She noticed the tension between them, and did not want to get caught in the middle. I tell her to go with the one who invited her first one day and the next day to go with the other. She goes ahead with that plan and the girls seem fine with that. She has to move on with establishing relationships. The first visit went well. They got on fine. They watched TV and her friend was surprised Amy did not recognize any of the shows. She got Amy involved in a discussion about the actors, and which one was cuter. Amy did not let on she had no attraction, but did put more effort into the dialogue about the actresses. She tried not to gush too much on this topic. I reminded Amy about Mom's school friend that had disappointed her by not telling her that she was gay. She thought that was for a good friendship, that had lasted a while. I agreed. I came to pick her up when she let me know she was ready. Her hostess was astonished by me arriving without being given directions. Amy covered it well saying she texted the address when she arrived. Awkwardness handled. We will have to watch that with the next one."

The following day, Amy went to the second girls house and saw in her a vision of herself in her past life. She was very attentive. Offering things nervously, trying not to spook her guest as if she was with a boy on their first date. The girl engaged Amy, but tentatively, trying not to seem to eager, but wanting to have her new friend show the same interest, reflecting the pensive caution. Amy wanted to have an amorous engagement. She wanted it so much she nearly ached with the restraint she was holding herself. She suggested games she liked to play. Her hostess found one of the games. Life, the board game was perfect to confirm your position of interest. They started in and as they came to pick a spouse each one in turn chose one of the same sex. With both cars having pink pegs, on both sides of the car, they looked up at each other and reached out a hand. Grasping one another's hand they stared bravely into each other's face. This wasn't going to be a forever relationship. It was however, going to cement them into a secret understanding. Now they knew they had someone that knew how the other felt and that they were no longer alone. When I came to pick up Amy they kissed each other goodbye. A kiss on the lips that said they were accepted for who they were.

"That was intense. I'm glad you found a confidante."

"I know she says she is gay with her actions. Still they can say one thing today and completely turn on you the next. I am encouraged. I can let my guard down a bit."

She was quiet all evening. Deep within her thoughts. Weighing the position, and living out her fantasies, with her compadre. I could see it playing out before me in the recesses of the mind, my mind and hers. She visualized walking, holding hands, stealing glances at each other, and stealing kisses when they were alone. There she would stop, and thinking of me, asked "Is this wrong for a twelve year old to be thinking this way?"

"To her parents, it may be. To your straight schoolmates, it would be. To me, I would be right there with you, with as much support as you need. Romantic things only though. I would not want you doing anything that you couldn't do with a boy. So, no sex! I was always after the girls and visualizing these same scenarios. I was too young and too eager. If you are prepared to accept the reactions you will get, I would not deter you from pursuing a love interest."

"I don't know if it is a love interest or not." she objected.

"I know it may not be a serious one, but it could be a casual one."

The next day saw the two having lunch at her paramour's house. With her parents at work, they had the house to themselves. They would lay on the floor beside each other as close as they could. They held hands. Thoughts of impulses, that she must not take as the sands through the hourglass, she saw them slip away. They did not whisper words of love, for they knew, they were ignorant of what is truly love. They did embrace. They were so enamoured with each other, that I took it upon myself to watch the clock and bringing Amy to see it when their time was up.

The day was awkward for them. This was the first encounter for both of them. Although Amy had lesbian lovers in her previous life, this one is with a new life. They now had to coexist without arousing attention from negative people. Other girls proposed get togethers with Amy but none showed the connection and were purely friend oriented. She didn't pay much attention to boys and was not cornered in showing any. The one encounter for lunch had to keep them, to keep them safe.

The love life showed promise, but cautious pursuit. When her parents were both away, she would ask Amy over. Those were not very frequent and that, they could handle.

The exams came with excitement for Amy. She had studied with her friends and felt confident that she would have no trouble. The girls were serious about their studies and helping their new friend get prepared. Amy was buoyed with the hope this would help her move ahead to studies by which she could be challenged. She was accepted here and cared for the friends she has made, but she knew she could flounder if she was not having to work at her class studies.

Marie and I were getting ready for our trip to Cuba. This has become an annual affair accompanied by several friends from around the area and from England. We number about a dozen. We wanted to go other places but have become friends with other travellers as well as some of the staff from the resort. Our company grows larger every year. There may come a time when we will move on to different places, but for now we find comfort in the group that we share many events throughout the year.

Amy is looking forward to seeing us off, so she can stay with Grace and her family. Up to now they have only met a few times. Although she knows much about them from our memories, she is anxious to have some first hand knowledge of the family. Her nieces are older than her, but they don't notice because she is so much more mature than her age suggests. On weekends one of the girls works at the mall nearby. Amy will have a chance to go with her sister, to pick her up after work, and even get to shop.

We don't go near the mall if we can help it. She is also anticipating having pets to enjoy. We haven't had any since our last cat died last year. He was nineteen and had been with us the longest.

We are concerned about leaving Amy so soon, but she will have both her sisters to help her if anything should come up. Realizing all the things I failed to consider, is giving me concerns as they add up. I faced so many things in my life thus far, that I thought I had it all covered. Simple, little things are making as much a difference as major items might. Having to deal with the characters she is coming in contact with, is showing me the plan is not that easily controlled. No matter how smart you think you are, there is always someone to teach you a lesson and if you are not prepared, it can send you off on a path you never knew existed.

Amy has started packing a bag to take with her, as we are packing ours. We never took the other kids on our trips. We didn't start until they were adults and could, and did, go on trips of their own. Nickolas had been to Jamaica on a location filming of a TV series. I had taken some of them on business trips, but that didn't count, so they said. Our vacations were camping trips with the kids, when they were growing up. Amy will likely miss out on that experience. Marie wants to sell our trailer and she won't go tenting. She has had enough of walking to showers and bathrooms. I still feel there is something left for me yet. I have been wanting to get a cottage, or build one. I would have great use for that trailer while building one. Even using it as extra rooms would be a great advantage.

I have trouble letting go of things I value, even when nobody else sees it. I guess that's why we've been married forty years. We are both to stubborn to quit. Time is slipping by so quickly. I still feel as young as my kids are. I wasn't very healthy when I was their age, and now that I have been retired, I feel younger than I felt then. I like to say 'age is relative, and I have a lot of relatives.'

As the time grows near, Amy has finished her exams and will be back to regular class times. I ask her to be careful while we are gone. I will still be in touch telepathically as usual, but won't be able to get in touch with Grace, or Faith, if there were to be trouble. I rarely worry as it is a useless thing to do, but this would terrify me, to know something is wrong, and not be able to help.

Amy has been invited for a sleepover with her confidante. She is anxious to go and I am concerned. If it was a boy she was having a relationship with, it would be a simple 'no', but this is beyond me to judge. I see the need to have her close to someone with whom she can be herself. I could ask her to have another girl there to keep things from getting strained, if Tanya's parents were to discover their love situation. I wonder if they know that Tanya feels she is a lesbian. That's what I need to do and surprisingly, Amy agrees.

"I don't want Tanya to come out, this way," she says aloud "when we have lots of opportunity to be together alone. I want to have her let her parents know, when there are no outsiders there. Then she can give her parents the opportunity to be calm, and ask her questions, instead of feeling like they were having things flaunted, in front of strangers."

"I think you have that well thought out. Or should I say we?"

"We, it is."

"Should you be the one to make that call, or should it be me?"

I really hadn't thought that part out. It had yet to be decided how the request could be broached. Amy and I had the same reluctance to being the one. We could ask one of her nieces to come. Or if she could be asked. We could have another classmate come. How do you put that to her parents, or her. Finally we have decided to explain to Tanya the reason we would like another girl there, and let her decide what she would be take comfort in doing. Amy feels better about making the call, and Tanya sees her point, and asks if she can have another girl join them. What's better is that her parents agree, without any fuss.

The sleepover was good for the girls to share and bond with the other girl, another classmate that was not one of the popular group. She was glad to have been asked and was a great part of the activities. Amy had Tanya close but was able to resist getting too close. The parents were happy the girls behaved well and the question of a budding romance, was a nonstarter. The other girl enjoyed being included in all the activities and had no idea that there was anything going on, between the other girls. Amy was extremely happy at the peaceful life she is now enjoying. This intimate party elated her so much. In her past life, the relationships were always out in the open, because many of the girls were known to be gay. There was always the threat of violence. She came home relaxed and hopeful for Tanya's chance to tell her parents calmly and without challenging them.

Chapter Fourteen

The Miles In Between

When we left for Cuba with our friends, we had dropped Amy off with Grace the night before. We had to be up around three in the morning and as usual we could not awake at that time if we could not sleep. We get as excited as kids on Christmas morning. We drove over to where we were to be picked up by the limousine. When we arrived they were all acting, just as we had felt. The anticipation was being fed by every one of us. I had to have a drink before leaving home and I was glad I had. I would have been collapsed on the floor from all this hype. I was able to relax and talk with them. The alcohol helps control my fibromyalgia symptoms better, than an anxiety pill would. It worked on gradients, smoothing out rough edges of the disease. It was better than the Atavan, I have to take for the dental appointments. My confederates were able to understand me when I spoke and I was able to remain in the group.

~

Amy had a great time after we dropped her off. The girls were busy talking about the two weeks they were to have together. Grace's girls were close in age and just a couple of years older than Amy. Joanne was sixteen, while Jayme was fifteen. There was a younger boy, at seven, and an infant that was a foster child. Bradley had been with the family since birth and, at the time he would be leaving, was adopted. There was a great connection with the family that would have had horrible consequences if broken. It was a unanimous decision to adopt. Grace and Brad worked wonders handling this busy group.

Marie knew Amy was gay but did not want it flaunted in front of her. Amy was fine with that, she did not want to flaunt anything. This wasn't common knowledge so, that did not play a part of any of the attitudes between the girls. It would have been awkward if Bradley had heard since he is very outright with his comments and questions.

Pets abounded in the house. Amy loves the little dogs and the cat. It raises serotonin brings your anxiety down, as well as your blood pressure, to interact with animals. Amy had no sign of allergies to the pets, so she could cuddle as much as they would allow. What is it about soft, furry animals that get you feeling so good to cuddle with one. I have had pets nearly all of my life, with only brief periods in between. At one point Marie and I had three cats, an older cat passed down from my mother after her death, and two tiny, terrible twins. They enjoyed terrorizing their senior relative. One rarely spoke, one could only squawk and one was bellowing to make up for the other two. After losing those, Marie said absolutely no more animals. She had said that before, but Grace brought over the first of the twins, the one we were to have with us for nineteen years.

Amy has one more niece, Briony who is thirteen, and two nephews, Christian who is fifteen, and Oscar who is an infant. She will likely see the older two during her stay at Grace's. Christian is a popular musician in high school. He gained fame in middle school and an instant following among the school's students and staff alike.

Briony is in middle school, but due to bullying from other girls has developed further, an illness becoming much too common among young girls. Briony had asked me a few years ago, about diets. I told her then that diets at her age were most dangerous and unnecessary. "You will gain weight to see you through growth spurts, which will leave you thinner. If you want to keep a healthy weight, eat healthy foods and keep active." This advice she used for a few years, until she encountered these bullies. Now she is under hospital care for Anorexia. She was pestered because she had a figure most women aspire to and the girls were jealous of it. She was critically low in blood pressure and pulse, when she was brought to Children's Hospital. She was there when Amy was there. They did not meet there because there was a greater need to keep Amy isolated for her to establish her case. Briony was too ill for visitors then and it would not have helped her at that time. Now when they are together, Amy will see the one of whom she was modelled after. Briony and Natalie Wood were the images I had pictured during my prayers. Briony had the dark colouring that our other kids had. For those younger readers, Natalie Wood was an actress of exceptional beauty that seemed never to age. She was drowned tragically, off the coast of California, at Catalina Island.

So it is that we left Amy to stay with her sisters and their children. We knew the experience would be monumentally bonding for them all. They all have such strong presence and the effect will be life long for her.

~

We have been squeezed into a stretch limousine for our trip to the airport. It is very chilly outside but all that body heat would keep us warm the whole way there, too warm at times. The last month has seen record low temperatures for the whole of eastern Canada and the New England states. All of us have been anxiously awaiting this respite to tropical climes. There is no quiet time for the whole trip to Toronto, just as there was none to have at our gathering point.

At the airport, we fell out of the car and were immediately bristled, by the cold stiff winds from the northwest. We clamoured through the cavernous expanse to the check-in counters. There we doffed the baggage and collected our boarding passes. Then off to the security entrance to the mall of the airport. The restrooms, shops, restaurants and bars awaited us there. Lots of time to waist and a great lot to waist it with. It never stays the same from one trip to the next. We now go on safari to find the place we would like to perch. Partings and rejoinings along the way, we unerringly lose track of some hoping that we won't have to send search parties about. This time it was me for whom the search was. The greater part of us are British expats which give out a homing cadence to help us manoeuvre with some sense of congruency. Those with loud voices raise the volume of the quieter ones, and echo among the halls and portals alike. We are not the only denizens present at this ungodly hour, but the rest won't dull the din of our voices. The gang finds a place not near as good as we had last year and have all the comfort necessary to see us through. It was right at the gate we needed.

~

Before we left, Faith brought Briony over, to have me load a computer game on her laptop. She was to spend the day at work, with Faith, the following day, and did not want to be bored, while she waited to go to her doctor's appointment. Amy had a chance to meet with her, and talk about the time, they had at the hospital. Briony was having a hard time. She would get angry when forced to eat, and was difficult to manage. She had been discharged from the hospital and her parents were trying to get her back in, before she hurt herself.

It hurts so bad, to think of the damage these kids do to themselves. It is so hard, to think that one of your own, is now battling this horrific disease. Briony is a very bright girl. As a baby, she was very neat. She would not throw food around and would wipe her mouth, when the food smeared around it. She didn't use her sleeve, but a cloth, or a napkin. She would talk nonstop, and now, is quiet and withdrawn at times. I have always wished to save the sufferers, and am frustrated that I can't. So many are suffering, and their disease is such, that they refuse help and fight those trying to take care of them. This is the harshest thing that healthcare providers can face, when they have everything to help them, with but they refuse treatment. It is hard enough, for doctors and nurses, to lose patients beyond their ability, but to have the means and not be able to administer it.

I am drawing attention to these ailments, to show how the world suffers, and how we must help rid ourselves of the causes. Some of these are our attitudes that are being passed down to our kids, who are using them to hurt and even kill, and we say 'but our kids are good kids, they would never do a thing like that.' Yet that is what they are doing.

'Where have the young girls gone, long time passing. Where have all the young girls gone, long time ago.....' If only it were just that simple, but the innocence has gone, long time ago.

~

The flight loaded quickly and ahead of schedule. The six of us were stretched across the cabin in one row, perfect. The plane taxied out for de-icing, and then we were off. We were upbeat all the way. Three years in a row now, there was a big winter storm in our area after we left for Cuba. This time I warned everyone two weeks ahead, that there will be a storm on the fifth of February, because we were leaving on the fourth. I was not wishing it on anybody. I was warning them to be ready. Sure enough, there was a storm that started on the evening of the fourth and into the fifth.

Landing in Cuba, we were there ten seconds and we were in the island way. It was like we were home. We knew the route. We knew the drill. We got out of the bus at Brisas Guardalavaca and we were home. Our friends Rosie and the Brits were there to greet us. The music was playing. There were Champaign and orange in our hands. We checked in and got down to the beach as fast as we could. Stress had no room that day. I could not hear a negative that could bring me down. We had been upgraded to ocean view rooms, and we knew the noise was going to keep us up, but that was not happening, until it was happening.

The water was like Lake Huron in July. It was cool to get in but oh, so relaxing. The rough and smooth belts of coral sands ingrained in us the tempo of the next two weeks. There were other large groups from all over, congregating in their little areas. We were no different, to start. We had an entertaining nucleus in the core of our gathering that tended to reach out into the crowds and spread.

The whole thing began several years back. One of the group of home based friends had suffered a loss that drove her to seek out isolation for her birthday. It was just two people getting away for a week. Soon it was decided that a few more would go and make it an uplifting holiday. There were the original two, plus two more from the home group, and a third addition from the UK. The UK was a long flight and one alone would be hard to cope, so they allowed her husband to join the otherwise all female crew. Thus, Bernie's Babes' was born. An unusual, international, entertainment entity, that would draw in the enthusiasm wherever they went.

The following year brought a problem. I was to turn sixty while my wife was to be away with the group. She felt that it was too much to leave me at home on this milestone event, so she was ready to opt out of the trip. The rest had really wanted to extend their celebration and keep it going. After much deliberation and negotiating, it was decided to allow me to come with them on their next journey.

I was to be an assistant to the other, original, token male figure in the group. The trip was a big success, as I managed to be an asset to the girls, and earn my place in future excursions.

The group had thus, broken the barrier of male access and grew from there. Some shifting of members took place but it was now open to others and it began to mushroom.

This year there was to be ten and an additional two for the

second, of the two week duration. Now you may be wondering about the title of 'entertainment entity.' The girls took it upon themselves to mimic the professional entertainers the day after seeing a 'Water Ballet' group perform. Their antics drew attention and attracted admirers of their incredible talents. With tongue firmly in cheek, they went through their paces and showed, without a doubt, that this was a small medium to be taken at large. The more room the better, to reduce the chance of injury to audience and cast alike.

~

Amy saw the dynamics of an efficiently run, full, family life. The storm gave her some time to help and learn. She saw how problems were handled and how the family tradition of double entendre and idioms, were perpetuated, in spite of the resistance of all concerned. She found the catch phrase, 'that's a Papa joke,' and how it didn't matter who said it. She still kept in tune with me and in spite of my partying, me to her. Our sensing was becoming less controlling. We felt the other and took comfort in the closeness, but enjoyed the environment in which we were.

School had been proceeding slowly and she was cruising through the curriculum. The test in showed that she had a prolific grasp on the program and more was asked of her but, the school board did not want to over promote, or skip grades of a student, so it was reluctant to take any action to place her within her experience level. Some cases where students were put into more challenging curricula, resulted in a lapse of studies of one aspect or another. So, to keep a rounded exposure the students are kept to the studies of the whole class. There is an exception where the board has one school that was progressive and let the exceptional student progress at their own pace. This, however, is accessed by recommendation at the end of the year. Some students can flounder in the course of the year and display a rebellious attitude toward the system for keeping them in the quagmire of unchallenging rhetoric.

Because Amy is in an unusual position, her teachers have taken action, to get the board to place her in the progressive school. The board, with some input of the CAS workers, and her doctors, decided to go ahead with the placement, on a probational term. If the results of her next assessment, are not up to the level expected, she will be returned to the traditional curricula. Anyone coming to know Amy, knows that will not happen.

The school she is placed in, is near the school her nieces attend. She is now able to travel to and from school, with Jo and Jayme. While we are away, the arrangement is smooth. They point out to her, where she would get the bus when we return, and where to get off. The new classes are a relief for her. She shows her aptitudes and is directed to the studies that fill her interests and she is quick to respond. The teachers move her through the range of their expertise and report that she is excelling in every aspect. They recommend a more accelerated venue. With this recommendation she is put into the same high school that Jayme and Jo attend. She is well suited for it.

~

I tell Marie what is happening, when we are in our room at night. We don't need to be notified to give our approval, since we are only her foster parents, and Grace is handling that position for us. We are beside ourselves with delight. This can mean great things for her.

~

Sadly, with this news, is the trouble that is facing Faith and her kids. We knew Christian was having problems with depression brought on from the stress he has with the family functions. Estranged parents and isolation from one, or the other. More disturbing is Briony's troubles and the effect it is having on Faith's health. Faith is getting run down, trying to access treatment for Briony. She is up all night and missing work. She will have no vacation after using this time to care for her daughter.

While she is busy in one part of the house, Briony takes a knife to her arm. It is almost more than Faith can take. She gets her admitted under psychiatric care, and this is the only relief she can hope for. She will still, likely spend all her time with her daughter.

~

Amy keeps us up to date on all that she hears. It is a weight we have to set aside, while we are on vacation. We can't talk by cell phone from where we are, because there is no wifi connection. Calling home won't help either. Faith is proud and would not want to have us disturbed on our trip. We decide to wait for Grace's decision, on whether we should be told. Amy will let us know when we need to take action, although there is not much for us to offer, except a shoulder and an ear.

~

The heat is satisfying, but a bit too much for me, as I feel heat stroke setting in. It is a familiar situation and I take immediate action. I handle it day-by-day. I have had many experiences, with sun stroke and heat stroke, in the last thirty years. We are prepared, with medications and a nurse within our group, to confer with. It means less exposure and more room time for me, but the others fill Marie's days. We gather for breakfasts and dinners, and see our friends on the staff. We are well taken care of and well fed. This year, I take the most time out, but the others have all felt the downside of tropical vacations, over the last few years.

I am used to napping at home, to allow time to heal, or just recharge. The room is good to relax in, and when I am outside with the group, they take care of me. This year, I have spent time in four hammocks, under palm trees or other tropical shades.

We have been well served by our friend, Johnny Cool, on the beach. He comes in often and remembers what mug, goes with what drink, for which person. Even after quick changes, in the middle of the day, he rarely makes a mistake and that is usually a small aspect of the order.

Our usual bar waiter inside, has moved on to another position, in another resort. Jorge -pronounced Horhay- has been replaced, by a variety of university students, on placement. Aliusca and Loami are showing much promise and have improved greatly, during our stay.

In the buffet restaurant, we have Suri, Maria, Olga and many others that go out of their way, to accommodate us, and the other customers.

Many of our hosts and hostesses, invite us into their homes, to see how they live.

We took a carriage ride to visit local schools. We had seen a remote village, last year and saw the need for school supplies, in their three room school. We brought some with us this year. The carriage was to take us to schools, but they were not as much in need, as the one we had seen the previous visit. We left some supplies with one school, but the next was very well supplied, so we went to a village that did not have a school, and handed out the rest, to the parents. Our driver, Jose took us to his house. It was a beautifully kept and decorated, in the Cuban style farm house. He had a beautiful flower garden, a sugar cane field and other crops. He had a one month old daughter, that had gone to the hospital, with the mother, for a check-up.

Jose's horse was a little rebellious. On our way through the village, we stopped to hand out gifts and the carriage wheel became stuck, on a rock, that was filling one end of a rut. He couldn't pull the buggy over the rock, with our weight. We got out and once the wheel was free, he took off, galloping up the hill. When he was brought under control, we had to climb the hill, to board the wagon. Jose told us, he changes the horses at one o'clock, but this one, had two more hours to go. We decided to return to the resort, and let the horse rest.

~

During Amy's commute, she would see what we had been up to that day. A glimpse back to little used technology, the rod Jose used, to repair the rubber strap tire, that had slipped off one of the front wheels. The modern and ancient equipment used daily, together in this struggling economy. The ingenuity of the poor families, trying to cope. A history lesson lived through, in our shared vision and memory, brings home the relative ease, we have in Canada. The simplicity of their lives, show us how much we complicate our daily lives, to lessen our labour. It is no wonder people are choosing to go back, to the harder, but simpler ways of life. Getting off the grid and back to nature. Amy sees the allure, as she rides the diesel bus, through heavy traffic and views our journeys, in Cuban rush hour. The bicycles, ox-carts, horse pulled, homemade, buggies with old truck tires, and modern trucks and busses, giving an insight into the choices that can be ours. I don't think many would give up our comfortable cars to ride horse pulled wagons like the Amish do in our frigid winters.

She sees this, but can't tell what, or how she sees. Imagine her telling her classmates, of her psychic connections. How much would be accepted, without ridicule? How quickly would they decide, she needs psychiatric care? It would be like saying 'I'm batty, not Batgirl.'

She can still tell something, that she knows of our trip, by relating a shared story, of previous trips. She can share her interest, in her fostered life experiences. Her nieces, travelling with her, would welcome and talk of these, at least a little while.

Have you ever wished, to be able to be in two places, at once? What you could do and enjoy, in one place, while your other self, could do the drudgery of your usual jobs. Two incomes, to help pay for your existence, would be easier and yet, still give you a time of relaxation, after work. Having help in all your endeavours, close at hand, without having to explain what you are trying to do. Oh, and playing tricks on people, like the identical twins do. Almost limitless possibilities, would be at your call. You could earn yourself a tuition, for medical school, at the same time you are attending classes. You could go on vacation, while not taking time from your job. Take the day off, and still go to work.

In a way, this relationship with Amy and I, is just that kind of opportunity. The many ways we see ourselves and our menu of life course selections, is twinned, allowing us to combine and broaden, the scope of our horizons. How we handle this, is the key of the magic of our imagination. The labours of hands, the enjoyment of vistas, the pursuit of perfection, the closeness of companions, are ours to travail and implement.

In the span of two weeks, Amy has gone through the labyrinth, we were hoping she could pass. Once the authorities set to work to place her, where she could fit in their boundaries, she was now in the position, to really expose her knowledge and experience, of three lifetimes. She is in a place, that can launch her studies, in any direction she would like to choose.

There have been claimants come forward, saying she is their daughter, but they can't describe the unique attributes, she possesses. What seemed like frivolous requests in my prayers, have set to work in keeping her out of undesirable handlers. Some of the claims were in hopes of finding a lost love one, but that is also a reason for those traits. They want their daughter, not Amy, after all.

~

Marie and the rest, took a walk up to the market and left me in the shade, to guard the encampment on the beach. On the way back, they walked along in the ocean. They were so pumped about the experience. They had a snack at a beach bar and found a pizza shop as well. One of the other guys had felt the heat too much, and had gone back to the hotel, for some cool shade.

Our reinforcements, are coming in on Tuesday and the girls plan some outings, for them to take with us. It is the first time here, for one of them, so they get one to stick in her memory. A cruise on a catamaran to an island paradise. We had taken cruises like this before and every time it was different. She had said, that was top of her list to try.

There was a run-in with someone of a nearby group. They didn't follow the established protocol, for keeping there spot safe, while they had gone away, and one of their chairs was put in our camp, for a member that needed some relief from the lounges we had. Heated words were passed back and forth, but it was left at that. The next day, with tempers cooled and needs understood, a better and closer entente was made. Both camps helped take care for the other.

There are many people who come back each year and the numbers grow every year. We greet those returning guests and share news, since our last meeting. Many have had big changes in their families and health, and the atmosphere sweetens, as we all draw nearer, those that are sharing an annual retreat with the same degree of attachment, as we have come to feel. Each group has grown as ours has, and some of us are there after infirmities, gave us need to get away.

We see weddings taking place on the beach. They always command the attention of some of our group. The carriages bringing and taking members of the events, get much attention. We meet some returning after having their big event of previous years, and those who are just planning a future engagement. One had even brought their newest addition, since their union.

The amount of life passing through and near our resort, fills our experience and draws us out to enjoy it. You feel the piece of the island and the people. You see goats herded past to graze in the park across the road, a variety of animals pulling wagons, buggies, and makeshift carts. People walking by, on their way to jobs, or the market. The pace is slow and easy. You see occasional soldiers walking by, without weapons. That one point, sets you into a feeling of comfort you would not find, in some of the other Caribbean countries, where you see guards in the resorts, with automatic weapons drawn. So many aspects of this island's life, makes you wonder, if your life isn't the deprived one.

We go down to the beach after breakfast, to the camp the early risers have established. There is shade for the fair skinned and sun for those that need to lay there and warm themselves. We talk of our plans for the day and wonder where Johnny Cool can be. It's almost ten a.m. and our blood/alcohol levels are getting low. We are reminded that Johnny doesn't start until ten, so volunteers get ready to make the run, to the rum, I mean bar. I know that's not much better, but it is afternoon somewhere. At home we rarely drink and here we rarely stop drinking, and the feeling is the same. Not one of us gets intoxicated and we function normally. One of the mysteries of island vacations.

The volunteers head off to the bar and Johnny meets them en route, receives the orders and takes over for the day.

Let me put this to you. How many times would you go into work, on your day off, with your family, to introduce them to your customers? Granted, it is a four star resort, but you may only get one day off a week, as some of the staff do, and it takes hours to get there, and back home. They even pay to bring the family in. These are wonderful people, we meet here. Would you bring your customers, into your home, of your own accord? Would you have an impromptu party, to celebrate them coming? These are not business people. These are waiters, bartenders, cooks, and entertainment hosts, for the resort.

This is a communist country, run by a military based regime. The country's economy has collapsed, time and again and is struggling. The people just keep going and it does not add up to the other, similar nations, that we see in the news everyday. We have to step back and congratulate the people, for their example of perseverance and co-operation to coexist and focus on an ideal, that is rarely able to function, without being corrupted. I don't want that for my country but, I can't help applaud the ordinary people, of Cuba.

We go out on the Hobie-cats with one of the staff, and they always joke about making a run to the U.S., or the Bahamas. The feeling of contentment seeps into you, every moment you spend with these people. You see their struggle and help them, with what you can and they love you.

I found a man that lives near the resort. He comes to sell his homemade crafts, that his daughter makes. His name is the same as mine and he has been through the same eye trouble, as I have. Can you not relate to someone, in your shoes, in this alternate existence? I was a bit unnerved by it. I tried to see myself, in his place and at the same time, struggled not to. I wondered if it was me, in an alternate reality, I stepped into. There but for the grace of God, am I, looking back at myself.

Along the shoreline, are big resorts like ours, and little homes of the people, who have lived there all their lives. They are farmers and fishermen, tradesmen and craft makers, that exist, on what they get from the ocean and their neighbours in business.

They have recently been allowed, to buy their land from the government. The government is taking land, from the coastal people and villages, to build more resorts. We hear this year, about the lives of the people, being moved into apartment buildings, away from the sea. The tourism that is helping to save their economy, is tearing down their lives. They are told that they will have new buildings and beautiful ones. Where will they raise their crops and livestock, that we enjoy seeing herded, from their little farms, to the park? Where are the resorts going to get the food, to feed their guests from, without the fishermen and farmers? Progress, if there wasn't the resorts, I would not have the opportunity, to care about these people.

Every tour we go on, takes us to see life that is disappearing and trying to be preserved. The beauty we see on the tours, is being eaten up by the resorts, that house the tourists, that pay to see these slices of the disappearing life.

The rising prices of the resorts and costs of flights, to get us here, are taking away the opportunity to keep returning.

The falling value of our dollar and rising cost of living, takes us from the beaches and people that need us, to come to support their economy.

How many catch-22s can we recover from? Our jobs disappear and our pensions are being eaten up and to keep the cost-of-living index from rising, the governments take factors off the list.

We need to get away to forget these things, and we find they come with us. That is how Johnny Cool gets so much of our business. "I'll have a Cuba Libre, Johnny!"

I keep looking into the future and seeing the things, that I saw in the past, that were going to keep me, from having the present, that I've got. How it all worked out, is completely beyond me, and I feel Amy getting a headache. "I'll try to stop all this analyzing." I say out loud. Nobody hears me because Johnny is back.

"Surround yourself with life and loves, Amy. You will get by somehow and so will I." I mumble aloud to Amy and myself.

~

Amy calls her friend, Tanya, to see how she is and get her up to date on her scholastic journey. She also wants her to know that she is thinking of her and cares what is happening in her life. She asks Tanya to tell the other girls what is going on, so that they will draw closer to accept Tanya more. She was popular and Tanya was more tolerated than liked. She asked about her parents and if they know yet.

"No, not yet." she replied, "Mom is in the other room, so I can't say too much about that."

"Do you still feel the same?" Amy asked.

"Oh yes. I think about it always. I'm a little preoccupied with it I think."

"You and..." she nearly told her about the secret life she leads. She has to be more careful when she gets emotional. "You and I are together in this and I want to help you, even if we don't stay together that way. I am your first and I can't be selfish, in thinking I would always be your only one."

"Have you had others before me?" Tanya asks.

"Not in this lifetime." she replies honestly.

"Can we get together? I want to see you and be with you. I feel empty and lonely."

"We'll have to wait until my foster parents are back from their trip. I am staying with my foster sister, and her family is busy. I can't ask her to take me anywhere, because she is always running around, doing things and I hate to impose on her. When they come back, I will ask them, if you can come to our place." she is asking me while saying this. 'We'll see,' I say.

They talk more about school and the friends Amy had made,

at Tanya's school. They talk about the bullying that goes on there, even though there is a zero tolerance policy. Tanya talks about Briony, although she doesn't know about the connection with Amy. The news that gets past around was blaming Briony, but that is just another side of it. Nobody is completely honest about it, so the truth is never really told. Both sides twist the stories, when they do tell. It is no wonder, the ban on bullying is so ineffective.

~

The arrival of our reinforcements, comes on the first of the birthdays, we are celebrating. We start the day off low key, just as the birthday-girl wants it. After breakfast, we hit the beach, and enjoy the bright 31 Celsius temperatures. We go up to the lobby when the arrival time is near and we wait. We sit and wait, we stand and wait, we walk and wait, and we wonder whose fault it will be when they do arrive. They are over an hour late when they finally get off the bus. The computer terminals were down and it put them all on hold on the wrong side of the gates. Three planes are held up by it and one passenger lost his luggage, somewhere between the two airports. He was not part of our group, but became part of the larger circle of acquaintances. We keep in touch with him during his stay.

The trouble with large groups, is the chances of relationship strains, being aired too publicly. The good thing about large groups, is the speed in which the tension, is eased and lost. We are all relationship counsellors, psychiatrists, and parish priests, without any of the messy qualifications to muck it up.

There is a restaurant on the resort, where all of the service personnel, are entertainers. They are operatic style singers, guitarists, folk singers, jugglers, and magicians. They are very good and we go there every year. We are there for the evening birthday meal, the choice of the guest of honour. We share this occasion, with a couple celebrating their first anniversary, and we find that some of us, had been present at the wedding. We helped them recalling the day and wish them well, when they leave the restaurant. We all recalled the day, and the couple.

The next morning we are up early, and waiting for the bus tour, the group is taking. It is a catamaran trip, to an island paradise, with snorkelling en route and a safari on the island. The tour company for our UK members would not insure the safari for their clients, so we were separated for that. We were riding in 1970's Russian military vehicles that, although gave a rough ride, it was smoother than the bus from the resort to the dock. The animals were all relatively harmless and could be approached at designated points. Many were quite entertaining. The islands of Cuba, were said to have no dangerous animals. The sea around them did have sharks lurking. The Captain of our boat watched the snorkelers and swimmers, so that they did not float away in the current, during our stop. He also kept watch for sharks, but did not advertize that. Some swimmers got carried too far from the boat, so the Captain jumped in, with a flotation ring you would recognize from movies, and swam out to get them. The rescuer, towed three swimmers back, pulling the ring a few yards behind him. Cheers went up to congratulate the hero and we continued our on board party.

The following day, we were traveling on foot through the resort, on our way to the market. A few were scattered around one of the pools and bars which we were passing. A man approached us asking if we needed help. We were just swimming across the pool so we thought it a bit odd. He asked us if he looked familiar and then we recognized Captain Roberto, the hero from the trip. He was visiting a friend, with his family and introduced us to his wife. He told us that, if we were to take his tour the next year, he would recognize the members of each trip. We would be easier, being in a group, but he could recognize all his guests. We continued on our journey and said we would stop by, on the way back.

Many of our hosts made it a point, to remember something about their patrons. One waiter/bartender remembered my bamboo cane that I got from my grandfather. Johnnie Cool, remembered the shape, or a symbol, from the mugs we used. For some it was the group as a whole, or one or two members, that stood out. They practiced this, to make all their guests, feel welcome and at home. Some will say after time has brought us together to share with each other, that we are a part of their family and you really feel that welcome.

~

Amy feels the warmth we are enjoying, as if she was there herself. She would lay in bed and feel the way we are. The soreness and the comfort, she enjoys the connection, when she has time to reflect on it. She is settling now, in her classes at school, and her family at home. They don't know how close they are, in her family, but they feel her growing close, and are enjoying the ease of care, she is needing. Grace is very perceptive and feels there is more, but we did warn her about that, just to keep her guessing.

I find it is better, to hide things in plain sight. Nobody ever looks there.

~

We stop by Capt. Roberto and meet the grandkids and some spend time there. I feel the need to get out of the sun, and head back to the room. I feel safer this year, because Amy will know, if I am in trouble. In spite of our secret, she would get Grace to call, in case of an emergency, if I am alone. I get into the room and lay in the cool air, from the fan. We keep the temperature turned up, to keep it from getting too cold in the room, but the fan, on low, still makes it too cool, for Marie. It is not very long before Marie comes in, to see how I am. We both put our feet up and relax, until it is time to get ready for dinner. We always eat with, at least, part of the group. It is a bit much, to ask for seating for twelve, at every meal.

Our time grows short here and we are looking forward to going home, but not too much to being there, in the frigid air. Two weeks is a long time to be together and we feel all talked out. We long to see our families and get working on saving up, for next year's trip. We have paperwork to give to Faith, so she can let us know, what we need to do with it. Faith is helping to get one of our friends in Cuba, a visa to visit us in Canada. This is carrying on from last year. Faith has so much to keep her busy. Well we will let her decide how to handle it.

The day before we leave, we see our friends and family from England off, for their trip home. Now we know it is over, and tomorrow, it is our turn. We spend some time on the beach and then head up to pack. The weather had been rough, on and off, for the last three days, since my birthday. I have a new cane to pack, to bring home. One of the others bent and is not too reliable, but only the new one, will come apart, to pack in the suitcase. We get showered and go down for dinner. Meeting in the piano bar before going in to eat. There is a huge line-up to go in for dinner. It's a struggle but we get word, to one of our servers inside, to let us know when there is a table, for the eight remaining members of the gang. There is a huge group that has come in to replace us. It is reading week at the universities at home. That does it, now we are ready to go. It won't be us attracting the attention now and we can't have that.

Up early, checked out and down for a quick breakfast, we gather in the lobby to await the bus. Many of our Cuban friends come by to see us off. Marketa, Rosi, Mike and even Johnny Cool are there for some hugs and handshaking. We move out onto the front steps for some parting photo-ops as gardeners and other wave goodbye, as they head of to work. The bus is late arriving so the rest have to get away to their duties. Another round of hugs and we settle down on the steps. When the bus finally arrives, we are loaded up and slowly heading down to the next pickup point.

The driver seems reluctant to get us to the airport. He waits for traffic ahead to turn aside and follows horse carts seemingly forever. When the terminal appears it is most welcome. Are we getting anxious to leave? I think we are in a bit of a hurry at this stage, as we hurry in to line up for check-in. We are in one line or another getting shuffled through all the stages. Some loud people are processed with one inebriated guy wanting to kiss all the women in the security check points. The officials step back and wave him off, being very patient.

We scatter to take care of all the last minute things. The restrooms and duty-free shop, along with the coffee shop are visited. I am assigned the watchman job so they don't have to wait for me. The board promises that the flights are on time. Gradually my companions all come around and collect the luggage and me.

One flight is loading and constant calls for its passengers to assemble, seem to be falling on deaf ears. The plane is being held up and people are being asked individually, if they are the wayward traveller. Our flight is ready and eventually starts loading. As our last passenger boards the plane, the previous plane is taxiing down the runway, to take off. A commotion erupts onboard our flight, as a man comes quickly, squeezing down the aisle. The missing person from the Montreal flight, has finally been located, on the Toronto plane. He is getting off ours, as his takes off, leaving him behind. How that happened, is being debated up and down the aisle. At last being shrugged off, with shaking heads.

We get in the air and on our way, looking out the windows, to watch Cuba, shrinking below us.

I am in the last row, up against the bulkhead and the window. I feel like a sardine. There is no room to move my feet, or just about any other part of me. I give up trying and watch the movie, in an attempt to get my mind off it. The movie ends and another begins and I wonder how I am going to stand, when we land. I thought the discomfort, is going to be the worst, and just bite my lip. Something moves behind me and I stretch my arm back to check it out. Nothing, it must be my imagination. Time goes by and I feel it again. I squirm around to investigate. The bottom of the seatback is frayed and open but I don't feel what was moving. Clearly there isn't enough room for whatever it is, to get out, so I sit back and try to ignore it.

Do you know the way your ankles swell, when flying? It doesn't hurt so much, but your shoes get tight and skin feels stiff. My knees must have been too cramped together, because it was my knees that were swelling, as we were descending in our approach to Pearson Airport. There was no room for my knees to expand so the pressure built up squishing against the nerves and veins. Amy was crying, with the pain she was feeling, from me. I nearly screamed out. There was no room to get up and it increased the pain with every foot we descended. We landed at last and the pain started to recede. As the others beside me gave me some wiggle room, I felt that this was not going to be easy. I was helped to my feet and got my knees locked straight under me. I lumbered down the passageway. The attendant asked if I would need a wheelchair, and I had to say yes. The other passengers with wheelchairs, were being disembarked ahead of me, and someone went off to get another chair. Marie had been sitting in the seat ahead of me, and she waited to follow me off the plane. Another chair appeared in the hall above us, and they waited for us to get to it. It felt so good to sit down, and flex my legs. They wheeled me up, to where I could be loaded onto a shuttle cart.

Marie and I were loaded onto the shuttle, and we scooted through the halls, to another man with a wheelchair. He had just returned from taking one of the loud passengers, we had seen in Cuba. He told us the guy was drunk and unruly and was being handled at customs. We were taken through the check points and to the luggage pickup, where we met up with our company. We saw the two that had been with us the one week, heading away as they waved to us. The rest of us were going home together in the limo, so we just returned the wave and let them go on their way. Once we got our bags, my escort led us through shortcuts and out to the area, we were to get the limousine. He suggested one direction for the limo loading area, but we were going in a private car. We got to our spot as the big white stretch limo pulled up.

"Ah, you're going in style." my escort said. and pushed me over to get in the car.

We were packed up and on our way. I texted Grace to see what plans had been made for my birthday celebration with the family. She said that was left undecided, so we settled on Friday night and left off to contact Nicholas and Faith. Faith had some disturbing news about Briony, that we had got previously from Amy. We let on that this was news and wished her well to handle it. Nicholas took a little longer to reply but welcomed us home and wished me a happy birthday.

Most of the friends and family at home had sent messages on my birthday, thinking I would be able to get them at the resort. Since we had no wifi there I got them all when I arrived at the airport or at home.

The limo got us to our meeting place where our car was waiting. Grace had told us they had put it there earlier that day. The snow was piled high and we had seen on the plane that it was everywhere. Amy was waiting for us at home, so once we were loaded into the car we waved goodbye and went off to get the groceries we would need the next morning.

Amy was so glad to see us pull in, that she came out to help us carry our bags in. We were home. What a relief. We were not happy with the weather, but we were home.

Chapter Fifteen

How Much More?

The CAS and the Police, had some progress reports for us when we called them, but it was not much more than we already knew. We were told of the school assignment they had settled, during our absence and that there had been some unsuccessful contacts, with hopeful claims for Amy. The news, we had to understand, they said, will take time. It won't do to get anxious, or upset. We had Amy and that is all we needed right now. We did show a little emotion, just enough that we would look concerned. We said that we were happy to take care of her, no matter how long it took to get this settled.

At home, we went over the information from the schools Amy had been through, and the one she is now attending. She was performing very well, in all the reports and was now settled in a course, that would take her to where she could decide, what path she would like to follow. What other course would they have? One to take her nowhere?

Marie went back to work the day after we got home. Her boss was sick and Marie said that she doesn't go to doctors, but to a Naturopath. I had been to a Naturopath and she helped me very much, but it took more than I could take. The results were overpowering. She is stubbornly doing without all modern, devices and shuns any attempt to force her centre, into the twenty first century. A week later she is still sick.

The extreme cold we were experiencing, is bad enough in a dry part of the country, but we live in the middle of the Great Lakes region. Humidity and wind chills don't make for happy campers. Unless you are a winter sports enthusiast, you huddle in your sanctuaries and dream of the warmth you imagine, should come with 'global warming'. Four of the Great Lakes are frozen over. This is a rare event, as these lakes are like inland seas. The only difference, is that they are fresh water.

Without my summer exercise program, I don't have the fitness level, to stand up to harsh weather. At home, the cold snaps and rainy intervals, are keeping me inside. In Cuba, the heat and strong sun kept me from getting the workout I needed. Heat stroke and ground floor accommodations, didn't help me either. I have gained weight and lost progressive momentum. We are to expect a cool spring, that might give me a break then, but that's two months away.

Amy and Tanya are asking to have a sleepover. I am supportive of Amy's being gay, but don't want to be conducive for sexual exploration under my roof. I have to ask them, again, to invite another girl to keep things innocent and above the covers. The opportunity for lovemaking was the main purpose for the occasion. They do consent to have another girl there, as they had before. I can feel the wheels turning, as Amy searches for another girl, for whom the encounter would be enticing.

"Amy, you, of all people, know you can't put that over on me. I know what you're thinking, as you think it. I have to live with my conscience, and you have to listen to it, stewing about this. Do us the favour of going with me, this time. You will have other opportunities to seduce and be seduced. Tanya is still inexperienced and you have the exposure of another lifetime."

"Yes, I have. A lifetime cut short and ripped apart. A longing to be held by someone that loves me in a physical way."

"I know you do and I sympathize with you very much. I feel your pain and your lust, and that is why I have to be the voice of reason." I feel like I have been robbed of that same closeness, by the medicines I have to take to protect my health. I know Marie has felt the loss, the same way. I know her thirst for it, was late coming and quick going. The natural rising of blood pressure, that drives your libido to its peak and also threatens your heart. The trade off of being responsible to your bodies health, at the sacrifice of its desires.

Amy can feel the lust I have lost from the innocent sounding 'water pill'. "I'm sorry, Dad. I'll ask someone to come who isn't going to want to 'play'." She gives me a grin.

"Thank you, Amy. I would love to let you 'play', but what kind of a dad would I be, if I allowed it?"

"A really cool one!" she grins. She gives me a kiss on my cheek and goes to call Tanya and give her the news. Tanya is disappointed, but is glad too. At least, She has the chance to be near Amy again.

Limitations that you must put upon yourself for the greater good. The lessons you must give and take, that steal the enjoyment you crave. Being responsible to keep yourself from being held responsible. I have tried to do it both ways and I know the results from each way to be, at once, both good and bad.

The sleepover is okayed by Tanya's parents and you know that she has not told them. You can't be the one to load that bullet. That is a relief. Stepping up to inform on another parents child, needs to be weighed carefully. Is this going to save someone from hurt, or cause it? Is it going to prevent a crime, or give rise to the possibility? Tanya deserves the right and responsibility, to tell in her own time. Likely, they will have already guessed of her orientation, if they are attentive to her.

I know Amy would love to be able to pull the wool over my eyes, and get another girl who would like to 'play', but she knows, that what she knows, I know, or at least, have the ability to hear it in my own mind. I have always been studying thoughts of possibilities. Daydreaming is what my teachers called it. Being open to new ideas, is more along the lines of what I would call it. It did make me idle of action, but not of mind. I never wanted to deny any possibilities. The existence of God, leprechauns, faeries, mermaids, or any other idea that was put forth, were held open for debate and rebuttal. Until something is proved completely, it will occupy a world in my mind where it not only exists, but thrives. Anytime another entity is introduced, good or bad, it holds a space in my brain, that is fighting for its survival, or extinction. I have, on occasion, tried to deny an existence, but once there, it can never be erased. If I cannot disprove it myself, nobody else can. Therefore all things exist. If they did not, I would never have heard of them.

It is a busy place, my mind. I need to get away from it, from time to time. I am still waiting for the first opportunity.

The night of the sleepover has arrived and the girls with it. I may not sleep at all tonight. I am on thought patrol. I have an idea that Amy would like to slip me a 'mickey.' She has the reason to want to, and the knowledge of how to do it. She also knows, that she could not try it, without me knowing, what she is doing. The other two would, however, have the means, by which it could be accomplished.

Amy introduces Valerie. She is a classmate from the progressive school that Amy had been to, before the high school, she is at now. Valerie was a shy gir,l that Amy hardly got a chance to know. She was surprised when Amy called to invite her. Amy told her that she wanted to get to know her, because she was also shy. In fact, Amy is more careful than shy. Marie and I are spending the evening in the kitchen, playing cards. The girls have an array of movies to choose from that my kids and grandkids have watched, or they have recommended. Now, with the snacks put out and the venues set, we each move to our appropriate locations.

We don't have a big flat screen TV, but we do have surround-sound. With the lights turned out, the furniture rearranged, and the girls in their places, the night watch begins.

The girls have chosen a tearjerker to start with. I would have done the same so that I could comfort the girl next to me. Good move Amy. Watch your arms don't get to sympathetic.

Amy is in the middle and they are on the floor on cushions from the chairs. She is keeping her guests separate and, she hopes, unaware of what she is doing with the other one. Another good move I will have to keep watch on. Amy and Tanya are holding hands out of sight of Valerie. Valerie, though is tight up against Amy's side, so she can feel any movements that are too pronounced. Did Amy find another kindred spirit, by chance?

I have to concentrate more on the game I am playing. I will leave them some room to enjoy the night. If I don't, I could go mad. I am, after all, a teenager of thought, if not body. I have vowed to never grow up. Besides, if I don't keep my mind on 'our' game, Marie will beat me, even more than normal.

Valerie seems to be content to be part of something, outside her family life. She is snuggled close to feel that there is someone there. Amy is sure that is all there is to that, and Tanya isn't sensing any overtures coming from that side. Amy is satisfied, for now, to have friends close and having fun. The warmth of the two girls against her sides is soothing to her loss of the romantic plans she had. The girls lean in as a particularly sad scene, is played out on screen. The timing of the film is pulsating in them. The romantic scenes tighten the lovers' grip and relax the proximity to Valerie. That is reassuring to me. It would not do to have a rivalry show itself, between the guests. A disappointing scene caused an audible groan to come forth and Marie and I look at each other and smile.

I realize Marie is smiling because she just beat me again. She will watch me when I am concentrating on something and she will grin at me until I notice her watching. This irritates me, because she will forgo watching the movie she likes, to watch me, watching her movie.

We go on playing until Marie is getting restless and wants to go to bed. Her legs get itchy when she is tired. Mine will too, from time to time, but not as often. We get ready for bed and don't say anything to the girls, until we are finished. The first movie ends, as Marie goes on to the bedroom. I take the opportunity to give the girls some instructions for the night. They can sleep in the living room, if they turn off the TV, before they fall asleep. They can also sleep in Amy's bed, if they can get room enough, to get comfortable. They are short and Amy's bed is a queen size mattress. I go to the den to work, and give Marie a chance to fall asleep. I usually do this for her, because I alternately breathe hard, or I snore. She does the same, but I can still sleep when she does it. She may not be able to sleep with the girls here. She often can't sleep, if her mind is to busy. I like to give her all the time she needs. After all, she has to work and I don't have that affliction. It is a Friday night, so she has the day off tomorrow, but she deserves to get a good sleep then, as well.

The girls put in a scary movie and turn their attention away from me. I am out of sight and they have to keep their secrets from each other so I can relax. Amy does take the chance when one presents itself to touch Tanya inappropriately, out of Valerie's view. They check out the room they will have on the bed, so they can decide, where they are going to end up. They also give each other permission, to leave the group if comfort is not attainable. They go back to watch the movie. This is an old one from Walt Disney, about a family renting a vacation home, that is out in the woods. It is an old stone manor house, that creaks and groans and gives an eerie feeling. It's called 'The Ghost Whisperer' and it is completely apart from 'The Lake House', they had just seen. It is scary, but not gruesome. I have to say, Amy did her homework. Valerie gets up to use the bathroom and Tanya wrestles with Amy, to take advantage of the chance to 'play'. I know this will stop when they hear the toilet flush or the door open, so I rest easy. They nearly miss the opening of the door and almost get caught trying to smooth their pajamas. Valerie is not expecting to see anything so she doesn't. She comes in looking toward the TV set. She snuggles back down beside Amy, and barely notices that

Amy is more tense. The tension eases quickly, so Valerie lets it go. They get into the movie and respond to the mood, close to each other. At some scenes, both girls grab Amy's arms, for security. Neither thinks anything of it and Amy takes what she can get. I can't help but feel proud of Amy's efforts to resist.

I realize that if I was to know of something happening, I would look suspiciously too much aware, if I came rushing in to stop it. I decide a preventative trip to the kitchen is called for to get some celery, or fruit to snack on. That would kill some of the momentum Amy is building, at least for a bit. I get up and go down the hall and watch the eyes turn my way and the expressions I get. Amy grins at my feeble attempt to spoil it for her. I think for her to hear, that she is quite well versed at playing as well as 'playing'. I disappear back to my hole in the wall.

The night feels more like magic for Amy and Tanya. They kept things out of Valerie's sight, but more and more, did not mind if they were found out. They were more risky, the more they weren't noticed. I would go into the bathroom to try to interrupt them and I could feel that I was failing. It would not surprise me now, to feel Valerie get into the act. I was very relieved that, so far, she hadn't. I ventured down the hall again and into the kitchen. On the way back, I walk into the living room, to look at the TV. Amy had her chin resting on the arm next to Valerie. They all looked up and smiled again. I felt, either Valerie knows and doesn't care, or she is really into this cheesy movie. The minute I left the room, I looked back at her and she ignored me. She was teasing me, like a little kid with a cake they weren't to touch. Poking at the icing.

I had to admit defeat and just save my efforts for stopping open acts of sex. I could shame her in front of the guests but don't want to alienate her from me. Harmless gestures will have to be permitted, without acknowledgement. I have to keep it from affecting me. I am an animal, so I have the problem of being adversely encompassed by the things I will not be able to stop. I just keep thinking, 'this is my daughter, this is my daughter'. Amy is beyond responding to my thoughts. Her own thoughts have control of her now. She could be my son in exactly the same situation and I would have no more options than I do now. It does not matter that I chose to ask for a girl. The only difference is that she cannot get the girl pregnant. Now I could break up the night and take the girls home, or forbid it from happening again, or accept that my twelve year old daughter is having a love affair with another twelve year old girl and let it happen. It could get messy for them when her parents find out and it would not help me if it did. I am beating myself up for things that have not happened. The actions are in her thoughts only.

I have asked for what I have received, simply because I did not consider all the ramifications. Maybe I did consider them and convinced myself that I did not. I do have the capacity for subconscious thought, especially with the overactive mind I have. I must be careful now, not to fall deeper into the animalistic side of the brain that could sink me into depravity. I feel a depression eating at me. What have I done. I am not one that is going to answer to that side of me. I am one who is going to do battle with that side of me. I turn to methods I used when I was younger and dealing with horrors in my mind. Horrors that would be written about by a fellow sufferer, Steven King. I chose to block them out with beautiful scenes and innocent excursions through my alternate dimensions. My journeys had to become increasingly deeper in detail and depth of understanding. I attempted to lose myself in those depths. I would stare into a face, shape, scene, or pattern until I could no longer see the room, but only the images I was projecting into that at which I was looking.

When I was young, I had been molested by someone that I had given my trust. It only happened once and I rescinded my trust. He had been placed in our house by the CAS. I kept it to myself. Later, he was removed from the house for turning a teacher's car over at a sports event. He was given employment at a garage we had connections with. He was under a car which was jacked up. There were no safety stands under the car and the jack slipped. The car landed on him nearly crushing him. He went into a coma for several months. He finally died and therefore was punished for those things he had done. I was able to forgive him, but not me. I gave my trust too easily and now I could not give it without feeling fooled. I did give my trust, but not completely. Many people have gone through similar trials. At this point in my life, I feel fortunate that I could minimize the damage. I still suffered. That is one thing we must learn to do, each by our own demons. We must learn this to learn to forgive and let go and continue on to learn to give. We must through all of this learn to love and accept love.

Amy's sins that night consisted of some stolen kisses and inappropriate touches. The rest was her imagination running wild.

Amy's night did not get out of hand. They felt satisfied before long. They opened up to be with Valerie who remained blissfully unaware of the actions of the other two. They still had their moments, as they had wanted, but they gained something for which they had not planned. They gained a friend. Eventually they would tell Valerie about themselves, but for now they thought about her before themselves just long enough to make a friend. All three had a time they would not want to forget. They would think of it whenever things were not as they liked.

Chapter Sixteen

Coming To Terms

After the sleepover, Amy and I had to get straight the things we needed to set down as rules of engagement. As one with some adult reasoning, she saw that she had unnecessarily, stressed our relationship. She knew she had overplayed her hand. She appreciated me for giving her the chance to make the right choice and salvage the occasion. She saw how much I was tormented, because, as it played out in my mind, it also played out in hers. This was the dynamic that was to govern all of our actions. It was up to both of us, to be together on our decisions. It was the game plan for the duration, until death do us part. We both had a say in the inception, and now we both have to see it through. This was not a life lived by one person. Marie, Amy and I, have all been connected until death parts us. Once Marie and I are gone, Amy will be just like our other kids, except for the life she lived attached to us. She will resume her considerate ways. She will put aside her attempts to resume, her previous life's path. At least for the next few years, she will not go looking for sexual gratification. She will pursue her studies, to provide more for herself, than we could give her. Like her siblings before her, she will have to provide for her own education, beyond high school.

Marie and I will stand by her, in all her trials, but she will be the one to pay the damages, in any mistakes she makes. We will lead her the best we can. She will have to rely on scholarships, to get her to college. We are in our sixties now and don't have the earning power, to fund her future. All she can count on us for, is getting through high school. We will take care of her needs. She will have to take care of her wants.

She is in a position to do great things. With her sensibilities in order, she can achieve them. Teenagers don't usually have the sensible attitude, to help them make good choices. In this family, there are many that have. I expect her, to live up to their examples. She skipped right over her childhood, but she had that in her previous life, she can draw on that, for the learning that that provided.

She is going to church with her mother and helping her with the things she does there. She is learning to do the baking, that Marie is known for, and craftwork as well. Marie has been doing craftwork, since she was a child. She has an eye for detail and a critical view of her own productions.

When Marie was a teenager, she would gather wood pieces from her travels and clean and preserve them. After that she did needlepoint and was always taking on more difficult, challenging projects. She learned to knit and crochet. She worked in a craft store and made samples of their patterns to display. She had a good eye, for colour coordinating and matching. She became known for her intricate examples of all her work.

Amy started learning needlework and used that, to relieve the tension of her school work.

Fathers' Day is marked by Marie going off with her girlfriends, to the cottage and return early enough Sunday, to celebrate with me and the girls at Grace's place. Amy and I are left alone and that is not a bad thing, once in a while. Movies are watched, pizza is enjoyed, and schedules are thrown out the window. Amy and I spend some father- daughter time together and do many of the things, we can't do when Marie is home. After all, she is partying heartily at the lake.

This year it is my son's first Father's Day. I hope he celebrates it with his son.

It wasn't all work for Amy. We would go to her aunt's cottage on Lake Huron and learned how to handle a canoe, with her nieces. They would take the canoe out in the lake and have a picnic, around the sandbars. They would stay on shore, on rough water days. They took long hikes along the beach, hunting for driftwood and rocks.

We had camped quite regularly, until it Marie was tired of it. Now Amy and I would go camping together, both in our camper trailer and in tents. She recalled the time, I had slept along the highway, next to a road sign for safety. It was in a sleeping bag, on the gravel shoulder. That was when I was a teenager. It was at the interchange of highways 2 and the 401. I had been walking home from a weekend adventure in Port Stanley. I had walked most of the night and needed the rest. The next day, I continued my walk back to Ancaster. She also recalled the trips to Algonquin Park, with my brother and the vacations at my grandmother's cottage, at Fawn Bay, on Lake Couchiching. We had time to relive and renew those adventures.

We went up to Georgian Bay. We went to the Castle Gift Shoppe. I had been there when her sisters were tiny. It was very different now. We had been there in 1978, while renting a cottage on Balm Beach, and it had not been open too long before that. We stopped in at Ste.-Marie-among-the-Hurons and explored the places there. I had not been able to drive for long periods, for quite a while. With Amy along, I could do things like that again, with frequent stops though.

All this we would do, during the school breaks and summer vacation. It was different with Marie working on most occasions. Marie had always felt, that setting up camp was too difficult and sleeping on the ground, was too much. I would struggle through it and be creative, each time we set up. Amy found it not too bad, when she got a chance to try it. I felt it was worth the effort.

I did have to be careful of heat and sun stroke. We took frequent breaks, to cool off in the lake.

It was fun doing these things with Amy. It didn't always, have to be away from home.

We worked together on projects at home, that were put aside frequently, before Amy came. We did some work in the yard, preparing to build the extension on the garage. We worked on building my model railroad, in the basement. Amy also helped clean and organize my spaces, in the house. Marie was very pleased with these things. She would not mind having people over, now that there was order.

Happy is the husband, who has a happy wife.

I had had help before for short periods, building the railroad. Christian had been interested in it, but he could not read my mind, and wanted to do more than I could teach, in the short times we had. Amy knew what she had to do. We moved along, without a word of instruction. When I moved to a different job, she knew where and why I was going there, and went right along with me. How many times have you wanted help, like this? No questions, no problems, just smooth, seamless, effort. It was like it was choreographed. If there was an injury to one of us, the other was already going for help, or the remedy for the problem.

We were looking forward to our next project, before we were finished with the one we had on the go. I had discussed build a hotrod, with my friend and next door neighbour, George. We had taken both sides of the argument, and explored the pitfalls and benefits. We had both discouraged and encouraged the other, on the task of taking the project apart and putting it back together. Now, Amy and I reviewed the discussion and were making plans to go ahead. After all, what was the point of extending the garage, if we weren't going to fill it up, with another enterprise? To address that, before we deceive ourselves, there was still no space in the garage, for something that big. Honestly, how could you put a car in the garage, when there is all the other junk, you want to keep? You have to give your head a shake, once in a while, just to clear the dust. So now we have to get a temporary canvas shelter. Who am I kidding? How could it be temporary, when you would not want your work to suffer the harsh sun and winter weather?

Yes, Amy has to be sensible about things. She will just be home with me, for three, or four years. How would she be able to accomplish all of this? She has this weird idea, that the hotrod will go with her, when it's finished. We better make it a truck, so she can haul all my other crap away, with it.

The trips we take and the work we do together, give me a real lift in spirit. The best part, is that I know, when she is doing it just for me, and when she really likes it herself. She has the inquisitive drive to do it all, even if I was just along for the ride. When I am just along for her, she knows it. There are no secrets.

Her sisters will do the same, but I can't read their minds. That's okay though, because they will tell me. No secrets there either.

I wonder if it bothers Marie, that I will go off with the girls and leave her at home. With Faith and Grace, they wonder too. Amy knows what Marie, is thinking about it. She told me, Marie would like to have the time to do that, if she wants to, but she doesn't want to, and it gives her a break, from me. Sometimes no secrets, isn't all that great.

I would like to have the choice, of whose thoughts, I can read. Somebody said, that it is none of our business, what people think of us. I really would like, to be able to fix the problems, some people have with me. Que sera, sera. I can't have it all.

Chapter Seventeen

Whirlwinds

On one of our trips, Amy met a girl that just blew her away. She couldn't concentrate on what she was doing and lost track of what was going on with me. She could not go anywhere unless the girl was going there first. Amy's every thought was of this girl. She was a pretty girl, but not enough that she stood out to everyone else. You didn't see people watch her go about like Amy did. She didn't seem to notice Amy. I knew what Amy was looking at and concentrating on about her. When I looked at these traits, it made me scratch my head. Tanya was lost from her thoughts, with this new girl. She was older, about sixteen or so. Her figure was average and she was about six inches taller than Amy's five feet. It was the way she moved, that got Amy's attention. She had a fluid movement, that was not exaggerated, like you would see on the runway of a fashion show. It was a subconscious thing. The girl didn't look, to be trying at all. I had to look close, to see it. Amy did not have to try one bit. It was like the close up shot, of the movie camera. She just zeroed in on the sway.

I know what she is thinking, but I don't really know why. I feel the stress in her gaze, at this girl. I see what she is seeing. The one thing I miss, is the chemistry that is going on. I get all the thoughts and feelings. The sights and sounds she gets, I get. I am missing this chemistry. I thought we would get it all. Apparently not.

Amy finally gets the nerve up, to approach her at a store window, she was staring into. She stood behind her, just to the side, and squeezes out a 'hi'. The girl turned and looked at her. She looked straight in Amy's eyes. "Hi. Do I know you?" she challenged.

"No. I'm just here with my dad and I saw you walking."

"I'm sorry. What do you mean?"

Amy was nearly choking on the words. "I was just watching you walk. You walk nice." She reddens.

"Thank you, but I don't understand." She looked puzzled.

"I was just wanting to meet you and get to know you." she stammered a bit. "I wondered if you would show me around here."

"Um, I don't live here. I'm just visiting my grandmother."

"Would you like to explore with me?' Amy was getting more control of herself.

"Uh, okay. Have you been here long? Where have you gone so far?"

"I've just been where you've been for two days."

"What? You've been following me?"

"Yes. I've wanted to have someone to explore things with.

My dad is a little too slow moving and I wanted him to just rest for a little while."

"Why didn't you say something before?"

"I'm a little shy and I didn't know what I should say. You are so pretty and I was afraid you wouldn't talk to me."

"I'm a little confused. You thought I was pretty?"

"Yes. I did. You are pretty and you walk nice." Amy seems to be acting more like the twelve year old than someone whom had more life experience like she has had.

"Okay. I don't know what to do with that. Would you like to just sit and talk so you could help me understand more?"

"Yes, I would. I would like to talk about it with you."

"Okay. There is a coffee shop on the corner up here. Lets go there."

"Okay. I'll just tell my dad to go relax for a while."

The girls headed to the coffee shop and sat by the window facing the street they had come in from. "Your dad looks a little sore. Is he okay?"

"He's fine. He's got vertigo so he uses the canes to steady himself."

"My grandmother has that too. She fell once and ever since then she's been really dizzy."

"Dad has lots of other things and it's all mixed up. I don't know what happened to him."

"Where are you staying?" The girl is letting herself relax more.

"There's a camp ground by the river. We have a trailer there."

"Okay, so you were watching me?"

"Yes. I thought you were beautiful."

"So are you some kind of lesbian?"

"Yes I am. I've always known it, but find it awkward to approach girls."

"I don't know what to say. I'm not gay, but I am flattered at what you said about me." Now the girl is feeling awkward. "Did you think I was gay? Do I look gay?"

"I hoped you would be gay, but you looked pretty. I haven't been able to think about anything else but you, ever since I first saw you. My dad said the only way I could find out is ask and he said if I told you how beautiful you were, you would be less offended if you weren't gay."

"That's true. I did find it hard to be offended by it. You are nice and we can still explore together, if that's what you really want to do."

"I do want to explore with you. I mean the town."

"Alright, let's go explore. I mean the town, too."

They spent a few hours together exploring and went to her grandmother's place to show Amy where she was staying. Just in case she wanted to explore the town some more. What Amy really wanted to explore was her. She walked Amy back to the trailer park and met me.

After that disappointment, Amy was looking pretty dejected. I tried to buoy her spirits, but wasn't too successful. "Would you like to go home? We could go somewhere else if you want."

"Let's go home. I'm tired and I feel ripped apart." So, home we went. It was the most quiet she has ever been. Even her thoughts were still. When we came in, Marie was talking to one of her friends on the phone. She looked surprised to see us so soon.

"Amy, I think you're getting confused with all the conflicting feelings your body is giving you. On one hand, you've got an experienced soul that has way too much information for a twelve year old. On the other hand, you've got an inexperienced body that is going through puberty. The hormones flaring are giving you too much push to get into the game your adult sex drive is itching to use. Your emotions are in overdrive. You have missed a big preparation stage. You're wanting to use that which you had from your past life. The trouble is, you have to get this slower and you still won't get it synced up until the hormones let up."

"You're probably right, Dad, but how am I going to put the brakes on. Especially when I don't want to."

"I guess you just have to make some more mistakes, until the fear of making mistakes will help you put on the brakes. If I was to go out now looking for someone new, I would be in the same boat. You were lucky to bump into Tanya right away. You got confidence that helped to push you to the crush phase. That is where we get our fingers burnt, but it's a necessary step. Hurt helps you learn how to take it, so you learn to heal."

"She did take me by surprise. I thought I was back in my old life. I did not expect not being able to tell if she was gay. I thought she would see me and fall in love and it would be perfect."

"That's the crush. You get sucked into the void, in front of the prize, and the earth just fills in, over top of you. Maybe she was curious, and had thoughts of experimenting? She might have been thinking, of taking an opportunity."

"I didn't think of that. Once she said she wasn't gay, I stopped hoping and just accepted, that it was 'her being nice.' I never thought of it, turning into anything. How do you know all these things?"

"I was a father. I learned when I was a teenager, what not to do. I learned as a father that you can't keep your kids from learning, what not to do. I also learned, that you can't tell your kids, what they don't want to hear."

"I listen to you." she objected.

"Yes, because you haven't learned, not to listen yet. Plus you can read my mind, when your hormones aren't blinding you."

"Mom hasn't taught me yet." she grinned. "I have been with you too much, to learn her technique for tuning you out."

"I did help you from getting hit too hard. That girl was nice enough to you to console, you after she stepped on your heart. I did feel that. If she had tried any harder, she would have been gay for a day."

"I think you're right. She was nice to spend the day with me. I really liked her."

"Chemistry momentarily misdirected, I suppose. Society has, for now, become considerate of most people. That is changing in some places. Hate is trying to take away, the power of love. There are too many people, wanting to let it. Enjoy the benevolence, while it is here."

Marie is off the phone now and wants to hear what happened. I gave her the Readers' Digest version and Amy filled in the details. She gave Amy a hug and held her for a few minutes. Amy lets out the emotions, she was trying to hold in. I walked away, to let them be alone. Well, as alone as I could manage.

Chapter Eighteen

Off On A Tangent

Amy never gave boys a thought. Boys, on the other hand, have been giving Amy a thought. She is a beautiful girl, and not all boys think that girls, may be interested in other girls. Naivety is still around, in high school aged kids. Loners don't get their buddies, telling them all about life's twists. When they take an interest in a girl, they follow her around, waiting for the nerve, to approach her. They don't want too many people around, in case they are rejected.

Amy has not looked so much at the girls, in this school year, after the crushing blow that summer. She is concentrating on school work. She has thought to focus on a career, and is trying to see, where she feels most comfortable. The social aspects of school, have been put off-limits, so she can delve into a serious future. The self-imposed limitations, are easier to stick to, than those put upon you, by someone else.

One boy in particular, has been watching her, with idolizing eyes. She is not yet turned thirteen, and is as developed, as a seventeen year old. He is as stuck on her, as she had been, that summer.

She had as much of an idea, of this interest aimed at her, as her prey in her encounter that summer, had had. It was her niece that pointed it out. She saw the guys looking, and the one boy, was noticeably more ensconced in his thoughts, while he took the bus, that she rode on. Jayme was one, to come right out and say what she thinks, and mentioned the boy's stare, when Amy was getting ready to get off the bus. She checked behind her, as she got out of the door and when she saw him, getting out at her stop, she looked up at Jayme and waved, so she could seem to be unaware of her follower. She walked up the street, without looking back at him. He had given her time to get ahead. He had been spooked a little, when she had looked by him, at Jayme. She was glad he gave her the space. She didn't know if he was stalking her, to approach her, or to attack. She walked briskly and listened for his footsteps. She did not panic. She was close to home and she knew I was there to help her, if he tried anything. Just the same, she looked for the Neighbourhood Watch signs, in the windows. She got to the driveway and turned in, keeping a steady pace. She tried to see, if she could see in some reflection, but the angles weren't right. She looked back, just enough to see through the corner of her eye. He was looking toward her, but kept walking straight past the driveway.

She breathed out, relieved that it was over. She saw me looking down the drive at him.

I let her know, he was taking notice of what the house looked like, and the address. I came forward to watch him, so she wouldn't have to. I had been readying myself, since the moment she started up the street. I felt her tensing up, and got out where

I could get to her, if she needed me. I saw him walking to the end of the street, and made note of which way he turned. I stayed watching the corner. I wanted to see if he would turn back. After an acceptable amount of time, I went back to my work.

Amy wondered what she should do, the next time.

"Just watch to see if he's getting off at your stop. If he is, you can stay on, if I'm not home, or if I'm home, get me to come to meet you. Another thing to do, would be to approach him and ask, if he would like to walk with you. If he is not out to attack you, he would take the opportunity to walk with you. In either case, I could come to meet you. If you stay on the bus, you can go home with Jo and Jayme. I'll come to pick you up, on my way home."

"What should I say if he walks with me?"

"Just find out his name and where he lives. If it is not around here, ask him why he comes this way. He might just be going to the recreation centre, or a friend's place. He might be following you, because he likes you and doesn't have the nerve, to talk to you. In that case, just make a friend, and let him know soon enough, that you aren't looking to date anyone. You can blame me. Say that I won't let you date, until you're thirty five."

"Thirty five?"

"Yes. It's a noncommittal number. He will know I am either, a super strict ogre, or I have a sense of humour, but that he shouldn't get his hopes up. That would keep you, from having to be totally up front with him. It's not so bad, to have boys that are friends. They can run interference for you, when I am too far away. Other guys might not bother approaching you, if you have a guy to challenge them. Eventually, you can tell him you're gay and you like him to stay close, but not too close. There are a few options for you. The 'make him a friend', is probably the best, but even then, you would have to be careful, that he doesn't think he has a chance at dating you. Then if you decide that you would change teams, you have the option."

"Oh, I won't likely be changing teams!"

"Never say never. Long shots do happen. If you're prepared to accept the possibility, you won't be as affected by the shock."

"Okay Dad. I will be open to the possibility, that I've been lying to myself."

"That's all I ask. Now, what's for dinner?"

"Well it's not crow."

Amy did have the opportunity to make a friend, the very next day. I was at home, when she was coming to her stop, and she went ahead with my suggestion. Jayme gave her a nudge, as she was about to get up. She looked over her shoulder and saw him standing up. She got off the bus and waved to the girls. Then she turned around to face him. She said hello, and asked him, if he would like to walk with her. He was startled, but accepted the honour. She made her enquiries and he admitted to living, close to the school they attended, and that he was coming here, to get a chance to meet her. That is what she was afraid of. She saw me coming, and had me stop and wait. She said she was flattered by the interest, but that she wasn't allowed to date boys, until she was thirty five. She saw his face change and his hopes sag. Then he seemed to get the humour. She said, she would be happy to talk at school, any time, so he didn't have to come all the way here, on the bus everyday. He showed some relief, and some elevation, of those hopes. She told him, she was only twelve, and that she won't be seeing anyone, outside of school, for quite a while.

They were just getting to me, when she finished explaining that, so she stopped and introduced him to me. He had to fill in the name, since he hadn't told her yet. We shook hands, continuing the walk to the house. Amy told me where he lived, just so he didn't freak out, when I offered to drive him home. It might have occurred to him, that we had not communicated. We drove Brent across town to his house. Now we have defused any fear, that he would become a threat to her. His father was in the driveway, so I got out and spoke to him, to let him know, what was going on.

On the way home, Amy and I laughed at the look of surprise on Brent's face, and how it got used so much, in that little period of time. She did feel better about coming home from school, after that scare yesterday. We enjoyed telling her mother about it, when she got home.

Brent did hang around Amy at school, after that and Amy did, enjoy the friendship. She introduced him, to her nieces, which left him open to Jayme's barbs. He didn't fare too bad, on that though. It only gets repeated, if it has some affect, the first few times. Having a guy around her, got her more noticed. She felt it was too much, but you can't really stop it, once it starts. Sitting on her own, she was nearly invisible. Sitting in a group, stood her up on a stage, of sorts. Guys noticed her, because a guy was with her. Girls noticed her, because anybody was with her.

We had some feelings flaring up, about the attention she was getting. I tried to get her to relax, and lose herself in her work, but do it in an open space, around lots of people. If she felt threatened, she should try to face the threat, like she did with Brent. I became more alert in the mornings, when she was at school and I tire easily, when that happens.

We had to sit down and get this stress, worked out. "It won't help any of us, if we can't function, when we need to. This is a different scenario now. This is not your past life. You aren't threatened yet. You can't jump at shadows. Be aware of what is around you, and where you can get to, for immediate help. Walk with somebody, when you are away from school, or home. If you are on the bus, and you feel threatened, stay on the bus, until you can go straight into a open business, or walk with someone to their place, where I will meet you. If you can hide anyplace, quickly, without being seen, do it. If you are caught, where you are cut off, scream and hurt the attacker, as much as you can. But, before any of this happens, realize one thing, you are not a target. You are not being threatened, and you have me, to witness anything, you can see, or hear. Before you panic at any time, take a deep breath, and ask me to come to you. Let me know, where you are, or where you are going to be, and I will get there."

Amy had been agitated so bad, she was sobbing. She kept seeing that same scene, over and over again. She saw the men surrounding her, and the woman she knew, from university, was egging them on, calling her a Lezbo, and taking the first swing at her. They raped and beat her, and the blows kept coming. Once they had violated her enough, they threw her to the street. They kicked her body until it was limp and lifeless. Then she saw herself, being pulled out of the river. She was bloated and torn. She had parts missing. Nobody knew her. They weren't even sure, if she was human. She was just stuck under a tree limb, that had fallen in the river. They didn't know where she came from. It was years before her attackers where found, and only then, because they were bragging about it in a bar.

I gave her something, to help her sleep and sat by her the whole night, ready to comfort her, when she would shake, or shudder. I had Marie call the school in the morning, to say she would not be there. I felt those attacks. Just as I had felt my attackers, fifty five years ago. I lived. She did not. Someone stopped, and called for help, for me. Nobody stopped to help her. My mother could not recognize me, when she came to get me, at the hospital. Nobody could recognize her, until an autopsy, told them she was human.

I have lived a full life. I hope she can, at last, do the same.

Chapter Nineteen

Back On Track

Amy was back to her normal, cheery self by her birthday. The day we 'found her'. We gathered her friends, Tanya, Valerie, Brent and her relatives, to celebrate a new teenager. She was thirteen and still no word from the search, for whom she was. We wondered how long it will be, before they give up the search, and allow us to adopt her. We were not letting go of her, until I walk her down the aisle, at her wedding.

The CAS have been keeping up with her progress. They did get the call, about her breakdown, and it was determined, that it was a past experience, that had been triggered by some, series of events, known only to her. She would now receive psychiatric care, for the episode and an alert has been flagged about the incident, and what it means to her present condition. Did it cause the amnesia, in a separate occurrence. There was an alert sent to hospitals, in a wide range, to see if a patient, suffering from this type of malady, had been treated and matches her description.

The same hospitals, that were initially contacted, plus those in a much broader radius. Still, there was no news to be found. It seems to be, that she had just dropped from the sky.

You know, that when professional healthcare providers, start mentioning, that people just dropped from the sky. It is thought, that it was them, on which the patients in question, had dropped. Thus, this line of thinking, tends to disappear, before it is reported.

Now Amy is back with us, and is ready to go back to school. She has her team, to watch out for her, and I am ready to get to her, before she has even alerted the team. Tanya comes to see her more often. They go out on dates, supervised of course. Yes, Tanya has come out, to her parents. They knew long ago, that she was looking in the other direction. They figured, that Amy was what she was looking for, when she stopped looking.

Now we take turns escorting them, to the assorted venues they find. Everywhere except gay bars. They will have to be patient, if they want to frequent those.

They don't advertize, but they do enjoy the times they have.

Brent still doesn't know and neither does Valerie. The family have been let in on the secret. Whether the family caught on, when they were told, is anybodies guess. Amy says her friends will be told, when they are asked to be best man and maid-of-honour, at the wedding. We will see, if we can see, that shocked look, on Brent's face again.

Her grades are not suffering, even without taking her absence into account. She is still up in the air, about which career to take. She has started to interview the professionals, in the family, and those that we use regularly. She called on her doctors. Her advisers and teachers, were pointing out options, that have promising futures. She is not piqued, by any one thing.

I'm glad I'm not looking for a career these days. There is nobody to work for, that can promise a lifelong position, anymore. Nobody but one. You. You are the only one, that can support your future. That means being the creator, of the product, or service, that will be able to keep you busy, for your life term, and provide a pension, from investments. The most negative part of that possibility, is that you are essentially, applying for a job, everyday. You have to sell yourself, everyday, to every customer.

She decides to put off the decision, for the new year. She takes a break for Christmas. We get working on our project, that was put off, during the summer. It is down to our model train table. We have decided to modernize it, to give it the reliability, of the new products available. I had already bought some of them, before Amy came, and now she will help me, bring it into the twenty-first century. That is what she spent downtime, at the summer excursions, reading up on. On this, I am the follower. After this change over, my skills will take over, with the scenery and details. Until then, I will do, what she needs me to do. Well as much as I can understand.

She talked to her friends about their hobby interests, and didn't get any volunteers. I already knew, the grandkids aren't going to jump at the chance. Christian had some thoughts on it, long ago. Nothing lately.

She had thought of posting a notice at school, but we both got anxious, thinking of new people coming in, to give us a hand. The local hobby shop said, they could arrange some help, rigging the old locomotives, to the electronics. We put that decision on hold, too, and got going on setting it up, for the ones that will work. Amy is great, at picking up new ideas, and going right into production. The table wiring, is easy to switch over. We switch four wires and we are on AC, all ready to program the engines. We have ordered the system, that works well with our equipment, and it arrives before the holiday break starts.

We are ready to go in a day, and now, we get to work, building the upper part of the table. This is where, we install the scenery elements. The track work is not very complicated. I had designed it to be easy, for me, when my health gets worse. If you are prepared, it doesn't come too fast.

The things we have to work hard at, is getting the table to look like furniture. That was Marie's main stipulation, that it looks like furniture. Amy devises many ways to accomplish that, and fit well within our budget. She saw one item, on the Model Railroader e-mail. She makes it, so much more fun, than it had been, in a long time. Doing things like this, with someone that enjoys it, as much as you do, is incredibly more satisfying. By Christmas, we have the table built and the mainline track laid. We finish the wiring by New Year's Eve. We get problems fixed, that I had made, before she came. A switch motor that should have been installed, two years ago, is finally done.

We call Marie down, to witness the maiden voyage, of our first train, across the whole layout. "Finally. How many years have you been working on that? When will you have the scenery done?"

"Never. I am going to be constantly changing the scenery, until I can no longer do it." I said as a matter of fact.

"We will both, be working at that, and it will look finished, soon enough, but it will be changing, as often, as we decide to do it." Amy jumped in. "I won't let him, get lost again, like everybody else did."

Marie was not happy with that remark.

"He has been asking for someone to help him, for years now, and nobody came down to see, what he needed doing. I will help him get it done." Amy was defiant. She knew when I had asked, and when some said they would help, and that they had not come, with any intention of helping at all.

Marie stormed upstairs and pushed the door shut. "You know she will be miserable now. I usually apologize right away."

"Well she may not remember, or admit to it, but I can see into her mind, and she knew, you had asked, for two Christmases, for someone to help. I know she did not intend, to help you. You always help, her with her projects. You help her figure out spacing, and patterns, and that isn't your hobby. It's hers. She said before, she could help you, but quickly put aside, any thought of doing it.'

"Maybe she can't remember. You can help her. But I don't think she will like it, one bit. It would be better, if you could apologize. You don't have to like it, but it will help keep the peace, around here."

"I'll apologize. Someone besides you, has to call them on that, because they all said they would and didn't."

"I know, but I can't force anybody. It's not nice to work with anybody, that does it under duress."

Amy grunts and heads upstairs after her mother. She apologized and then told her that, she can look inside her memory, and find every instance. Every time when something was said, and then denied. She explains how she knows, and that it has been a source of contention, for years and even that, was denied. She didn't want to pick a fight, but she did want to keep me, from being pestered about things, that I had asked for help for, and not received it.

It is strained for them for a time. Going back and forth in their thoughts, about injured pride, accusations, facing up to guilt, and finally coming together to hug, hold onto, and forgiveness. It is never who is right, and who is wrong, weak, or strong. It is love, and how to come back home. How do we get back, to where we were? How do we undo, the hurt? How do we own up, to what we really want? Holding onto each other, they let themselves let go, and then the tears come, and wash it all away. The hurt, the pride, the waste of time, trying to get back. They think, could we not have just, done this earlier. Long and short answers, are no. We have to go through it all, for it to really bring you back home.

Now that it is done, the recovery begins. The rebuilding of energy reserves. The refilling of emotions spent. The regaining of strength, in the overdrawn tissues of the body. The propping back up, of the facades. The hiding away the wreckage, of memories. All stored up for the next time. Never wanting the next time.

'Come to my window. I'll be home soon.'

The good times we remember, to bring us back, after the storm. Back, through the broken doorway, of the heart.

Chapter Twenty

The Health Of The Hearth

Patch up the spaces, between the logs of the cabin. Seal up the gaps, around the windows and doors. Replace all the shingles on the roof. Stoke up the furnace, in our souls. Now reach out, and share the home we've built, for it is just a pile of wood, if we don't open it up and welcome someone home.

Amy is back in class, and sailing through the lessons. To where? She does not know. She has canvas filled with wind, but no port, to set the course for.

You think about the more fortunate, that spend their lives floundering, just outside the harbour of success. They have so much, to get them there, but they can't find the entrance to the harbour.

Then you see the dingy, struggling through the surf. Rowing and bailing. Rowing and bailing. Coming straight and true. Straight into port, in tattered and torn sheets, streaming from the hapless mast, held on by hopes and dreams.

The fuel grows stale, in the tank of the vehicle, with no place to go.

"Is it too easy?" I say out loud while I sit alone in my den. "Where do you want to go, in your life? What do you want, to get out of it all? What was your goal, in your past life? Did all you want to do, was breathe?"

Amy hears me talking, over all the noise, of people filling the huge room. She is at lunch. Sitting by herself, waiting for the answers, to appear in her mind. She is oblivious, to the others at the table. Perched on a tree branch, high on a hill, overlooking a wide valley, full of life. She can't see past the leaves.

'I don't know what, I want out of life. I can't think of what I wanted, in my past life. I came into this one, for your dream. I didn't have one, of my own.'

"Well you can't get far on my dreams. I have enough trouble, getting anywhere with them myself."

'But they were so clear. Clear to me.'

"Yes dear, they are very clear to me, but I only have one oar. You know how fast, you can get anywhere, with only one oar, don't you?"

'But at least you are going in a straight line. You are getting somewhere.'

"Well then try switching sides, now and then. Pick two choices, and aim for them both. That is how I got here. Look into yourself, and see the kind of person, you want to be. Then look to see the kind of place, you want to be in. Then see what kind of path, that can take you, to both places. But remember, every paradise has its poisons. There are faults in every masterpiece. They are just covered up, by a masterful stroke, of genius."

'Okay genius. Start stroking.'

"Did you know that the great artists threw away most of their work, because they were not happy, with how it looked. Make a mess and see if you can find, anything, worth saving from it. Then make another mess, and find something in it. Eventually, you will find out, what it is that you like, and how it is, that you found it."

'Okay Dad, I think I can do something with that.'

"Just remember to start over, when you can't see through the mess."

'I have to be someone who cares, about those around me. I want to have a family. I want to help people, that can't help themselves, and people that don't know, how to help themselves. I would like to have somewhere, that I can go, to recharge myself. Somewhere that I can be alone, with God, and the people I am doing it all for. I want to be like you. I want to help point people, in the right direction. I want to help them get up, and walk on their own. I want a girl, who is like the light, and the air, to me. I want to look into her eyes, and see me there, right in the middle of her heart.'

"That is what you need to aim at, but I was a lot of things, before I became me. I was innocent. I became evil. I went through hell, and dragged people with me, because I thought, I was going in the right direction. I took up peoples' time, that didn't have any left for themselves. I got through, by talking to God, and listening for His voice, wherever I could find it. I let Him, lead me back. I brought people back with me. They didn't know, whether to trust me or not, after what I had put them through. They came with me, because they loved me. I kept talking to God, and I knew His voice. I could hear it, through all the noise and clatter, of the steel mills. Through all the voices, the words came, in answer to my prayers. I heard Him in church, on the street, from the song on the radio, from someone talking in a restaurant. I knew His voice. You know it's God talking, when you hear words of love, hope and direction. You know it is not Him if there is pain, fire and retribution. He needs no one, to deal out harm. He told us that, through His Son, Jesus Christ. He will only tell you to love, and care. I came through the dust, up from the pit, listening to Him. I was not saintly, not even good. I can't say 'I did it my way,' because I only fell through cracks, crawled up, and hid behind God's hand, and let Him, take me, where I had to go. I started to show the good, He gave me, when I started to love. He cleared away the soot, and crap, and scars, and made me look good. I smiled and tried to make people feel better, about themselves, and that made them feel better, about me and the others around them. I didn't save anybody. I just opened my eyes to people, and let them see my heart. When you do that, it helps them find their way, back to God. You don't go out and drag them. You show them, He is there."

'I don't know how, to do all that. It hurts, just to hear it.'

"You don't have to do, any of it. You already know God. Just keep Him with you, and show Him to others, by letting them, see Him, in your life. I turned my back on Him, and that is why, it took so long, to get back."

'What do I do about school, and what to go for?'

"Look at the things that help people, and decide which ways, fit best, with what kind of help, you want to give people. Counsellors, psychiatrists, doctors, nurses, mechanics, actors, singers, writers, composers, sailors, carpenters, brick layers, they all have different ways, that they are helping people. Pick something, that fits well with your strengths, and will help your weaknesses, improve. If you go with something too easy, you won't try hard enough, to succeed."

'I have to go to class now, Dad. Stay close.'

"Always."

When Amy left school that day, she was still mulling over the things I had said. The bit about, all those different jobs, and how they all, helped people. She could see it and she was still confused. I didn't interfere with her thoughts. I had said enough. Probably too much.

I listened to her. I thought back to myself as a kid. I was in love with girls. I saw them in so many ways. Some were scary, and could break you, with a look. Some were dull and lightless. Some shone so bright, it dazzled me. Some were clear, and open. And some were dark, and mysterious. It was those last three, that got to me. There were so many of them. How is a kid to decide? What can you do, to narrow it down? Why would you want to? So I started out with three. There was one of each. The one who dazzled me, was always bright. We played together, with the one that was clear and open. They were with me, for quite a time. Then I started school and met 'the mysterious one'. As close as I could get, I was never close enough, to keep with her, and had to move on. The one who dazzled me, moved away and dazzles me, to this day, just as the mysterious one vanished into mystery. The clear and open one, was with me until my grandfather died, and we had to sell the property, and move away. I saw her again in high school, and she was still clear and open. I was eight by the time we had moved. I was at a new school, with new girls, and there were so many, of all three types, I was lost. So I let them come to me. I could never figure out, how they were so beautiful, and amazing. How could I have them all? When one would call, I would answer, until another called. I could not deny them. They had a hold over me. I was never one to believe, I had a hold on anybody. After a lot of running, this way and that, two of them faced me in the hall, and told me, if I couldn't decide, I could not have either of them. 'I can't have you?! It's you, who has me!' Many, many, many girls, had me going all over the place. When I finally settled down, it was by accident, that the one that kept me, got me. She was and is a combination, of all three. Don't get me wrong, I am still pulled from this one, to that. The difference is, I stopped going.

Now it is my daughters and granddaughters, that dazzle me. Marie keeps me, now and forever.

'Dad? I think I have got this narrowed down to three.' Was she mimicking my story? 'I think that psychology and theology, are the ones I want to study. The third is carpentry. I need an outlet, for the frustration, from the other two, just to keep me sane.'

"Good choices and they fit together so well. Congratulations, on getting past the first step."

Chapter Twenty-One

Moving On

Now that Amy has chosen a career to pursue, she starts evaluating and organizing her thoughts, ideas, and memories, that will be useful in that area. She gets very focussed on her plans, when she has a definite goal to aim for. She has Marie's dedication and attention to details. She has my imagination and ability to create, from the abstract images, she forms from it.

I don't know how much, she will be able to stick to her studies though, with us going away to Cuba again, next month. She likes it at Grace's, because she can go to and from school, with her girls. It is difficult with Bradley and his activity, that can make it hard to concentrate. It is only for two weeks. She could let up for the time she's there. He has, calmed down some.

She has been thinking about summer school, to get her a head start, on next year. Jo is taking extra classes, to shorten her high school time, by a year. Amy has been thinking about that, too. She is planning on going to her advisor, to check out the list of courses, she will need to take, and whether she can get those scheduled, to double up on them. I ask her to be careful, she doesn't burn herself out, but teenagers don't listen, when their busy knowing everything.

An interesting development, has come to my attention. The weight that had left Marie and I, when Amy was created, has snuck up on us. The experts always say, that no matter how you lose your weight, if you haven't changed your habits enough, it will find its way back. You have to keep moving fast enough, that it can't catch you. The cold weather last winter, kept us in most of the time. Once you have been idle long enough, inertia keeps you from getting started again. With all the same problems affecting us, there wasn't enough change. We have had some good results, lately, and if we can keep the momentum going, we might get back to where we were, fourteen months ago.

If Amy takes summer school, we may not have her with us, for the cottage time. I know she will be disappointed about that, but she wants to get scholarships, to put her through university. Her cousin did it, and she feels up, to the challenge. She says we can do the weekend trip, that we did last year. We might even run across that girl she met last year. She would like to further her friendship with her. She would like to get in touch with her, even though, it wouldn't be a romantic affair. If she does go to summer school, she would still like to see, if she could find her again. She would also like to go farther, with our plans to build a hotrod, this year.

Oh Amy, why didn't I pray for you earlier. Okay, I just opened that can of worms, so lets see, if I can settle them, back in the can. When you start asking for something, you have to build that desire, until it starts burning. Once that happens, you get to the point, that separates the wishful thinker, and the truly desirous. When you reach that point, you start turning to prayer, and letting God in on the deal. That is where it starts. You now need to build the desire, to a white hot need, searing all the other wants, until it is the only want, that hasn't been consumed. That is where you start asking others, for help. When you can get three people, to agree on that prayer, and do so, in the sight of God. He will answer your prayer. You have to show your determination, in getting that, which has consumed you with desire. It has to be right with God.

If your prayer is for someone else, and others are praying for the same thing, in their favour, you will set the direction of that blessing, by specifying where it should go, and whom shall enjoy the blessing. In a case like that, you will also reap the benefit, because of your selfless action. These are the parameters, you need to work with, in getting a prayer answered.

As it was said before, Marie and I, had agreed on the prayer. According to the parameters, we needed an extra, third person. We just had us who had agreed. When Amy came, she told me, that she was the third person, because she volunteered for this experiment in creation. An experiment that would see, if two people can remain connected, psychokinetically, to each other and also have another person, that will provide another complication, being connected to one psychically. Can this be done, without causing irreparable harm, to any of the concerned people?

So far, Amy, who is the most connected in this relationship, has only suffered, from the memory of her death, in her previous life. Other than that, she was the same, tortured type of person, you would find, anywhere on the planet. Marie has only an outgoing connection, in that Amy, can access her thoughts, but Marie, cannot access Amy's thoughts. I am in the middle position in involvement, being only psychokinetically connected to Amy, and that is a two way connection. Up to this point, we all have acclimatized ourselves, so that we are not overly sensitive, to the arrangement.

Brent has expressed some discomfort, being in close proximity to Amy, and not being able to interact, romantically, with her. Brent is seventeen. Amy is thirteen. She does look more like seventeen, so I can see his problem. Amy doesn't want, to tell him she is gay, but how else, can you cool someone's desire for you. An argument might give her some room, to come up with a more permanent solution. Perhaps a confrontation, on the subject at hand. Complaining about him, being overly focussed on his sexual image, of her. If not that, she could complain that, she has to focus her energies, on preparing for a career, and doesn't have room, for romance in her life. ... Oh, that might do it. A two stage frontal attack. It is harsh. It will probably send him off permanently. Does she really want that? To lose a friend, because you don't want them to know, about your most basic desire. No, she can't do that to him. If he is truly a friend, he will accept her, for whom she is.

She decides to confide in him. She states up front, that she does not want to lose a good friend, and would be as close a friend, as she could possibly be, if he could understand, and accept her, for whom she is. "I do care for the friendship we have. It is more than I ever had with a guy. But, it is also as good a friendship, I could ever, be able to have, with a guy. Brent, I am gay. I have always known, that I was gay. I will always be, a lesbian. You are closer, than any brother could be, and I love you more deeply, than I would, ever, be able to love another guy. I hope you will remain, my best friend. I hope I can help you, accept me, as your gay friend. I do have something in common with you. I love girls, as much as you do."

Brent looks dumbfounded. He swallows hard and looks at her. It hurts to hear, that he can never taste her sweet lips, or touch her body, as a lover would. He does not want to lose her friendship, but he always wanted her so badly, that he would get angry and hit a wall, with all he could gather of his strength, just so that it would hurt more, than this emptiness within his arms, and his heart. "Amy, I do want to keep you as a friend. I don't want to lose your friendship. But, I have such a desire to hold you, that it makes me livid, with rage, to think I could never have you, as a lover. I don't know how, I can answer your revelation. I feel like I have been gutted, and hung up in the sun. I am empty."

Amy holds him in her arms, pressing herself on him, as if to imprint her form on him. He has nothing else he can do, but to hold her close, and he does, hold her closer and closer. He realizes what she is trying to do for him, and it fills his heart. It takes away the rage. It fills him. He doesn't feel the emptiness, that has been eating away at his heart, these last few months. He bends his head down to kiss her head and rest it against her. The time is lost from him, and all those around, have vanished. It is just her, in his arms. There is nothing else.

It was more than he could have asked her for. It was more than any sexual act, could have touched. It drew him closer to her, than he could ever hope to be, to anyone. When he finds a mate for life, it will be pale in comparison, to this feeling deep within him now. She has given him so much of herself, in that short time, that he can never hope to get anything, deeper, from anyone else.

"Maybe we can double date. You can be my wingman. I can never be anything closer to you now. I am happy to be your friend."

"Back atcha bro." She stretches up to kiss him on the lips and then turns away. She felt like she won the lottery. She was glad that she had done the hardest thing, she thought she would ever have to do. To come out, to her best friend and keep him.

I try not to spoil the moment, when Amy is interacting with someone. She had chosen well in her method and I was proud of her.

Chapter Twenty-Two

Holy Days, Batman

The annual trip to Cuba is upon us. There will only be ten in all this year, and it's all out for the two weeks. Amy will be deep in thought, for her school work is a big priority now. Grace will handle the authorities, while we are gone again. This is starting to feel like a rut, to some of us. Oh. the problems you have to bear in paradise. We are going to make it to the little village we went to two years ago, where the school there, was in real need. We have stocked up on items for the school and the village as well. Marie and I are really in need of the break. We hope to get up on the top floor to maximise the exercise. The sand is calling us home and the surf is singing harmony. There are a lot of changes going on down there this year, and we just hope that we can still get the feeling we have come to expect from it.

It has always been a pleasure to encounter the Cubans in there daily lives. It shows us two things; 1. There is need everywhere. 2. We can live simpler lives.

I have brought some tools to give to the people of the village to help them create better crafts. They sell them near their harbour and can use some variety. We hadn't got any of the trinkets yet but we will be sure to get them this year. We may not come back there again.

Marie and I are both in our sixties now, and we have only so long, before we won't be able to enjoy these trips. I am already needing a wheelchair for some places I need to go. We are feeling our age, despite the relief we got with Amy's creation. They say you're only as old as you feel. Well, we feel old. We don't act it, if we can help it, but the miles you travel take their toll. We are about to leave middle age. In mind we are much younger. In body we feel ancient. The time to retire is not close enough, for Marie's taste. We want to enjoy our time and that may mean selling our home, to get our pension out of it. We bought it for our retirement. The best you can do, is the best you can do.

When Amy, came into our lives, God had used flesh from our bodies, to create her. It was an exhilarating feeling, to have that weight removed from our tiring frames. We became fifty pounds, lighter and thinner, in such a short period of time. We looked six years younger. Considering that I was looking around seventy five, I looked closer to my chronological age. Marie was looking about fifty and instantly, looked like forty again. Women always look younger, in my opinion. But, that lasted for such a short time. Once the stresses, of handling the attention, that came along with Amy, took its toll, we were very nearly back to where we were.

If you know the Bible, you know that Eve, was made from a rib, taken from Adam, while he slept. After using the 'Prime Rib' from Adam, Eve was instrumental in the downfall of intelligent

Man. Eve spoiled it for women for thousands of years. Since Jesus died for our sins, He took away the curse that had defiled Woman, in God's eyes. Still men have held Eve's sin, over the heads of all women, even unto this day. They are still fighting a fight, that was called off by God, two thousand years ago. Jesus died for all our sins. Not just man's. Women can no longer be subjugated in God's sight. This was ordained by God, Himself.

I think a whole lot of women just began to feel better about Christianity.

I must clear up what I had said earlier. I said 'Intelligent Man'. I said this because we know there is irrefutable evidence of many of the Bible's stories. There is also, irrefutable evidence that man has evolved from other primates. Here is the kicker. God would not allow Eve's sons to enter into more sin, to do His will, of being fruitful and multiplying. The boys did not have any sisters. This leads us to believe, or should I say conclude, that Adam's sons, mated, with the offspring, of evolved men. Adam was Created in God's own Image. When his offspring mated with the daughters of evolved man, they completed the evolution of prehistoric man. Prehistoric man was never a fully intelligent species. God's creation of Intelligent Man, in his Image, became the fulfilment, of the creation He had set out to do.

I think a whole lot of apes just thought, I knew it wasn't all our fault.

Now that I have put forth the only possible explanation that would tie in the whole of man's history and explained the elusive, missing link, I will say, "You're welcome." God had explained it to me, while we were talking about my suggestion for Amy's creation.

I know, so many of you are saying, "You're kidding, he

couldn't come up with that on his own. He isn't that smart!"
Yeah, I know.

Is it that easy? How do you correct a defect in your bloodline?
You mate with a family line that doesn't suffer that defect. You
can't help the members that suffer now. What you do is helping
your grandchildren. How do you improve the animals in your
stock? You breed with a healthier stock. How can it not be that
simple. Intelligence added to a strong sturdy stock improves at
least fifty per cent of the stock. Proof is in the improvement of
each consecutive example of developing man. Introduction a new
and healthy line will push the existing line further ahead, enough
to skip an evolving stage, because it infects a stagnant line, with
energetic genes. If I'm wrong, all I did is get your attention and
made you take a break, from the same old way of thinking. If you
are faced with conflicting evidence supporting differing concepts,
rethink your concepts and look for the unifying concept. The
evolving species was not equipped to move to the next stage. So
a new line was divinely created to unify the aspects needed to
continue the needed development.

How do you create a bad bloodline? Practice inbreeding.

Chapter Twenty Three

Cuba Again?

I enjoy leaving for places new and diverse, but I also enjoy making friends in the places we go and return to their happy faces. I may not have a lot of time to do a lot of both. Just for now, we will see how things go in returning to our friends.

Amy can get to work lining up her qualifications and building her interest and knowledge of her chosen fields. I've let her know the things that I know on the subjects, so that leaves lots of room for her to discover. You know? The blank slate effect.

We get off in our usual way and make sure I get better seats. I have no problem when I arrange for wheelchair assistance this time. I did preselect the seats and made arrangements to have the same going back. Whether I get those seats going back, will have to be revealed in Cuba. I have faith in the system to mess it up. I mentioned earlier, that the group was smaller, this year. The expectations are for a less rigid management of our activities. We aren't waiting some things for newcomers to take them with us.

The feeling is relaxed but we will miss the ones that aren't going with us.

Amy wasn't dating Tanya when she was last staying at Grace's. I told Grace, that Amy can go out with Tanya, if she wants and that Tanya's parents will likely go with them. She also learned about the other friends, that may be by to see her.

Grace didn't know about Amy being gay, and wondered why I was preauthorizing Amy and Tanya's going out, and with Tanya's parents along with them. I thought I should tell her but was hesitating. As it was, she came out and asked. "Is Amy dating this girl, Tanya?"

"Yes, she is. Amy is gay and Tanya's parents with Mom and I are chaperoning their outings to keep them in line."

"She's only thirteen. Why is she allowed to date?"

"She would hang out with her friends if she was straight, so we want to keep them on hold, by not letting the romance go too far. We are keeping it to the buddy stage, but do allow them to hold hands, hug and kiss, like they would if they were just best friends."

"Okay. Do the kids at school know they are gay?"

"One boy who was in love with Amy, and wanted to go farther with her, was told. He was her best friend and is now watching out for her at school, to keep her from being bugged by anyone there. Just keeping other guys away."

"Didn't he know how old she was?"

"Yes, she told him that a little while before she turned thirteen."

"Do my girls know?"

"I don't know that one. I know Amy didn't tell them, but they figure these things out sometimes. I don't know how to find out without giving it away."

"I'll see what they know."

"Okay, careful."

"Girls, what do you know about Amy and her friends at school?"

"What do you mean?" Jo was thinking, something was up.

"She hangs around with us and the guy who followed her home on the bus a couple times. He lives over by the school. I figured he was like her boyfriend, or something." was Jayme's offering.

"Oh, that. She has a girl she knew in her other school, that started last September. They hang out with that guy, Brent. I think the girl's name is Valerie." Jo says.

"So is this guy Brent her boyfriend?" Grace asks.

Jayme speaks up, "Someone said she saw them hugging one time, really long and they kissed. They don't do that now. At least I haven't seen them, when I was around."

Jo asks, "Why?"

"We were just wondering." Grace says.

"I guess the word hasn't got around. Somebody would have said something to your girls, by now. I'll tell Amy to let your girls know, if she feels the kids at school, might find out. If they want to have a sleepover. It's alright if your girls are with them."

Once we were on our way, we didn't think about Amy. We knew Grace could handle it. I would know immediately, if anything went wrong. We enjoyed the enthusiasm on the way. This may be out last time for this place. It is our fifth year this time. We come bearing gifts and will get down to that little schoolhouse this time. I am looking forward to getting a room on the top floor. That would give me lots of exercise and help keep the weight coming down.

When we land, we are all walking stiffly. Each time we fly it's getting harder to move once we land. Swollen ankles and sore butts, are getting to us. We are hoping to get some better seats on the beach this year. We've brought some foam cushions to soften those resin beach chairs. Another hour in the bus and we are home, to our winter place. We hit the beach as fast as we can. I picture movies about march break, and teenagers running into the surf. Then I picture us. Me with my canes, and the others all strolling down to the beach. Both groups thinking the same. Freedom! No work, no cold, no snow! The teens thinking that thirty is over the hill. Us thinking, next stop, under the hill. Both groups reaching for the warmth and expression of life is the goal of the adventure. It's odd that we should garner more attention than the teenagers. We joyously romping in the surf. We aping the musical movements of the ballet artists, so well trained and dedicated. We, performing the farcical picture that could offend, but glorifies their perseverance and sacrifice.

We escape reality, and face an alternate reality. We flee the struggle of the wealthy north, to the embattled reality of the struggling south. Standing on the feeble limbs that are gasping for oxygenated blood. Resting on puffed out flesh that is crying for the merciful relief of that which a little padding can provide. Elevating swollen appendages, to gain some breathing room, for tight shoes, that might give a semblance of youthful virility. We cling to the middle agedness, that we did not want to enter, and yet do not want to leave. Each supporting the feeling, that we are alive and virile, despite all the evidence to the contrary. From the youngest to the eldest, we hold together the illusion of the life we reach for. If there is none, there is none and we are none the wiser. If it is to be had, we will have it on our own terms. We have no choice. If we do not reach, we throw out all the hope that brought us to this stage in our existence. All the times we planned for our retiring years, were a lie, if we cannot grasp them, while stealing these years before the scheduled appointment.

Gathering in the extended members that we have shared this, supposed utopia, unto this date, to once again flaunt ourselves, in the eyes of the angels saying, 'we will not come easy.'

How can Marie and I, at this stage of life, enter into this experiment of creation, with our God? How do I have the audacity to propose it? Now, how can I walk off and leave it in the hands of the innocent and properly begotten children we have raised. Did they not have there own paths to lead? Did they not struggle and triumph on their own? We showed them and taught them well. Why are we saddling them with this extraordinary position? Why have we not given up our rewards, whether earned, or stolen, to care for this, our own device?

We are, undeniably, responsible for this situation. We have only ourselves to blame for its success, or failure. We have not really, given a sacrifice for our children, and offer still, no sacrifice for Amy. We stand by our commitment to see it through, but only, with ourselves, to suffer our own, designated penalty. We leave Amy, as well as our other children, to live their own lives and chose their own paths, as only they can, to live as they deem fit. We offer no sacrifice, but will collect our due suffrages.

The carousing we participate in, in this our paradise, is to celebrate our victory, over the hazards, of living within our means. The annual tallying of debt over assets, is yet to begin. We choose to celebrate the victory now, before we realize our defeat.

We fool ourselves, into believing that we are saving up for this trip, when we are just allocating one debt to another. Bringing it about, is still a victory, over our undermining reasonings. Enjoy life before the bill arrives, for you may not afford to pay it. Do not save your experience, to when you have the time. You will find you cannot save the time, to when you can experience. One will not support the other.

~

Amy has committed her time to studies and forsaken the divergences. She wants to achieve in this life, that which she was denied in her last. She has a goal of establishing herself before her mid twenties. If this can come to fruition, she will be able to provide for the children, she dreams of having.

Tanya's mother phones Grace and asks to have Amy come to stay a weekend. Grace, in turn, asks that Jayme accompany Amy. This is accepted, but when the time comes, Jayme can't go. After agreeing to the arrangement, Grace could not bring herself to call it off. Tanya's mom assures Grace, that she will be there and attend them, to ensure they behave.

Amy finds that they are covering for the drama that is to unfold within the home. Brenda, Tanya's mother, had been having an affair with one of the neighbours. She had been caught and decided to use the girls, to keep the resulting row, to a muted confrontation. When Dave, the father, arrived home for the scene to unfold, he launched into a rage. The girls slipped out of the house to call for help. The Police arrived in time to separate the couple and avoid the brutal engagement from escalating. Grace had also been called and offered to take the girls to her place.

There had been no intimations about this impending forum. Neither Tanya, nor Amy picked up on it. The parents were almost always working late, from what Tanya could tell. In reality, Brenda had been going to her lover for an interlude before heading home. Dave had been legitimately, engaged in business. He was a workaholic and did not apologize for it. Once the affair had been revealed, it put a strain on Tanya and Amy's relationship. Brenda had been seeing her best friend and maid of honour, from their wedding, fourteen years ago. Now Dave resented Tanya, for emphasizing, the hurt he was feeling. He turned his back on the family and left the city.

Grace had a problem that could affect her own family unit, so well knit together. The CAS had an obligation to remove children from an abusive situation. Although it was not in her home, it could have some negative results for her. It depended on the state of mind Dave had developed. Grace returned Tanya to her mother and hoped to save anymore intrigue in her own home. Amy tried to be the epitome of virtue for the balance of her stay. There were no more outings with Tanya for the foreseeable future.

Tanya was troubled by this split of her family life. She could not reach her father and blamed her own orientation for causing the break. Brenda continued to see her lover and was trying to bring her into her home. The house had been rented and did not cause a disruption in living arrangements. Dave had very nearly taken himself off the radar. Neither Tanya, nor her mom, could discover his new residence. Everything was left to the lawyers.

Hearing this from Amy, made the holiday, a shadow of what it was intended to be. I had tense moments during the unfolding of the dramatic revue. It was like watching an old movie. I had little I could do to help. I had to rely on the judgement of my daughters.

When Amy tried to call Tanya, she was unable to get through. Fearing the couple may not reconcile, Amy continued into her studies, with greater depth. Until we returned, there was to be no talk about it. The aura surrounding the event, struck Jo and Jayme with a darkening cloud over their aunt.

Bringing the household out of this funk was proving most difficult. Brad had nothing to say about it, after the warning Grace had given him. He just carried on with work and let Amy alone. This in itself was a great accomplishment, as Brad was known for his outright handling of any occurrence.

Amy's other friends had called but did not come by. There was no hint of them having any knowledge of the incident in 'birdland'. There really was no connection between the two areas. Valerie had met Tanya, sure enough. There was no rapport between them. Brent had only seen Tanya at Amy's birthday celebration. Other than an encounter with her and Amy downtown, he had no further contact with her.

~

Marie and I decide to get more out of this trip, than the other years. We may not be able to afford another one, and feel we must see more islands and cultures. We get out on kayaks, despite Marie's fear of deep water. We go on the Hobie-cats, and take a glass bottom boat ride. We walk along the road to see the houses and drop in on one man, that I recognized from the last two years. We get to the fishing village and the school we we're looking for. We also, went to the Indian camp. We waded through the seas, along the route to the market and purchased the items, we had put off from previous years. Life may not cooperate with us much longer, and we deigned, this is the most important thing we can do for us, personally. At home we will tend to the charges we have there, but here, this is our time.

We are enjoying our room on the fifth floor. It's on the end of the hotel and looks up into the hills. Below is the parking lot, where we see the old cars coming and going. There was a 1927 Model T touring. It's being used as a taxi and stops along the main road, with the other classic cars. Also across the road, is the park with a forest beyond. I shudder to think, this could all disappear with further development. Until then, we enjoy the serenity the views give us. We also have a terrace beside our room, that is ours to enjoy in private. From the terrace, we look down the coast and out on the sea. There is a beautiful coral reef and the catamarans stop there for snorkelling. We had stopped there two years ago and on the way back, had encountered a large shark. I mistakenly thought it to be an Atlantic Bull Shark. I found out later that it had been a Great White. I didn't know about the drama, that enfolded at the stern. The Mate had thrown out a line, when we saw a school of tuna feeding. I saw him reeling in the line empty and left it at that. Marie had been sitting in the stern, and saw a tuna on the line. She watched, as the shark lunged, and took the tuna off the hook, straightening the thick hook as he did.

I was enjoying a respite from my vertigo. It had been so long since I had been able to stand out in the open, with the wind blowing and not affecting me. Just standing there without the use of my canes. The gentle rocking of the catamaran in the low swells. I could close my eyes and feel as if I was the axis, on which the ship was pivoting. The feeling passed and the reprise faded, a few weeks after returning home.

This year and last, we attempted to repeat the feat. Going out on the ocean and lounging on the nets, as the rest went to snorkel the reef. With the rum drinks in our mugs and gazing down through the netting. Watching the marine life below, Marie and I felt safe and dry. We did not get a close up view of the reef and all that were dwelling there. We need not worry about the dangers either. I had gone in before to enjoy it. Now I prefer to enjoy laying beside Marie and watching the live performance, unfolding beneath our craft. I think of the comfort of watching TV in the living room at home, resting on hammocks, with the TV lying on the floor below us. Marie would never go for that. It's better to leave the antics here.

The Indian village was nice to see. It was up in the mountains. They showed off their ritual dances, displayed their crafts and showed the old hunting method. All dressed in the traditional outfits, baring from above the waist. The girls had red paint covering their breasts, prompting our resident painter, to jot down an order for red paint, in his imaginary note pad. Several guys offered to help apply the decoration for our girls. That's not going away soon. It had only just died down from their visit without me, two years ago.

We got out on the old train ride at the abandoned sugar cane processing plant. Children would line the route for the tourists to toss out candy and colouring books, with crayons and pencils. It was like this on every tour. Wherever we would go, the families with their preschool aged kids, would gather for the loot. It was joyous to see them scrambling to get the prizes being tossed. It was also sad that there were so many. You try to concentrate on the carnival type of joy, you see on the faces and not on the wide spread poverty. There is much less of it here than on other islands.

Here there is free health care and a free education, even through the university level. The only obligation they have, is to spend two years in the military.

They are allowed to leave the island to work elsewhere but must return in two years, unless on government business.

Life in Cuba, overall, is like a low key version of life at home. Much less income, but they are happy in what they do, as much as we are. Some are not so happy, but we have that too. The rush hour traffic here is comical in comparison. It takes hours of their day getting to and from work. They have long work days for some, that leaves little time for sleep and family. We also, have those that put in workdays so long. Even with the emissions from traffic, there is very little air pollution visible here. I can see why some people would come to Cuba to live, from other countries. Life is so much simpler here. It is stepping back, about a hundred years, from our lifestyle. They do have TV and computers, but so little stress on their faces. They do push themselves, at times, to keep up the pace, but such a leisurely pace. They still need blacksmiths, cowboys, and they see animals working the fields. You might feel sad, to think of this life disappearing.

Our time here is gone too fast again, but as before we are ready to go home. We miss the family life. We may not see the grandchildren often at home, but they are close at hand and that makes a huge difference. We are prepared to leave, in no time. We prepared weeks in advance, to pack everything to come here. It takes less than an hour, to pack to come home.

There are no big delays getting through the rites at the airport, this year. We have better seats this year. There is still very little legroom and elbowroom, but we are with friends all in a row and such quiet friends they are. All talked out, which is extremely rare for this crowd. No drama this time. All is peaceful. So much so, that you wonder, what is wrong here.

Getting through the airport at home is equally smooth. We will be spoiled for next year. The weather has followed the usual path while we were gone. A storm the day after we left and one to welcome us home, is forecast for tomorrow. Ah yes, we are home. Back to the 'great white north.'

Chapter Twenty Four

Home Again, Home Again, Giggedy Gig

Amy was waiting for us and even had dinner made. She had gone out shopping with Grace and picked up all the necessities. I was not surprised but I had kept it from Marie. I did say that we wouldn't have to stop and get anything, because I had asked Grace, to drop off some milk for us. When she saw the meal waiting, Amy and I shouted "surprise!"

What I didn't know, is that Grace, had brought everyone in and hid them from us and had not even told Amy. She had them come in and hide in the 'dungeon', as Marie called the basement. They waited until we shouted 'surprise', then they did the same. Grace had told Amy, that she would wait until we came home, to see how Marie would be, when she saw dinner made. We all jumped, when we heard that coming from the stairwell. They came up with more food and wish me 'Happy Birthday' and a big 'Welcome Home' for us both. They even had Nicholas and his family, come up from Toronto. The celebration of many things, went on for most of the evening.

Nick and his, went home early. He had to get home for work. He has a demanding job and although he works from home, he needs to get a good sleep. He may have the problem that lies at the bottom of my health problems, but getting good sleep and staying fit, will minimize the effects and may even keep him from having it diagnosed.

Gifts had been given back and forth. We had bought trinkets that were made by the people, whose villages and homes we visited, and brought them home for them all. We didn't do that every year, so it was a surprise for them. We wanted to help out the people we had seen, too. They weren't big expensive things, just things that help support the villagers.

After they had gone home, we collapsed in the living room and talked more with Amy. She told Marie what all had happened with Tanya's family. The news bothered her and I was glad I hadn't told her, while we were away. We can't help what happens, with other families. We were not responsible for any of it, but Marie still, takes it on as if she had encouraged it, by allowing Amy to go out with Tanya. It has nothing to do with Amy, or Tanya. It had been going on for years before Amy was around. The two women were a couple, before the marriage and did not end their relationship afterwards. Tanya did not even know about it, until the discovery had been made that day. Her mom had just taken, too much of a chance, as many, that carry on secret liaisons, do. It has gone on for decades. Tanya's being gay, was not predetermined by her mother being gay. It was something from inside Tanya, that made her make that choice.

It will be something, we all have to deal with over time. The question of sexual orientation, is personal and it does not make it go away, to fight it. Just as it will not go away, if we hide it from the world. Hiding it makes it worse, for the families to deal with, than opening it up, to allow for acceptance. People think you are ashamed of it yourself, if you don't own your decision, and let it be open. You may have problems from outsiders, by being open, but those are not people you have to live your life for.

Amy has work ahead for her to dive into, and escape the controversy. She isn't going to do anything outrageous, to make it known, that she is gay. At the same time, she isn't going to deny it, if she is confronted by her classmates and friends. She has friends and family that will stand beside her, and she makes the decision, to announce it to the family. The first to hear are Jo and Jayme. They are with her most often and will be challenged, by others at school and so, should have the facts. The sisters, aunts and uncles are told next, and friends that haven't yet heard, are the last to be told. Anyone else is not important and doesn't need to be told. There is no use standing up and shouting it out. The world doesn't owe you, and you do not owe it.

There will come times, when you have to face up to it, and if you have been open with your friends and family, you will not be facing it alone.

The things I expected to feel from my connection to Amy, are minor now, to the prospects for her future, if it is like her past life. I had visions of my life, taking that path of violence, that had happened to me, when I was young. I was able to sidestep that, by becoming as quick with the tongue, and be on a friendly level, with as many people as I could. I helped out anyone, before they needed to ask, once I knew what to do for them, and the more I did it, the more I became accepted and protected, by them.

Being open to people, was one of the fears I had to face. Just like I faced my fears of closed spaces and heights, I had to face the fears, I didn't know were fears. I had not thought to treat them like that. I did face them and did well, in conquering them, except for the fears I drove deep inside myself. I started to get anxiety attacks, once I backed off from attacking the fears. I thought I would be fine. I found that I still needed to face those fears daily. Anxiety still took control, but I found a way to cope, by giving it time to pass and be comfortable while doing it. I let the nature of it go through me, instead of letting it grab hold and take me. I kept the sanity I still had left, and managed my life around these times. Some people thought, that I should stand up and fight these things. I knew it could break me, if I didn't bend for it. I would go to work and prepare for the whiplash, that was always coming, to hit me and I was in comfort as it passed. Sometimes it would pass quickly and sometimes it would take hours. I then, could get on with my day. I had other obstacles, that came in the form of energy crashes. I would collapse on the floor if I wasn't ready for it. If I was, I would collapse in a nearby chair. My workmates would be able to see it coming and help me get to a chair. I had it covered and it was less destructive, because I did. I eventually had to leave work, but stuck it out as long as I could. I had gone to many specialists, that could offer little help. I eventually showed them how well it could be handled, and over all the years of treatment, I could finally pare back the prescription drugs and take some control. It had come to being unable to work for anyone, but still do things to be productive. I called it therapy and created great things, for my self-esteem. The big thing I learned, was face the fears and duck the battles.

Learn to like as many people, as it is possible. It takes less effort to accept, and like those that surround your daily life.

Amy has been wonderful for me. I have her with me to fill the times, when there is nobody else around. She is there fore me to see through her eyes, feel through her touch. She has opened up a whole new world to me. Getting a girls perspective, freely given, because it cannot be hidden. I feel the discomforts she has to put up with. See the view points and hear her friends issues. I am allowed into the realm of feminine behaviour. Guys all over the world have wanted this kind of insight, and would love to be able to understand their ways. I now have this privilege. I am going to enjoy it, but feel I might get more than I would want.

Just the monthly emotions and aches are taxing. It explains some of the moods I've witnessed before, and not fully understood. I feel these things and am glad, that I did not have them to feel, for the first sixty years of my life. Girls do have many perks to enjoy. They can wear just about anything and not get too much flak for doing it, especially in these modern times. They have an abundance of choice available for them, including all the men's choices. There actually was a law against that, at one time. It may still be on the books.

I appreciate the feeling that I get from Amy's lack of pain. She, however, does not like the constant pain she feels through me. She knows I don't have to do anything, for it to flare up. She also knows that it would go unnoticed, if the pain went away for a short period. By holding up to the pain, you are so tense, that it doesn't register a lapse, in the intense feeling. That is how those who suffer constant pain feel. The millions that go through it daily, have no recourse. They either get used to it and stay off pain medication or take the medicine, become immune to it, and finally reach the point, that has no better drug to handle it. Once that happens, they are no further ahead, than the ones who just came to live with it.

I know that I may not live long enough, to fully experience the results of this experiment. My fear now, is that I will.

Amy has not shown signs of having fibromyalgia. Faith and Nicholas had but Nicholas has kept his fitness level up. Faith has worked at it from time to time, but one aspect of the disease, is that it causes you to try to escape from physical fitness. You have low overall energy levels. You think, that the less you do, the less you will suffer from. That is the opposite, of what is truly needed. To keep the pain points down, you must move more, to oxygenate the muscle cells. Those that know what they have, possess the tool to overcome it, but not the will, to use that tool. This disease mimics so many other deteriorating ailments, some of which exercise is harmful. The earlier you find out what you are suffering from, the better. The trouble is fibromyalgia is usually diagnosed when all others with similar symptoms are ruled out. MS, rheumatoid arthritis, lupus, and Parkinson's, are some of these other autoimmune diseases that are misdiagnosed for those that have fibrositis, another name for fibromyalgia.

Amy's lack of pain, is acting like a pain killer, of sorts, for me. Touching the softest, smoothest, things, have helped me on my own. Now I have Amy, with her ability to do things and touch things, without pain. It helps to release endorphins in me, that displace the raw nerve signals. How I wish I could bottle that feeling. I start thinking of other things, that can release the endorphins. If she and I were to combine our efforts, separately, to create these releases, I would be able to increase my exertion level, to bring more results faster. To lose weight and give energy, would bring pain down, and energy up even more. This is exciting to imagine. Getting Amy to enjoy the fun things available to a thirteen year old, will keep her from feeling symptoms, if she has the disease, and be fit enough to minimize it. It will be a blessing for us both.

Amy does suggest something to help, but I have to remind her, that she is only thirteen, and that is not allowed. She has a giggle at my response.

Imagine if I had had the knowledge, she now possesses. What mischief I could have caused. What troubles I would have gotten into. I thank God for the innocence and immaturity that I had. I think back to my molester. I see that he had possessed that information, and look at the mischief he got into.

This thought has given me a new and different appreciation for Amy's lesbianism. She will not be passing that carnal knowledge on, to a boy that might impregnate her. With the clouds, comes respite, from the harsh sun. Life's little mercies. When things viewed as problems, present benefits.

Amy has once again, been allowed access to Tanya. She had been away visiting her grandmother. Space to allow her time away from prying neighbours. The affair was hardly noticed at first, but the ones that did, spread the word so few of the residents had missed it. With it all out in the open, Brenda had little to lose, in bringing her girlfriend to live with her. The girlfriend owned her place and wanted Brenda and Tanya to move in with her. This would bring it even more out in public. That was the better living arrangement for finances, but it would emphasize the status and open Tanya up to ridicule from schoolmates. With the zero tolerance of bullying at school, it helped to shine a spotlight on the bullies and bring them to accounts for the actions unnoticed, until now. Another case for negative things bringing positive results. With the spotlight on the bullies, Tanya had been empowered, to admit her own sexuality. Good or bad, it was out in the open now and she had the spotlight on her, that would keep the bullies at a distance.

Tanya and Amy were able to resume their relationship. It wasn't a long separation, but it was a welcome return to normality. Amy spent the weekend with Tanya and with the pent up emotion, let loose the restraints. Much to my chagrin, they had their first full encounter with their sexual nature. As much as many would like me to reveal, I feel that I can't put the event out on display. She is my thirteen year old daughter. I am privy to the ordeal, but not licensed to make it a spectacle. I feel both the shame, for being a spectator, and the release of sexual tension, of my own that I struggled to control, and at the same time, ignore. I am afraid that my carnal side, took the day and I was reduced to tears, from the realization of my more baser emotions. Amy had paid no attention to my struggle from my perspective. She, in fact, felt the struggle, and it increased her desire, and response. She was unapologetic about the union. She had wanted it for so long. She felt that, to not give in would cause her further distress. Brenda had her own agenda that night, and scarcely noticed the girls in the other bedroom.

I could hardly come rushing over with accusations, toward the girls' relations or activity. I would cause more harm than good. The girls are both underage and can't be held accountable. My ability to perceive them, in the act, from a different neighbourhood, would make me suspect and cause even more consequence. My battle with my daughter's morality and sexuality, suffered a fatal blow. I would not be able to keep her from her chosen path. It will be up to her to control herself. She has accepted that mantle, in the past, but she is at the mercy of hormones, driven on by her past experience and now her coveted reward.

Now I ask you. How would you handle a situation like this? To let the event go on, and even reoccur, is detestable. To run in accusing minors of having sex, from not only outside the home, but outside the neighbourhood, is insane, and would keep you from doing anything to stop it, or affect change. The very first thing that would happen, would be the removal of Amy, from my home and from my influence. I would in fact be placed in a place, where I would be seeing it all happen, just as it had. I had to go to the agreement we made with Amy, in the first days. That she would have to accept and try to ignore, Marie and my own sexual pleasures and relations. I would have to do the same for her, when the time came. I really didn't think it would come so soon.

So, you've been warned before, and I am warning you again, always, and forever more, be careful what you wish for.

All these things, that have occurred to people, to ask for, in wishes and in prayer, have led to complete confusion, and destruction, of moralities and ethics. The benefits of the knowledge and production possibilities have been there, but at such cost. The evil of it all, is that it cannot now, or at any natural point, be discontinued. We are, as stated before, joined together, until death do us part. God, of course, knew the answer. He knew, that man was attempting, to create and control life, and will eventually achieve it. He has shown, through this experiment, the calamity it will cause, if man is allowed, to continue on this path. The freedom of choice, that we enjoy, is destined to destroy us, as it had the dinosaur. We will have to be miniaturized, or lobotomized, to allow for us to continue to exist. As these things, are not likely to take place, I fear for our future.

I have gone through all the options available to me, up to this point, and all the foreseeable future holds, and I am forced to take the roll of a peeping tom, when it comes to Amy. I can't escape the position. I would have relished it as a youth, without morals. Now as I am a father of four, and a grandfather of six, I have seen the morality and embraced it. I talk to my God. I admit to Him my shortcomings, and do my penance. He does not ask of me, more than believing in Him, and coming to Him through His Son, and that I sin no more. I admit to Him that I am weak and prone to repeat my sins, He has comforted me still. I now see, that beyond those sins I have piled the sins that have come from this piece of work, that He has allowed and put before me. All I can do is, to further my efforts, to detach myself from emotion, and carry this task through to the end, with as little response as I would have, if Amy had been born unto us, without these connections. How many of these conditions, I can carry through, is only for me to attempt, and bear the result, with surety, that He will forgive me yet, my failures.

Chapter Twenty Five

Where Have They Gone?

The release of emotions and lust, that Amy and Tanya enjoyed, was over now, as Amy returned home. She came in the door with a guilty look on her face. She looked at me and then at Marie. Marie asked "What's the matter, sweetheart?"

She looked back at me and I at her. She realized that I had not told on her. "Oh, nothing Mom. I'm just tired that's all." She gave Marie a hug and then came to me and hugged me and whispered "Thanks again."

I gave her a playful, but firm slap, on the bottom and went to sit in the living room. I did tell Marie in my thoughts and vehemently ranted about it. She was feeling so guilty that she did not try to see that Marie had not heard any of it. Score one for Dad. That is about as much as I can expect to get. The little things mean a lot in relations with your kids, as they do with everyone. I have said this before and will say it again. It is an important part of any type of love, and love is our most important job.

"Have you had your dinner, Amy?" she asked her.

"Yes, Mom, we ate already."

"Have you had your dessert?"

I heard Amy thinking, 'not my just ones.' "No I haven't. What are you having?"

"Just berries and yogurt."

"I would love some thanks." she peered in at me sheepishly.

I just smiled. I had given her the scolding in my feigned harangue to Marie. There was no use adding more. She saw that she would suffer greatly, if I had told Marie. She came in and sat on my lap. She leaned her head against mine and whispered "I'm sorry, Dad. Can you forgive me."

"I can, but am I the guy you need to ask?"

"I have asked Him."

"Well then, you're forgiven." I know that she will try, but I also know how easy it is to forget yourself, and stray again. I am not the most religious man on earth. I know that I am not even half way there. I try and just as Amy did, I know that I will fail again. Amy got up to eat and left me wondering 'how long will it be?'

Many thoughts pass through this brain and it is quite tiring, to be monitoring the issues I am concerned with at any one time. Amy listens to it and looks at me and shakes her head. "Try to relax, Dad. You don't want to wipe yourself out."

"Oh, sometimes I think that is what I need, is to wipe myself out. So I can rest."

"I know, but you really don't want to do that."

"I really do. that is the only way to get a break from the constant thinking and the pain. If I can drop off from exhaustion, I could be free for an hour, or two. I could be at peace, just for a little bit." It's not that she didn't know what I was thinking. It is like that in my mind. I can be very aware of every inch of my body, one minute, and not know where I am the next. I can feel when this stage is coming on, so I stop what I am doing and wait for it to pass. At this point, I can't walk. I can't talk clearly. I drop away from my reasoning, into a cloud. It is comical, the things I say at this point, when I'm trying to find where I was, or where I am. In good shape, I can concentrate on several things at once, but that is just a short period now. Most of the time, I can follow the conversation. But when I enter that fog area, here is nothing. Fibro-fog is the term used by one specialist. There is no defence for it.

If I could just check out, for about twelve hours. I am done in and I need to have an uninterrupted sleep. I would still wake up tired, but at least, I will be half way there. I could rest on the bed for a couple hours, after waking up, to charge the rest of the way. That is another effect of fibrositis, your body muscle tissue, is being signalled to work, by a chemical transfer in the mitochondrial part, of the cell's nucleus. This goes on, even while you're sleeping. So when you wake up, your body is still tired.

Amy comes over and stands by me. She helps me up, and down the hall to her room. I lay down on the bed and fall asleep. "Mom, I'm sleeping in your bed tonight. Dad's asleep in mine. I don't snore, so I won't keep you up." she calls out. She covers me up and goes back to the living room.

"Why is he sleeping in your room?"

"He was about to collapse, so I put him in my room, so you could get to sleep, and he can sleep right through. He was beat and I knew he wasn't going to last long."

"How did you know that? Oh, I forgot. Silly question. Good

thinking. If he's that tired he will be impossible to sleep with. That's handy. Being able to know what he's thinking."

"Not so handy when you want privacy. I see what he sees, hear what he hears, and know, what he knows. He can do the same with me. I can also, do the same with you. You are lucky, that you can't do that. You would know what he needs, and what he is doing, but you can't shut it off. It's inescapable. He feels everything I do, and when I have a shower, he feels it. When he does, I do too. It's like we are stuck in each other's mind, and can't get out."

"Is this how it has been, since you arrived?"

"Yes, Mom, it's been like that, almost, from the very first moment. When I get my period, he knows all the details. When someone kisses me, he feels and tastes it."

"That's disgusting. How can you live like that?"

"It's no picnic for him either. We both realized the problem early on. We can't do anything about it. If I get passionate with Tanya, he has to feel the passion too. He tries to shut it out. He plays loud music through his headphones, but that doesn't work at all." Amy looks down at the floor. "When he gets passionate with you, I feel it."

"Ewww, that's disgusting. At least we don't do that very often."

"No, but you know what I mean. When Tanya and I get married, he will be right there, on our honeymoon."

"Oh, wouldn't a lot of men, want to be there."

"Ugh, then I'd be a porn star. It's forever, Mom, until death do us part. The three of us are stuck together. One consolation is, that I know what you think, but you can't hear what I think."

"That's good, now that I know what it's like for you. I'm glad."

"I hope you can forget about that. It will help you to go on about your life without feeling on display."

"You're right. I never thought about it, when we were talking about it. Before you came that is. He mentioned it, but I didn't think about that part of it."

"I know. Nobody thinks about the down side, as much as they think of the benefits. I think this is why God went along with it and asked for volunteers. It is to teach mankind a lesson. You've heard the expression, 'be careful what you wish for,' a lot before, but who goes to the trouble to think about the down side? Nobody."

"I wish I had been able to talk about that before it was done."

"Everybody does, Mom. Hindsight is 20/20. Shoulda coulda woulda. I can see the positive, and I know how much it would be, to be able to keep people, from comparing their troubles with others. Never do that, by the way, because everybody suffers, and to them, it's bad enough. When someone says they suffered more, it's belittling the anguish that they felt. It's okay to have compassion and to say, 'I know that life gives us great pain to bear.' That is helpful. Saying 'that's nothing. Look what I've gone through.' You are saying, that you are better than them. Listen to people and care about their trials. Tell them about yours, and let them make the discovery, that maybe their troubles weren't so bad. Dad goes through a lot of pain. When it starts to get to him, he thinks about the children with Cystic Fibrosis, and what they go through. He thinks about people paralyzed, and their hell. This is why, he talks about what he goes through. To help people know, what it is like, and to help them, appreciate their circumstances. When he says he knows how it is, he means it, to help you through. Nobody should feel that much pain. Millions do. He feels the pain of others now. When someone tells about their suffering, he gets a sample, of the pain they have, to show him and help him offer help, or prayer. I wish everybody would only compare, to be more sympathetic. It doesn't help you, or them, for you to say, 'my suffering is worse.' To say, 'I know pain too, and I feel for you,' is what they should be saying."

"I agree. If people thought more like that, it would make me feel better."

"I could use a drink. How about you, Mom?"

"Hahaha, you're thirteen. You're not getting a drink, unless it's tea, or how about hot chocolate?"

"Hot chocolate, please. It would be nice to have a fireplace to sit in front of. That would make it feel, just right."

"Dad and I have talked about getting one. We both want it, but have been putting it off."

"You should do it, and get that TV to go with it. Then you could read, what is on the screen."

"You know about that?"

"I know about everything you have ever said, or done, or thought about. I know about your old boyfriends, and when you broke your wrist. I know how much it hurt you. I know how much it hurt, when you went to that dentist, when you were a kid. I know about you getting you boots stuck in the mud and your pirate ship in the trees. I know how you care for Dad, and how he cares for you. I'm a regular know-it-all."

"Wow. I never imagined."

"The good part is, that when I tell your grandchildren about you, I will be able to tell the whole truth, or not, if it is too embarrassing."

"Wow."

"If you ever think about being able to read minds, remember there is a down side, and it is bad. There is good too."

In the morning, the girls were up and Marie was going to wake me but Amy stopped her. She said I needed to sleep. They left me alone. Amy was off to school. Marie went out to shop and went from there to work. When I awoke it was nearly time for Amy to get home. I had slept for twenty-one hours. I must be sick. It is so hard to tell, when you have those symptoms, all the time. I get up and have a snack, to get something in my stomach. I really don't feel different. I go do some things that I was wanting to do that day. I can do the shopping tomorrow. I check myself in the mirror, and I just look like, I had just got up, after sleeping for twenty-one hours. Maybe I was just beat. I will find out tonight, if I have to go to bed early, or if I can get to sleep at all. I really can't tell. I take certain vitamins and mineral supplements that were prescribed for certain deficiencies. I raise up the vitamin C, when I know I am sick. That helps me minimize the effects of a cold, or the flu. Other than that, I stay on the same routine.

Autoimmune disorders can do that to you. Symptoms of other illnesses, can be hidden, even from someone, who is so in tune with their senses. Early detection of other ailments, can make the difference, in recovery time, or recovery at all. When I have something different, or even similar, but stronger symptoms, I check with my doctor, before discounting them. I give it a day, or two, to see if it is not just a twinge of something, and then call the doctor. I don't want to ignore something, that might be crucial, but I don't sound the alarm, for something minor. You have to treat the small infections properly. Once they get out of hand, they can cause all kinds of trouble.

I get the okay from Amy, when she sees my reflection in the mirror. She is just coming up the road and Brent is with her. He's just going to his job and coming by here to keep Amy company. He keeps a close eye on her at school, to keep trouble away from her. You can tell by the way he looks at her, that he cares deeply for her.

Amy comes in and we chat out loud, to give some semblance of normality. It helps me feel, more in touch, and the sound of another's voice, means so much to a shut-in. We still don't have a pet, or if we do, I've forgotten. I always make Amy laugh saying things like that. Laughter is, the best medicine, after all. We never talk about the disagreements we've had, because that never offers any help, with what we need to do right now. If you remind people about the bad, it gives new life to it. Talking only, about today's needs, gives new life to you. It keeps the brain growing positively.

It is nice to be in touch with Amy, when she isn't with me. The things I learn from her school work, help me to keep my mind sharp. I still have trouble remembering short term, but the information will be there, readily enough, when it moves to long term. Amy and I can help bring that out earlier, by recalling it often, to imprint it in our more long term memories. It is important to keep learning, and using your mind more, to keep things like dementia, and other social disorders, from coming on. I say social disorders, because they are affecting you socially, and are affected, by how much, you are interacting with others, daily.

I do have people I could call, to talk to, but I don't often think of that. I am in my own little world at home, and if it wasn't for

Amy's connection, I would lose track of other people. It helps them, as much as it helps you. Someone caring for children all day, can feel relief, by hearing an adults voice, once in a while. When it is not normally heard. Like at an unusual time. The surprise lifts their spirits.

Amy and I go downstairs and do some work on the scenery, we've been working with. If we do this before Marie comes home, we have more time to spend with her, and make that time better for her. This also makes our alone time, more enjoyable. When we hear Marie coming in the door, we leave the scene, and make the 'scene', with her. Amy could tell me she is coming, but lets me hear the sounds, to keep me listening for them. That helps me keep my senses alert.

We do most of our cooking, on the weekends, to use hydro, when it is cheaper. Then we eat leftovers, or prepared meals, during the week. We started doing that, before Amy came and decided to keep it up, after she was living with us. We have more to cook, with her here, and she enjoys helping, to do some of the cooking.

Grace did much of the cooking, while Marie was working, when she lived at home. When she left I tried to get Faith doing those things, but it was easier for me to do it. With Marie's present job, we never know when she will be getting home, and after some disappointing meals, that I tried to do, that practice stopped. If we don't have a meal prepared for one night, I would go out and get something. That way, Marie would not have to cook and it breaks up the rhythm, of the routine. Amy will, now and then, help me get something ready, that is not so disappointing, and helps her work on her cooking skills. Grace's girls do that too, and Amy got doing that, from their example.

I enjoy my life, in spite of the things that have resulted from this escapade. I know God knew I, of all people, could handle this, without going insane. Amy reminds me, that it would have been a short trip anyway. It's nice that your family keeps you grounded. I wish more people had a support system like this. That is, without the special dynamics, that I share with Amy.

'Look through any window. Yeah. What do you see?'

Chapter Twenty Six

Chronicles

"You're writing about us, aren't you?" Marie confronted me.

"Yes I am. What would be the point of it all, if I didn't record the results? People need to know, what comes of these things they wish for. Others have written, about winning the lottery and how badly that turned out. I feel I have to reveal what some of the more wild wishes, would bring about, and what they would entail. I have often heard someone say, 'I wish I could be in two places at once.' Well this is just like that, and all the other weird things people wish for."

"Are you writing down everything we say and do?"

"Only the relevant things. I won't use our names. I'll change the names of all the guilty ones, because the innocent don't need protection, if they're innocent."

"What name are you going to give me?" Marie actually looks interested.

"George." I have to do this. At least I can amuse myself. "What name would you want?"

"I don't know."

"It will have to be something I can remember. You know I'm not too bright."

"I'll let you do it. It's your idea."

I hear Amy thinking, 'maybe you can write a sex manual, about Tanya and I.'

'You know, I wouldn't do that. Just a hint of it, is all it needs. You can write your own version, if you want to.'

'I think I will. I'll call it "Amy's Story". How about that?'

'If that is something you would want people to read about. You go "write" ahead.'

'You do entertain yourself don't you?'

'Uh huh. I do, indeed I do.'

"I don't know what I'm worried about. Just because you write it, it doesn't mean anybody will read it. Just look at all the people lining up, to hear what you have to say now." Marie pipes up.

"Way to inspire confidence, Marie."

"If you ask me, you have too much confidence."

'It reminds me of the dropped knife incident.'

Amy bursts out laughing.

"What is he thinking?"

"He thought about the dropped knife incident. The one at the townhouse, by the sink."

Marie laughs. "That was funny. After that I grabbed the tea towel from him and threw it behind him. When he bent down to pick it up, I got him with my wet towel. You should write that in there."

"It's no wonder, I stopped helping you with the dishes."

"Wah!." Marie did like to tease me. I tried to be the heavy, so the kids would not blame her for any punishment issues. I'm glad that I did. The girls said they left home because of me. I wanted them to go to Marie for consolation. They come to me now. They know I was a fraud. I am, really, a soft touch for the girls. They each came home, after their first car accident, and I give them a hug, instead of a lecture. They know who to ask when they want something. Their mother, since I won't remember them asking. Things are a little different with Amy. I can only get away with so much before I show my hand.

"I was thinking of getting a little dog, like Grace's." Amy is testing her connection with Marie. "How about a Lhasa Apso?"

"No pets!" Marie barks at her.

"Aww, please? Maybe a Shih Tzu? How about a Peekapoo?"

"No!" Marie insisted. "No animals!"

'Nice try, Amy. Maybe another day. I'm pulling for you, although I think you're doing this for me.'

'For us both.'

Spring was starting to show its face. It feels like it will be better than last year. Amy and I, want to go hunting for a cottage property. While we're at it, Amy would like to run into her friend, at her grandmother's house. I would like to find something I could afford. I would go for a run down shack, if it had an indoor bathroom. I would park our trailer up there, and use it to live in, while I build a better cottage. Amy has to finish the school year first.

I think Brent got this job over this way, so he could walk with Amy. Amy is starting to wonder, if he even has a job. He walks her from the bus stop, every day. I think she has to produce Tanya, to convince him that she is a lesbian and not just trying to ward him off. Amy agrees with me and invites Tanya to go with her, to see Brent, where he says, he is working.

The two girls go out to find the shop, to see Brent. Amy is glad to find him there and brings Tanya in, to introduce her to Brent. He wasn't put off by meeting Tanya. He seemed rather pleased, that Amy would come by, to show off her girlfriend. They chatted for a time and the girls left to go home.

"I hope he believed you. It creeps me out, to think of you, with a guy." Tanya let her green streak show.

"Aww, I wouldn't want you creeped out over anything." Amy is all of five feet tall. While Tanya is five seven. Tanya's arm goes up around Amy's neck. "I should get him and Valerie together. That should make you feel better."

Tanya looks down at her, checking as she did. "That might help. At least you didn't show much off to him."

"I didn't want to make him suffer."

"Well, you can make me suffer a little more."

"We have to take it easy. My Dad always seems to know, when we've been doing anything."

"We can't get too hot and heavy. Dad seems to read my mind, and he's threatened to tell my Mom."

'Atta girl, Amy.' I offer some thanks. 'Don't think she will argue with that. Many parents seem to be able to do that sometimes.'

"Is there anybody home now?"

Tanya shakes her head sexily. "We'll be all alone."

"Ooo, I think I'm in trouble." 'Dad? Try to get busy with something.'

I tried to get working on something. Nope. Not working. I got out my book and started reading about the Tudors. Man, that's no help. They're as bad as the girls, for crying out loud. I'm sixty three years old. I got out an old horror movie, shoved it in the player and turned on the TV. I turned up the surround sound, went and made some lunch and back to the movie. It was tough going but I finally got distracted by this dumb movie. Elvira, thank you very much. She will keep my attention.

Keeping my thoughts busy, was one thing. I will still, have the memories of them.

Marie comes in and hears the sound, "Do you have, to have it so loud? What are you watching?"

"Believe me. It has to be loud. It's 'Elvira, Mistress of the Dark.' I'm trying to keep from seeing Amy with Tanya."

"What? You can see them? Where are they?"

"Tanya's house."

"You can see them? How?"

"I see what Amy sees, feel what Amy feels, and taste what Amy tastes. I've told you that before."

"You pervert! She is your daughter!"

"That is why I'm watching 'Elvira', to block out those senses. That's why it's so loud. I just ate my dinner, to keep my taste buds busy."

"Oh. Can't you just tune her out?"

"No. I can't. If I could have, I would have. I can't."

Amy and Tanya have stopped, at last, but I am concentrating so much, on the dumb show, that I don't realize it. Amy is walking home and meets up with Brent. They stay together until she makes it home. They talked about Tanya, and he thought her to be nice. Amy asks if he remembers Valerie. He did, so she said, she thought he should take her out. He seemed a little reluctant, so Amy offered to double date. That made him more interested.

When Marie saw them approaching, she came in and turned down the TV. "They're finished. Amy is just about home. She's with Brent."

"Do what you want, with her. I've tried, to keep her under control."

"What can I say?"

"Just having you know about it, will make a difference. I think she knows now."

"How can you tell?"

"I know, that she hears our talking, through our thoughts. Since we just started talking about it, she will know."

Amy walks in and looks straight at Marie. "I know, I'm not supposed to do that, but she's so...... She just.... I can't resist her."

"You are only thirteen. If it was a guy, you could be looking, at an unwanted pregnancy. People would be calling you a 'slut'. If you are found out, by your schoolmates, you could be in for a really bad time at school. How could you concentrate on your work, with the bullying, that would be nearly constant? Them knowing, that you are gay, is one thing. Them knowing, you are having sex, with an underage girl, is quite another thing."

"But I am the same age!"

"That doesn't matter. You are still, 'contributing to the delinquency, of a minor'. She can also be viewed in that light. It doesn't matter to adults, who they blame. They can accuse, either one of you, to be the seductress. They can blame Tanya's mother and her girlfriend for your actions and that would put them in line for a charge of 'contributing to the delinquency of a minor'. Tanya could be taken from her. You could be taken from us. I would really hate, to have them take you from us." Marie is in tears. She doesn't breakdown, like that, often and Amy knows that.

Amy's head dropped and she ran to hug Marie. "I'm sorry Mom. I will tell Tanya what you said, and that we can't, be alone anymore."

"That would be a good start. Until you're eighteen, you will have to be very careful, where you are, and what you can be seen doing. You don't want to lose Tanya. Do you?"

Amy shakes her head. She is still holding onto Marie. It's like a fighter, in the clinch, to get a break from the opponents punches. She is starting to clue in, to what her mom is saying. She is wishing, someone in her past life, could have explained this to her. She thinks back. It was like a battle ground, on campus. The gays in their group and the straights in theirs. If the straights could get one, or two gays alone, there would be a beating. If it was one, it would be left at that. If there were two, it would be hard for them, to leave two, corroborating witnesses. These girls were tough. The ones that were leading the assaults. The debs would go along with the insults and pestering. They would not be there, when the beating took place. It would be a mystery, why these young girls, would leave campus. What ever became of them? The inner-city gangs, were no tougher than these bitches. There would be no trace. Not for a long time. What would they care? They had a job to do. Get these 'things' out of their world.

It was very sobering. Amy could see the faces. The two girls that had disappeared. What ever happened to them? They weren't tough dykes. They were like her. They were like the debs, but without the attitude. They were sweet young girls. Is the world changing? Has it accepted them, for the people they are? Or, is it just making it look all pretty, and holding hope, for the ones that have a different view of love?

Amy says, "I think I need to go to my room, for a while." She's still holding her mother. She's almost afraid to let go, in the vision storm that is taking place, in her mind. I see it vividly in mine and now, I want to go to my room.

'Safe in my garden, an ancient flower blooms.'

Chapter Twenty Seven

Schools Dazed

The time keeps moving on. Even if we don't want to go, it keeps ticking. Can we have what we want? Can we afford innocence, or the innocents? Can we afford the loss, of the ones we love, to the world, we hope not to know? Sexual discrimination, anorexia, bulimia, and all of the diseases that lurk in every turn of the clock. Is there room, for us to hide them away? Can we guard them from the assaults? Only the bravest of souls, choose to come, to live life again, here on earth. Those timid ones, come reluctantly. They are glad, to have their memories, of the past journeys here, erased. The times we have, are teaching us, how to love, care, teach, and help others through this gauntlet. Most of us, lose sight of our purpose, or never really find out, what our purpose is.

It was out there, already, that the girls were lesbians. They had told enough people, to have it become common knowledge. They were keeping well away, from being seen as actively, living that lifestyle, in a physical sense. They studied with their straight friends and it wasn't hard. They were still in separate schools. Next year they will be together, at the same school. They will be tested of their willpower. They will see each other and remember, the times they had each other. The warmth of their bodies, will be like magnets, drawing them, to feel it again. Will they be able to resist, when they could not, before?

Amy has real doubts about that. She has the most experience, to both abstain, and know why, she does not want to. Tanya hears and sees her mother, with her girlfriend, living openly, in her lover's home. She has the most temptation, to throw all caution, out the window. How can we expect them, to overcome themselves?

We have lived here, in this house, since the older ones were younger than Amy is now. Grace was eleven. Nickolas was five. I've lived in this house, longer, than I have ever lived, in any other place. It is the same for Marie. Could we, move away, to avoid the lessons awaiting these two young women?

They are just taking on womanhood. They have every reason they know, why they should go for it. They have every reason they know, to abstain. What we say now will not make a shred of difference. We have laid it all out there, for them to see it clearly.

If I was Amy, the way I was when I was her age, I would be all over Tanya, every chance I got. Amy knows that. Marie, at that age, would be sore tempted. How can we think, they could do, what we could not? The one thing they have to stop them, that we did not have, is Amy's past life experience and understanding parents. I'm afraid that Tanya has nothing, but Amy's will, to stop her.

Amy's figure, has filled out to full bloom, with an hourglass shape to die for. Tanya has started to look more than a woman should at thirteen. They are both beautiful girls and if you saw them on the beach, you would think them to be college girls. Tanya is the only person, outside of the authorities, that knows the anatomical abnormalities, that Amy possesses. It is even, an additional turn-on, for Tanya. They will be fourteen this year. Still too young, for the knowledge and exposure they own.

Amy wears baggy clothes to make herself look fat. Her appointments go a long way to put that impression out there. Brent teases her about being 'chunky', to keep the other guys disinterested. Amy has suggested to Tanya, that she bind her breasts, to look lean and lanky. She has started getting use to it. They go from sex goddesses, to bland and homely. No make up to draw attention. Hair in knots and gnarls. Who do they hope to fool? Everybody, including themselves. Their look should be accepted, by the time Tanya arrives at school next fall.

Amy is taking summer school again, and we will be taking the weekend trips, as well. If we can keep them apart, it will help shorten the torturous time, they can see each other. We head up to look in on her 'chance meeting' target.

Amy needs a distraction. As I set up camp for the weekend, Amy visits the grandmother's neighbourhood. She steps on up to the door and rings the bell. She gets a wide grin on her face to see her intended. Her friend recognizes her and hurries to the door.

"How are you?" she says as she opens the door.

"Good and you?" Amy replies.

"Well enough. I am so surprised to see you again."

"My dad and I are still looking for cottages. I thought I would look you up. You look good."

"Thanks and you do too! Won't you come in? I'm taking care of Grams, so I will be here all summer."

"How is she?"

"Not too well, she's napping now. Come sit in the parlour. Can I get you anything?"

"No thank you. I just want to catch up. You were so nice to me last year. I hoped to find you here this year."

"Well, it is nice of you to come. I thought you looked lonely last time. You don't look lonely this year. You can come by anytime, while you're here. So tell me about your year."

"Well I got through another and then went to summer school."

"Summer school?"

"Yes. I want to get the extra credits to move on to university, as soon as I can."

"Oh! So you didn't need to repeat a course."

"Oh no! I just try to get ahead. I have a heavy choice of careers to pursue. So I need to get used to a heavy study load. How are you doing in school?"

"Good I will be going to college next year. I'm going to study medicine. How is your social life? Are you still convinced that you're gay?"

"Yes, very much. I have to avoid being with anyone during the school year."

"Oh! I thought you would have someone for sure, with the way you look."

"Thank you! Are you seeing anyone?"

"No. I'm like you, a bookworm. Are you sure I can't get you anything? A glass of water?"

"Yes, that would be nice. I just realize that I don't know your name!"

"Gloria. I'll get you some water." she goes into the kitchen and fills two glasses with water. When she comes back, she hands a glass to Amy, and sits down right next to her. She places a trivet on the table in front of them, for the glasses. They take a sip from their drinks and set the glasses down. Gloria asks, "Is your dad expecting you back anytime?"

"Not for hours. He usually takes a nap, after working on the camper. That could take a few hours."

"I don't think I got your name, last year."

"Amy. It's Amy."

"I've been thinking about you quite a bit since you left. You left so quickly."

"I felt down, after you said you weren't gay. I was so, hoping that you were. I had a big crush on you."

"That's why I thought so much about you, I think." she reached for Amy's hand.

Amy couldn't help looking at her strangely, "I thought you were straight." She looked down at their hands.

"I'm sure I am, but I felt something for you, too. I didn't know what it was. I was thinking of you, and I felt jealous, that you were with another girl, and that it wasn't me. I am questioning myself."

"When my dad said that you might be curious, I didn't believe him."

"You talk to your dad, about this, and about me?"

"I told him because, he was worried about me. I was smitten by you."

"Your dad was right. I was curious and I still am." She leaned in and kissed Amy on the cheek. Amy took control, and at the same time, lost it. They acted out and Amy did not honour her promise.

I was asleep in the camper and saw it as a dream. I thought

it was just a review of the memory about Tanya. It troubles my sleep, but did not wake me.

Amy and Gloria didn't hear the restless grandmother. It was the squeaks of the stairs that finally alerted them. Gloria jumped up and ran to see to her Grams. Amy straightened her hair. She could hear them going back up. She walked to the hall, at the foot of the stairs. She saw Gloria peek around the landing wall. She was signalling for Amy to come up.

"She was sleep walking. I put her back to bed. She should sleep another hour. Come on. We can go in my room."

"You sure she won't get up again?"

"My room is up in the attic. We can hear better up there." Gloria grabbed Amy's hand and towed her up the stairs. "I want to know"

"Are you a virgin?" Amy asked. She still was, and just took it for granted, that Gloria would also be.

"No. My uncle took care of that. He snuck up here one night. He was drunk. He didn't listen to my refusal. He just went ahead and took me. He was too strong, for me to fight him off. I was eight years old. That was nine years ago. You are the first person to be with me, that way, since. Are you a virgin?"

"Yes, I am." they did have sex, or at least, they started, until they heard Grams, on the move again. Gloria went to check her.

"Grams is up and resting in bed. Do you want to leave now, or would you like to see Grams, and say 'hi'."

"I'll say hi and then I will go help my dad." After a short chat with Grams, Amy kissed them both on the cheek and left for the campground.

When she got back to the camper, I was just waking up. I had done most of the work already but still had a little to do yet. Amy helped me finish up and get supper. "Did you get to see her?" I was still groggy and didn't see her memory yet.

"Yes, and she was very glad to see me. I saw her grandmother and we talked."

"I'm starting to see that I missed a lot while I was asleep. You were sowing your wild oats, I see."

"It help quench my lust and I'm not known to many people here and you were right. She was curious."

"Do you want to leave yet?"

"I want to stay. Can we stay, please?"

"Okay, we'll go home Sunday. Just remember that Tanya, isn't getting it out of her system."

"I'll have to be strong for her."

"Why do I feel like, I just brought you to a brothel? I'll be looking at properties while you are busy 'playing.' Please, don't get carried away. You are, still, too young."

I left the camp after noon. I hadn't slept well, with Amy's busy dreams of Gloria, invaded mine. I really doubt, that my dreams of finding a cottage property, were invading hers. She was busy 'playing' with Gloria and listening for sounds of Grams stirring. I kept giving as much attention, to what was around me. Secretly though, I could not help wishing, I was Amy. I am only human and a man, so you know what's bringing those thoughts on. It's just the wish to be young of body. No, it's more than that. It's to be her, young, knowing, and free of pain. I have longed for the day, when this body, would give up and let me go. I will not bring it about, but I will welcome it. I know there is still work for me to do. I must finish this, before I am allowed to leave. There is much to do and I am the only one, that will do this part. Amy must experience life and I must record that which I feel through her. If I do not, it simply did not happen. The records show, that mankind forgets, as fast as he learns, without history to remind him. God allowed this to happen. He does not intend to do this again. I am certain of that. Amy's dalliances are the fly in the ointment, but flies do love to get in the ointment. Am I supposed to allow this? I doubt that I am. I am weak, God knows this. I can't stand myself any higher than any of my family. I have not earned that. I saw throughout history, men being brutal in His name. They tortured and killed their own families, in the name of righteousness. I have, all my life, wanted to save the sufferings of the innocents. I could not become a priest, since many of these history lessons, were carried out by priests. I had to be a Christian. I had to humble myself. I am meek at heart, but I do not want to inherit this earth. Not after they've got through with it. I just want to help people learn to love, and care for each other. I want to see people laugh, with innocence and, if they must cry, cry with love and tenderness. I can only do this by example. I don't have the strength and energy, to get up and spout off tomes of rhetoric, no matter what their value. I will help to sharpen the tongues of those that can. Even if it is to condemn me for my views. At least I'll have made them think and examine their own beliefs. That is something we all must do, to be sure, of what we do believe in our hearts, and make us stronger for it.

I have seen many places in this area and noticed that, I don't think this is the area I want. I think I only came here for Amy. Dag nab it. Oh-oh, I'm really getting old, recalling Stubby Hayes. Dag nab it. I know you can hear me, little one. Do you see, what I do for you. If that isn't love, it must be insanity. I have serious ideas, it's the latter. I seem to have brought the classroom along with me, because I've just been schooled.

I go on back to town and get some food, for now, and for dinner later. Amy is still with the 'I'm not gay' girl, who was so excited, to see her back on her doorstep. I can feel the softness, of her touch, on Amy's skin and the softness, of her skin, on Amy's touch. I am so glad she's not a scratcher, or a biter. I resign myself to experience young love at work. It is so much more than 3D TV. I can't shut it off. Deep inside, I must not want to.

Chapter Twenty Eight

The Many Lives

I have always enjoyed history, even when I failed it miserably, in tenth grade. I identified with it, and came to the conclusion, it was my own family history, that brought that connection to me. I found that when I studied the books of my family, we had caused much of it. The Vikings, the Normans, the aristocracy, all contained in my own garden of family trees. No matter where I looked there were famous names. How in the world did I fail it so badly? The answer was in those family trees. Many of my ancestors had not learnt well from history.

Now here is my Amy. Her soul has not lost its memory of her lost life, and yet, she is repeating some of those same mistakes. She is driven by the rising blood pressure in her veins. The endocrine system at work. All those hormones, taking us both, on an unending rollercoaster. I got off that rollercoaster, years ago. Now here I am, riding shotgun for my daughter, and I am bound and gagged. When she gets in the vicinity of one of her girls, --yes, she is just like her father was,--she is lost to my influence. Gloria and Tanya are ruling her mind. Amy is acting like I had been, at that age. The trouble with that is, she's doing much better than I did. I had wanted a daughter that would be able to listen to her father. I got a son in daughters clothing. With one exception. She has me wrapped around her little finger, just like the other two. Curses, foiled again! My job at this point, is to keep the miles between the three lovers, numerably great.

Could they just come to the point where they can see the dangers? Short answer is no. They can never see it, because they're too close. I could point it out, with instant replay video, power point presentation on Hi-def 3D-TV 70" screen. What will they see? The warm flesh they felt and concentrate on feeling again. The dangerous curves that could hurtle them into the chasm below. Will they slow down? Not as long as they are within sight of one another. I can only help Amy. The other two are on their own. With Amy as the common ingredient, I know she will be the one least affected after the dust has settled. She will be the most affected in the transition. I never had a long time without female attention. It was not always the way I would like it and I was torn so many ways, but the hurt only lasted until I saw another female. Hormones are great pain relievers, but they cause some bad tension pain, at alternating intervals. They drive you on, when there is no place to go. You are starving for the slightest touch, and you don't really care, which of the nearest focal points, are involved. Gone are the days, where you try to see the girl, because your hooked on the sister. The sister that always gets into the next relationship, while you blink. You would love the one that's free, if it wasn't for the blind image of the one you saw first. When all hope is gone, move on, as quickly as possible.

Do not pass go, it's too far out of the way. When you ever see the one that got away? Acknowledge quickly, before you have a chance to breathe, move on, especially if she was the one, to cut you loose.

All those years, you spent on the trail, of the tail, that hypnotized you. They go by in a flash, after the emotion is gone. You remember, the ones you never asked for their names, the ones you talked to, while waiting for the next one. You wonder how it would have been. The collateral damage you caused, when you weren't looking. The one you hurt and forgot from shame. They are all in front of Amy, but way behind you. If the silver lining seems too bright, your too close. You wonder, how long it will take, to come to a head. The chances you take are best approached, with a mapped exit plan. If you were faced with a chance to do it all again, I seriously doubt you could change anything. Things happened for a reason. The ones you lost, were for training purposes. You may have wanted different results, but you would not likely, have been able to see the chance, to take to change it. We see all the benefits now, of each of the ones that got away. Pity you hadn't thought then, before you dismissed them. Just maybe, you could see how, they dodged the bullet. The prize that you are.

Children are the justice, to the parent. You see them and wonder why did I get a child like this. It was the curse you got from your folks. They said 'I hope you have a child just like you.' That should have given cause for better birth control. You thought 'I would never treat my child like that.' Then you realize that you have become your parents. Children are the best reason for birth control. You hope they get all your good traits. There is that chance. If it happens, stop there. The next one will have all your bad traits. If that one comes first, then by all means, have another. What ever you do, remember your promise, that you would never, treat your child, like your folks did you.

Amy gets a call from Gloria. Her Grams has just passed away. "Can you take me there? She wants me to come."

"Sure I can. When do you want to go?"

"Right now. She was all alone when it happened. She can't get hold of her parents. They had just left, on a trip to Europe, and are between stops."

"Of course, sweetic. We'll go, as soon as I let your mother know." I text Marie, while Amy packs some things. We hop in the truck and head north again. Amy wants me to leave her there. I'm debating. I can't just mull it over, since Amy, is right there in my head. "Okay, you win."

The drive is not good. It is raining hard. The day seems dark, and the headlights are only useful, for others to see us. They don't even reflect, on the lines of the road. If it gets any heavier, we wouldn't be able to see anything. Is the world weeping, for this life so recently lost? Gloria's family were expecting it at any time, but the trip had been planned since last year. They only decided to go when Grams had rallied and seemed to be her old self. That was three days ago. Gloria had instructions on what to do, and how to get through to them. She had called the doctor, who had been treating her. The doctor would be sent over, as soon as possible. He is in transit to a meeting and the reception on his phone is bad, due to the storm. It takes us two hours to get there.

When we arrive, the coroner had just gone in the house. Amy grabs her bags and runs in. I hobble up the walk after her. Gloria bursts into tears at the sight of Amy. They get inside, and hold the door for me. I will stay with them, until Gloria's family can have someone there for her. Amy knew I would, and had packed something, for me. I watch the girls huddling together, both in tears. It seems as wet in the house, as it does outside. It seems to be like this, when something like this happens. It is as if the rain is to float the spirit off and keep the family from following. The phone rings the long distance ring. Gloria's father is returning her call. She tells him that we are here with her, and will stay until they get back. He asks to talk to me and I assure him, that I have no reason to get back, and am prepared to stay. He will call, to start the arranged proceedings, and will finish the week long journey. It is half over, and he cannot do, anything more, if he were there.

I don't mind the stay. There is nothing to do but be a comfort to Gloria, and Amy is taking care of that. I call Marie, to let her know, that we both will be staying. She doesn't know why, the parents can't come back early. I remind her of the scenario, that had been laid out for her own mother, when one of the sisters was away, on the same trip. She sees the point and agrees, that it is best, that I stay with the girls. The romantic feelings aren't coming into the picture now. It's the friendship that is in charge of their actions. Amy has only fleeting sparks of desire that are put aside instantly.

The mood is sombre and rightly so. We try to get some cheer to her. She is afraid that this will end her feelings for this place. She enjoyed the summers with Grams. It is not long before she is going to be on the busiest part of her education. Is this closing this chapter in her life? Will she be able to see Amy again? She is lost, it seems, and we are trying to show her that things are not so final for her. Grams was not the key to her journey, but the catalyst, that opened her world, to show her the choices she has. It gave her time to see things, apart from her parents' input. Amy's intrusion into her life was a small part of that. It didn't mean she has to follow Amy's path. The exploration of this side may just be to give her understanding, toward that lifestyle. Nothing is irreversible, in the matters of the mind, or the heart. She doesn't have to remain Amy's lover, but she would always be a part of her life. It could be an ongoing part, or just a memory. The need is being fulfilled now and it may only be the reason, we entered her life.

We all have relationships, that are there only for the purpose they were made for. Whether it is to open windows of opportunity, or close the door to temptation. It could be forever, or for now. How many lives have touched yours? How many hearts have you touched?

Amy and Gloria are taking a walk through the town, to enjoy the sunshine that has cleared away the clouds. The clouds are clearing in Gloria's mind. As they walk arm in arm, they aren't thinking of their amorous adventures. They are thinking of their friendship, and how this interval is cementing it. They talk about Grams and what she was like. Talking of what she liked to do and how she influenced their lives. The things she taught her granddaughter. The way she was taken from her conscious control by the illness that had gripped her. It had only been the last six months. Before that she had been busying herself with needle work. She did not have a big family and donated much of what she made. She was a comfort to people she would never see, through her gifts. Marie did this as well. Sometimes the recipients get her a message of thanks, for the beautiful work they were able to enjoy. It would be nice if Grams, had had such tributes. She knew that her work would be welcomed, and that was enough for her.

Gloria's folks get in after their trip, and thank us for being there. We stay for the funeral and then say our goodbyes. More tears, to wash away our footsteps, as we leave. The drive back is more enjoyable, without the rain. Brief conversations out loud, as we momentarily, forget the mental link. Our thoughts are of the family we just left. The endearment of her Gloria. The feeling that she was moving away from her, and that the escapades have ended. The friendship is strong still, but has left the impression on her heart, that it will only be that, from this point forward.

This is a relief to me. I will only need concern myself with two girls. I start to think of Amy growing up as she sits beside me, and I wish she could drive, because I am near falling asleep.

We pull into a restaurant in a village, just off the highway. The 400 is a long stretch to drive. We get some food and fresh air. Stretching our legs and looking at the scenery we miss, on these treks along the arteries to the northlands. It's a transition point here, going from the country to the city.

"Is it ever going to be finished? The struggle to get things right and sit back and relax."

"You have to learn to do that, as you go along. The struggle only ends when you do, like Grams. It is over for her. For us, it will slack off and speed up, but always go on. You need to sit back and relax, whenever you feel the need. Don't wait for a sign, or for permission. It will be easier, to ask for forgiveness, when you are rested."

"I don't know why I am drawn to the north, when I hate the cold, and the long drive. I love the scenery and the atmosphere. I love the sandy beaches of the south. What am I doing up here?"

"Looking for a better deal. The plots are bigger up here and they are cheaper."

"Thanks, Amy. I like talking to myself, when I don't have to listen to my voice."

"You're welcome."

'Did you ever have to make up your mind? You pick up on one and leave the other behind.'

Chapter Twenty Nine

Let The Games Begin

The time has come, to think of many things. The girls are back at school and both at the same school. Amy will turn fourteen this fall. Tanya has already done so. I said before that I had been like them at their age. I was wrong. I was two years older at least. They say that girls mature earlier than boys. Although I was a skirt chaser since I could walk, I hadn't been afflicted with the hormone challenge until about age sixteen. At least, the raging part had not got hold of me. Tanya and Amy should not be so absorbed in it, since they had made use of it already. It does not seem to be so. They haven't the alcohol to blame it on, like the college girls you hear talk of. Come to think of it, I didn't either. Oh, woe is me. I here the timer of the bomb, ticking away.

Tanya is in grade nine, while Amy is in grade eleven. They should be moving about in different parts of the school. That would help me. I hope with Valerie and Jayme there, it would help keep them from getting together alone. Am I naive to think like that? Brent and Jo have gone on to college. Jayme is going to graduate this year and I'll be down to one, to stay with them. I hope they have got some self control by then.

I breathe deeply and let it go. I have my own things to do. Marie is frustrated with me for not selling the trailer. I just feel I need to have it, if I need to fix up a rundown cottage. I don't like to sleep in a tent for that long a time and my help won't either. I know my sister's cottage won't always be there for us. I'm holding out for an adventure. Amy and I are both seeing the possibilities and planning the creation of something unique and a place for my family to spend. I was supposed to sell it two years ago. I just can't let go of that dream. Amy and I have been using it for our search getaways.

I still have other projects to finish. The model railroad table in the basement, made a lot of progress with Amy's help, but it is far from being completed, as if it ever could really be finished. I love the scenery and detail work and that makes it last so much longer. Marie would love to hire someone, to help it along, but that is just not the way it goes. The most enjoyable part is all that has to be done. That part is reserved solely for me. As I descend deep into the bowels of the basement, I become transfixed on the scene that has not yet taken physical form. I see the detail that is to go into it. I just have to get the general shape of the land, to portray the settlement that is to call it home. This part can't come from somebody else.

Amy has just seen Tanya. She is not binding anymore. She can't take it, she says, and wants to just put it out there. She doesn't want to hide herself and wants Amy to do the same. She has just come from gym and won't let them see her binding herself. She wants to take part in the team sports and she wants to look, like she belongs on the girls team. I don't blame her. Both girls are tomboys, but very plainly women. They like being feminine. They are attracted to girls and it doesn't make sense to them, to make themselves look like boys. They discuss the problem of attracting too much attention from guys. There are many hormone controlled guys here and the girls have all the shape, in the right places, to rev up those testosterone engines. Amy doesn't feel like attracting that kind of action. It feels alright in her baggy clothes. She doesn't like the boys checking out her girlfriend, but thinks it is too much, to ask her to hide under bandages. I don't know how they can do that, myself. I am not going to influence Amy's decision. I allow myself to just observe and as long as I just watch and listen, I won't be making my views come forward.

They have left it at that. Amy will continue wearing the form hiding baggy clothes and Tanya will let her figure loose, on the overzealous, hormone driven, guys. Heaven help them.

The word has gone around, that Tanya is gay. There is not much mention of Amy, yet. She has let people know, to a certain extent. I guess her clothes, making her look fat and shapeless, has not given fuel to that fire. But oh, that smouldering fire beneath those rags. Thank goodness, for the limited imagination of the average guy, as far as seeing past the obvious.

I guess it's a good thing we go to the beach farther away from home. The cottage is over two hours away. It is remote, too. A large stretch of beach giving, heavenly, private views. I hope ours has such privacy.

With Brent away, I am counting on his history, of association with Amy, to keep away those, a little more imaginative and curious males. You know the kind. Shy, brainy, inquisitive, nerdy types. I was one of those. Intelligent, but not smart, as far as knowledge retained goes. I was always on the trail of tail. Not that I was thinking of sex, right away. I loved the female company and was too polite, for my own good. I know there are more like me out there.

A father's pride shines brightly, next to his accomplished children. I stay away from the school, because of that. I don't want to shine the floodlight on her, unless she needs me. There is really no peaceful moment, to speak of, when I am on call every waking hour. Asleep, I am still on call, but she would have to differentiate between dream and reality, to get me going. I have very vivid dreams.

I feel more at ease as the year progresses. Tanya has kept herself well under control. Amy is enthusiastic for her studies. She and Tanya had double-dated Brent and Valerie, but there was no attraction for the intended couple. Amy was disappointed. She had hoped to keep them close and thought that as a couple they might keep in touch with her after high school. Now Brent could be drawn away by anything from his job to a love interest. She enjoyed having him there for her. Close friends, are hard to get and harder, to let go of. Valerie was not as close. She was not a social person. That is why, Amy had asked her, to join them that first night. She did come around, when Amy was waiting, for classes to change, or start, after a break. She mainly, just was there. If she had someone else with her, Valerie would not even join in on the conversation. She was the quintessential wallflower. Jayme would join them when she saw them and she had her friends that came with her. I suppose that things were pretty quiet there and that, was what I was hoping for.

Tanya did not want to stay away from dances and insisted that

Amy take her to them, but not in those fat clothes. Okay, here it goes. I have Amy go all out. She may not even be recognized if she wore all the makeup, form fitting gown and her hair done up just right. She could be like Cinderella at the ball. Those glass slippers, needed some height. It was a good plan.

The night of the dance, they arrived in a limo. Stepping out, they looked like movie stars on the red carpet of a big premiere. There was no photographers, flashing cameras. There were many eyes flashing their way. It was magical for them. Amy did not act like she did at school classes. She became flamboyant and energetically charged. Tanya was in her glory. The girl she loved was back and on parade. Nobody recognized Amy. Jayme was not beside her to make the connection. It was just the two of them sticking together and living it up. The danced like there was no tomorrow, and for Amy's flamboyancy, there was none. It came and went with the limousine. They drank in all of the excitement and the attention they garnered. The prom was an elegant day for young women. They dressed the way they dreamt of, since they were little girls. Amy's gown was a sweetheart, floor length, chiffon in a rich burgundy. Her hair was swept up but allowed to settle over the tips of her ears. Tanya had on a matching gown in an aquamarine blue. Her hair was drawn up tighter, to display her smaller face, with her fine features. They glided around the floor with such grace and elegance. Nobody else could bring themselves to get in the way of such finesse. They could only hope to match the scene they were viewing. The jaws were slung low, and eyes were strained, to see these two girls display such pomp. The only thing missing were the tiaras. Where had they seen this kind of spectacle before. It was so engaging to behold. The waltz was supposed to be a joke. Tanya was completely satisfied in their dazzling performance and once done they immediately left the venue to give mystery to their true identity. As the limo drew away from the entrance, they burst into laughter and Tanya rewarded her partner, with an ever so long kiss. She could not have hoped to top that performance. That made the event epic in, not only theirs, but the eyes of the whole population of the attending student body. The chaperones were dumbfounded, at the ostentatious display they had the privilege of witnessing.

Amy went back to school the following week with no trace of her sophistication. She was back in her disguise, looking frumpish and nerdish, to throw the school completely off her trail. The tall spike heals, that had been so treacherous to manage, in their performance, had hidden her diminutive stature. The makeup gone the hair loose and dowdy. Cinderella was back to scrubbing the fireplaces. How enchanting it had been. Tanya was more willing to keep her distance from Amy, now, to complete the mystery.

The talk about Tanya's guest's identity was rife in almost every corner of the school. Jayme and Valerie were not forthcoming with the valuable intelligence, about the vision viewed but not believed, at the prom. The balance of the night had been dislodged from its itinerary. The music played to too few on the dance floor. Most were trading guesses as to whom it was that they had seen. Tanya was recognized and is continually pressed for answers. She remained very tight-lipped. It was an event to remember. I dare not go near the school now, as my pride would glow rings around the couple, and they would be completely undone.

'I'm looking through you. Where did you go?'

Chapter Thirty

The Decision

The CAS has informed us of the courts decision, to allow Amy, to become a crown ward and therefore, she will be available for adoption.

We have been waiting for this for two years.

There had been no attributable response, to any of the advertisements and searches, in all that time. The court felt, that Amy must now have a settled family life, without question of her identity. She had been given a temporary I.D. and now, she will be given a permanent name.

We have petitioned the court, to allow us to adopt Amy and give her our name. The court asked Amy, for her thoughts on the matter, and she told them, she could not want any other family, than ours. The court agreed to our petition and she became ours, permanently, legally. We no longer received assistance from the CAS, and could now take Amy anywhere we go.

We had a celebration, with the extended family, after which we told the immediate family, the whole truth, as to whom she really was, and where she came from. She displayed the unusual traits, that would bring them to believe our fantastical story.

We changed our Wills and Power of Attorney, to reflect our new family, and also changed the secondary beneficiaries, to include Amy.

Amy chose to have an unusual name, to hint at her mystery. She chose to be called Amethyst Wrent. Her everyday name would still be Amy and she would refer to herself, as she has always done. The registration at school and in all her documentation, was changed, and her life seemed to her, more settled. Tanya, of course knew of Amy's special qualities and now, she was told the tale behind them. She was thrilled, to be included in the family secret, and vowed, not to disclose this information to another living soul.

They had become quite involved in the secret identity, of her date at the prom. The intrigue was intense. The wonder of the mystery girl, gave way to many theories. One said that Amy was a celebrity, but they could not recognize, which one it could be. Another said that she was a college girl, from out of town. The stories were funny to listen to and laughable to imagine. Tanya let slip, that she was from another school. Which, if you trivialized it, was the truth. Amy had gone to another school, before this one. They all had. They were anxious to have another dance, that might bring back the mystery girl.

The mystery about Amy's life was growing and blossoming. Nobody had the whole story but Amy and I, and we weren't telling. There was always something missing from each persons version.

Life seemed better for Amy. She didn't have anything hanging over her head. She was, finally, whom she was. She can say to anybody, anywhere, what her name was and where she came from. She had never had that before. It's such a simple thing, but until now, she could not do that. She can now say, that she was born in her parents' backyard, on the grass, by the swimming pool. She could say, that her father delivered her. It was such simple things to be able to say. If she wanted to, she could say, she was one hundred pounds, when she was born, but that would be too much. What a joy to have an identity. To most people, that is such a basic thing. To some people, they don't want their identity and want to steal someone else's. She is just overjoyed, to have her very own, 'identity'.

Some day she will be able to tell her story, but for now, she will be happy just to live it.

'You don't look different, but you have changed.'